EXTINCTION

Also by Bradley Somer

Imperfections
Fishbowl

EXTINCTION

BRADLEY SOMER

HARPER
Voyager

Harper*Voyager*
An imprint of
HarperCollins*Publishers* Ltd
1 London Bridge Street
London SE1 9GF

www.harpercollins.co.uk

HarperCollins*Publishers*
Macken House
39/40 Mayor Street Upper
Dublin 1
D01 C9W8
Ireland

First published by HarperCollins*Publishers* 2023
This edition 2023

1

A catalogue record for this book is available from the British Library

ISBN: 978-0-00-846752-4

This novel is entirely a work of fiction.
The names, characters and incidents portrayed in it are
the work of the author's imagination. Any resemblance to
actual persons, living or dead, events or localities is
entirely coincidental.

Set in Minion by Palimpsest Book Production Limited,
Falkirk, Stirlingshire

Printed and bound in the UK using 100% renewable electricity by CPI Group (UK) Ltd

This book is produced from independently certified FSC™ paper to
ensure responsible forest management.
For more information visit: www.harpercollins.co.uk/green

1

'I heard voices in the valley last night. Didn't see a fire or flashlight or nothing.' He keeps the transmit button pressed. 'I heard 'em though, talking . . . I know I did.'

The cigarette burns. He hunches tighter against the wind. The jacket is fine with the bitter temperature, but the cold seeps down the collar. His legs prickle, numb. Exhaled smoke, exhaled heat, both from inside his body, swirl before his eyes and then are gone.

'I'll find them.'

He releases the button, ready to hear another voice now, the first in days. Seconds pass. None comes back. He realizes he isn't just ready for another voice; he wants it.

'You there?' he asks the walkie-talkie.

The speaker shrieks as he adjusts the frequency knob. He jams the button repeatedly, a cricket clicking. Only static remains between.

'Fuckin' . . .' He lobs the walkie-talkie onto the nearby moss and turns his back to the sunrise. The sky is bright, but the sun hasn't edged over the mountains yet.

He flips up his hood. The fur fringe ripples as a gust strikes. Down the slope, his shadow crawls over cobble till dotted with moss and rusty lichens. Contorted pine trees anchor in rock and sand, bent from the abuse of cold and altitude. They took hundreds of years to grow waist-high. They look in agony.

He pinches the bridge of his nose to chase the tingle away.

A clear creek runs near his camp, trickling from a pale blue glacier farther up the valley. A breeze whips cigarette ash toward a sawtooth mountain looming on the far side. The rock is black, turned purple in the rising light. Purple eases into grey in the minutes the earth spins and he waits.

The last smoke trails out long before he hacks a divot in the gravel with the heel of his boot. The frost crust is deeper than it was yesterday. The creek will freeze soon, maybe another week, at most. He drops the cigarette filter in, fills the hole with the toe of his boot, and tamps it down.

A failing campfire smoulders in a shallow swale, a tombstone boulder for a windbreak. He hovers his hands close to the embers, then adds more sticks. Those wiry pines grow thick as metal and burn long, a testament to the density of time. He sets a blackened pot in the middle of the coals. The water sways and hisses with a few spilled drops. He surveys the camp once before grabbing the walkie-talkie and his rifle from where it leans against his backpack.

Scree slides from under his boots as he ascends. He shoulders through the low growth, then stumbles when a rock rolls from underfoot. Numb hands press flat against a frozen limestone outcrop for balance where his path narrows before finally reaching the razorback ridgetop. The land slants away danger-ously on either flank. Another massif towers on the far side of the valley; the rift between is deep.

The gale is worse on the ridge. The cold claws so deep that it's quickly in his bones. He whips his arms back and forth in an attempt to stimulate circulation. His fingers will ache more warming up than they do freezing, and he muses that he should let them stay this way. They only seem to thaw in time to freeze again, anyway. Without the headache, he probably would have remembered to grab his gloves, left drying by the fire.

There is more shelter from the wind closer to the ground, so he sits on his heels, hugs the rifle between his knees, and stuffs his fingers into his armpits. The feeling returns. It is pain, but it fades.

He hunches over the walkie-talkie to shield the receiver.

'Emma, you there?'

No reply.

'Emma, you hear me?'

He taps the button a few times, hoping the clicks will be picked up on the other end. Sometimes Morse still gets through, even when the mountains block their voices – four quick, two quick, spelling 'Hi'.

He turns to a new frequency.

'Nordegg Base, come back.'

With a glance at the peak behind, he figures climbing any higher would require mountaineering gear. A gust shoves him to his knees, where he stays, c⟶ and turning the handset's volume, but it's alre⟶ usts the frequency back.

'Emma, you there?' he says⟶

Again nothing.

'Emma?' His voice cracks⟶ ward, fists balled in his lap for warm⟶ ouches the gravel. He brings the walkie-⟶ ietly, 'Come back.'

His hood is a cave, dark and warm, and ⟶ ks to just stay there on the ridge forever. Nobody will find him. The fur fringe writhes side to side, blinding him to everything except a thin line of light between it and the ground.

From clamped eyelids, a tear runs up his forehead to the ground and he wonders if a tree will grow there now. He tucks tighter, grits his teeth, and grunts. His mouth is sour from sleep and cigarettes.

The howl comes constant and blasting up both sides of the ridge, nudging him to one side and back again, its touch ceaseless and unwanted. It brings the patter of ice pellets and sand against his jacket, loud enough to compete with the wash of static from the walkie-talkie. He wishes for silence, just peace, so he could concentrate on the electronic hiss, on willing Emma to respond.

A pattern forms from the static, four quick, two quick.

He laughs, sniffs, and swallows until his nose is clear. He opens his eyes.

Again, clicks, four quick, two quick.

'Hi,' he says to himself.

Then, three long, two short.

The number eight.

Sitting back again, smiling at the ridge dropping into the shadows on either side, he decides he won't just stay here forever. Emma's found him. She always does. Wiping his eyes with the back of his hand, he squints and spins the frequency to channel eight. The cricket is clicking stronger there, so he presses the button and says, 'Good morning.'

'Is it?'

He smiles. 'It is, thanks, Emma. You?'

'Fucking cold one here.'

'Yeah, a little nippy here, too. It'll get worse, don't worry.' He shivers and sets the rifle by his side.

'Forgot you're not a morning person. Where are you, Ben? Sounds like a clipper.'

He looks into the blurring gale. A swoop of white jabs his headache, making him wince, ancient ice slung over a sag-backed bedrock saddle. The ragged glacier edge has retreated far up the valley from the end moraine, leaving a glistening thread of meltwater tumbling across the barren rocks in its wake. The remaining ice is the same pale blue as the sky.

A scoured landscape of ranges sprawls out to the horizon, the peaks catching the morning sun in serrated white lines. Between them all lie topographies of shadow. He imagines the valley bottom, still in the dark. This late in the year, there are only a few hours of direct sunlight down there.

He tucks in again, sheltering the handheld. 'I'm up Mallard Peak way, near Baby Elephant.'

'Where?' Emma's voice fuzzes out with a pop.

Ben clears his throat and draws a firming breath, smiling at the sound of her. 'The glacier. Back in the two thousand aughts, some hunters found the ass-end of a baby mammoth hanging out of the glacier. Archaeologists came and chipped it out. They found a spearpoint in its side and tundra flowers in its stomach. Said it was two years old. But also sixteen thousand years old.'

'Fascinating.' There is silence. 'Is everything okay? You don't sound right.'

He sways back and forth, tapping the handheld against his forehead, four quick, two quick. Then he presses the button. 'Can we talk?'

'Sure. About what?'

'Anything. Just . . . it's good to hear you.'

'How many cigarettes do you have left?'

He pictures the battered packet. He knows exactly how many are inside, counts them hourly, or so it seems. Nineteen filters. He wishes he had packed more than one cigarette a day. Seemed like a good idea, cutting back and all. Emma never complains about his smoking, but he knows she hates the smell of it on him.

'Nineteen days,' he says. He releases the button and says it again to himself.

'How's it working out?'

'I have regrets.'

Emma's laugh crackles through the speaker. 'Where's your truck?'

'At the dam near Cache Cave.'

He blinks rapidly. There is grit in his eyelashes.

'You gotta help me out here,' Emma says, her voice barely audible.

'Uh, I parked where the rockslide blocks the road, past the far end of the dam.'

'You're like talking to a stone.'

He grins, thinks to tell her that he's out of practice, but she knows that.

Emma sighs. He hears it, which means she's pressed the transmit button and intended for him to.

'Did you see the moon last night?' she asks. 'It was so clear you could see the lights of Copernicus—'

A gust sneaks under his hood, bringing dirt, the smell of earth.

Emma always talks about the moon, its exotic names made familiar through repetition, like places she could vacation. He doesn't want to hear about the moon. She is still transmitting though, so he has to listen. His fingers hover to turn the volume down, but don't. When they start to ache from the cold, he makes a tight fist and clutches it to his chest. He concentrates on her voice.

'—I want to go,' Emma is saying. 'I'm going to. I want you to come, too. Last night was so clear you could see the web of lights in the shadowed part. People up there. More every week. It was beautiful, the stars in the background, the moon, and Mars a tiny red dot, all so close together, like an arrow pointing to the next stop. No more People's Front, no more swine flu, no neo-socialist austerity, no history . . . nothing but possibility.'

A click and he waits a few seconds to make sure she's done. The updraft moans in an icy blast.

'I heard voices,' he says, 'in the valley last night.'

He releases the button and listens to the static. He read once that the squeals and squawks are solar interference, fragments of all the time between the first light and now. That waver coming through his handset, there curled in a ball on Mallard Peak, is the entire universe murmuring.

'I heard voices,' he repeats. 'I didn't see flashlights or a fire or anything. I went to look, but couldn't get very far. This valley's a hard place in the day. Worse at night.'

He clicks off and wills Emma to say something. The waiting aches, much like the cold. He closes his eyes when her voice comes.

'You should head to Poppy Freedom's cabin.' Her breathing, like she's walking. She says, 'Poppy's old. You should check in on her, make sure she's all right. Maybe she'll make her stew for you. You could play some cribbage. Poppy'd love the company, I'm sure.'

Ben knows what she means. It's not what she says.

'She's a hermit,' he says. 'And it ain't for the company.'

His chest cinches tighter as the static stretches on, solar flares and black holes, billions of years to the edge of the universe. He grips the button as tight as he can, to still the tremors. She can't talk until he lets go. He says, 'When was the last time you heard from Nordegg Base? I tried all morning, but nothing.'

'A week, maybe?' Patience returns to her voice. 'I'd have to check my log. Why?'

'I haven't been able to raise Chuck since day two.' He smiles. 'Thirty-one cigarettes ago.'

'Hold on.'

The radio squeals and he's suddenly scared she is gone. 'Emma?'

'Wait. I'm digging out my logbook,' she says. 'You talk for a change.'

He searches for something to say. Then, 'I don't want to play crib with Poppy. I swear, that woman has no soul. If you think I'm wrong, you've never played a game with her. Ruthless.' He laughs, but it ends too quickly, leaving only the hollow wind chattering across his transmission. 'Her stew though . . . Remember that first time we visited her? Love the stew.'

He stares out across the ranges, the most distant peaks incandescent now.

'I don't look at the moon anymore. Last time was when the lights first went on. It made me dizzy, like I was falling into it,' Ben says, squinting into the wind. 'I felt like puking. I hear the only smell is of people, because there aren't even any bacteria in the dirt. I hear people take shifts sleeping until their shuttle goes because it's too crammed and there aren't enough bunks. I hear the scrubbers can't cope with the regolith seep, that it's in air. Breathing that stuff gives you cancer. Hooks into your lungs like asbestos.'

He breathes in the raw cold and coughs.

'I think about everyone up there, packed tight and waiting to head out to the deep colonies.' He shakes his head. 'I hear the spinning colonies are never quiet, that there's always the sound of machines running behind the walls. I hear the Martian sunrise is blue.'

Ben looks out again. All around is big sky, the slight curve of the horizon, the wonderful curse of the frigid air.

'It'll be a nice day, here,' he says with a quick nod. 'Better than anywhere. This is the only place for us, but everyone's leaving anyway.'

He releases the button.

'Only you and Poppy Freedom left, then? You're not very good at this . . .' Emma's voice fades.

He brings the speaker to his ear, bows forward again to shelter the receiver, but can still barely hear her.

'—reported in with Base thirteen days ago,' she is saying. 'Got a weather forecast. Chuck confirmed he'd relieve you at the end of your shift. He was fuming about more budget cuts, nobody left to tax. Who knows, maybe they finally pulled the plug and he just left without telling us.' She laughs. 'I thought he'd at least say goodbye.'

'I gotta find whoever's in the valley,' he says.

Emma says something about ghosts, but the transmission cuts out.

'They weren't ghosts.'

'You sure? These valleys are full of them.' Emma's voice sounds sad. 'Be careful, Ben. Find your ghosts. Then go see Poppy. You need—'

Only the wind remains, buffeting him from side to side. He stares at the handset and turns the volume dial until it clicks off. He slips the unit into his coat to warm the frozen battery. It presses like ice against his chest.

On his way down, plates of limestone skid loose from underfoot and clatter down the steep slope. Ben falls heavily onto his back, one hand clutching the radio to his chest, the other holding the rifle out to the side. The breath is knocked from him. He lies still, sipping air, and stares into the clear blue. He sets the rifle on the ground beside him and holds his hand up between his face and the sky. The heel of his palm oozes sluggish blood from a grey flap cut deep into the flesh.

The cold is good for something, then, he thinks. I'll freeze before I bleed out.

He flexes his fingers. The grit-speckled wound opens like a mouth.

A black dot drifts between his index and middle finger. A blink doesn't clear it. The dot circles in lazy loops. It grows larger, but so slowly it's difficult to register the change. A crow, from up high and spiralling closer. Another drifts in from the edge of Ben's vision. It corkscrews, counter to the first. A third and a fourth arrive, as if in response to some telepathic call, that there is a wounded animal below, the potential of a meal, if they are patient. And they are.

If I lie still for long enough, he wonders, will they be tricked and come for my eyes?

Ben draws a slow breath, thinking of what he and Emma had talked about, and what they hadn't. Her voice had sounded good. It had chased away the hollow loneliness, at least for a little while. And it sounded as certain as those voices he heard in the night. Men's voices, two or three, he couldn't tell.

His lungs full, he holds the air.

Just hearing ghosts, she said. But then again, what had her voice been, floating in the currents that scoured the ridge?

Ben lets the breath out slowly, waves the carrion birds away, and chuckles, 'Hang tight, fellas.' He gathers his feet under him, swipes the blood from his hand against his pant leg, and continues downslope.

His camp sits on a narrow bench, run through by the creek. Steep rock rises on either side. His bedroll lies crumpled like a shed skin. Beside it, a breeze riffles the curled pages of a paperback Poppy lent him. He read it last night until it became too dark. His pack sits nearby, on its side, where it served as a backrest to watch the fire after he'd put the book down.

The little fire still crackles. The pot has bubbles clinging to the inside, the water hot enough to stir a spoonful of instant coffee granules into and warm his hands around. He sits against his pack with the rim of his coffee cup pressed to his lip, entranced by the flames, breathing the bitter steam rising from under his nose.

A stick pops, kicking out a few embers. He peers through the woodsmoke, the smell of it stirring something deep and familiar in his genes. He thinks of the voices, of how his pulse hammered when he'd heard them.

The creek gurgles.

When the fire has died to ash, he remembers to drink. The coffee is cold.

When he thinks to look up, a single crow still circles. He squints at it. 'Persistent, aren't you?'

A blood smear on the cup reminds him of the gash across his palm.

Ben draws a first-aid kit and a protein bar from his pack. The cellophane crackles and he eats only half of the bar, then stuffs the rest in his jacket pocket. He takes a pill for his headache and washes it down with the last of the coffee.

Ben swipes grit from the wound with an antiseptic pad. The white gauze turns pink. The pressure from the tensor wrap feels good around his hand and the waste flares in the embers, belching up a smear of black smoke. He kicks a few other scraps of garbage into the fire pit, an empty tuna fish can, an empty mickey of whiskey. The bottle is plastic and ignites in a greasy flame.

Poppy's going to kill me, Ben thinks as he tries to straighten the paperback's cover by pressing it against his thigh. He stows it tightly in the pack, hoping it will get pressed flat again there.

Lifting a flap on the top pouch exposes a small bank of solar panels and Ben unzips his jacket to retrieve the handset. He draws two thin cables from the panels and plugs one in, clicking the volume on so whenever it has enough charge, he can listen to the universe again. There's a space for the handset in the main pouch, where it will rest against his back and keep the battery from freezing.

From the same spot, he pulls out the tracking unit. He pans the wand around and scowls at the controls. The switch is on, but the unit hasn't chirped in days. He bumps it against his knee a few times and it squawks. Ben flicks the display. Nothing happens. He plugs it into the panel too and returns it to its place.

After a final scan, Ben hoists his gear onto his back with an involuntary grunt, then grabs his rifle. He twists the bolt to check that a bullet sits in the chamber before setting the safety and slinging it over his shoulder. The strap squashes the cigarettes in his breast pocket. He slips the crumpled packet into the opposite pocket, then sets out, following the creek down the valley in the direction he'd heard the voices.

2

For stretches, the creek cuts up against the steep valley edge. Ben wades ankle deep rather than scramble to higher ground to avoid it; the weight of his pack makes it easier to have wet feet than to climb.

Sunlight crests the peak behind him and paints the rock walls pale grey. Shadows, cast out long at first, begin to shrink, an imperceptible change in a moment but obvious over time.

The valley widens.

The vegetation is thicker now that the altitude and soil are more accommodating. A dusting of frost melts from pine needles and the broad yellow and orange leaves of the understory, soaking Ben's clothes. Mist hangs knee-deep in the bush, fogging the angled light into hazy, drifting lines.

It will burn off in an hour.

It will be a nice day.

With movement, the chill retreats from Ben's body. His muscles loosen and his headache eases. The wind swirls high in the treetops, a white noise that's easily forgotten now that it isn't biting at his face and hands.

His feet are only cold when he wades into the water, and just wet the rest of the time. Discomfort has grown so common, it has been ignored since he stepped out of his truck, crossed the dam, and hiked south, first down the steep spur of a logging road, then struggled through the wreckage of an old clear cut. He'd passed the burned-out ruin of the logging camp and pushed into the woods, unnoticing, hunched under the burden of a full pack, his rifle, and his thoughts.

That was thirty-one days ago.

Nineteen days left.

The walking is always the same.

The meditation of movement robs his mind. Thoughts always flee in front of the monotony of a trek, through the forest, up slope, down slope, over boulders and fallen trees. The only distraction is found in stopping to parse an unfamiliar noise, or looking back to watch a stone clack down a rock face and land with a distant splash. Even mountains fall apart, slowly and always and mostly unnoticed, except in such rare seconds.

'Move,' Ben tells himself and shakes his head.

Finding a game trail, he slows to a more cautious pace. The trail was likely carved by mountain goats over the course of a thousand years, moving from where they used to overwinter in the main valley to some alpine meadow that once existed above. He notes the growing unease coiling in his chest, each step taking him in the direction of the voices.

The creek flows more rapidly and notches deeper into the bedrock until it becomes the three streamers of a waterfall, pitching over the escarpment that marks the entrance to the main valley. Ben scrambles down, his pack pulling his centre of gravity away from the rock face, as if wanting him to fall. He knows the climb well though, where the deep toeholds and chunky cracks for his fingers are. It only takes a few minutes before his feet touch the ground again, landing beside a blackened circle of cobbles that wasn't there when he'd ascended the day before. The remnants of the fire pit are surrounded by fiddlehead ferns lining the waterfall's pool.

Ben bites the fingertip of his glove and slides his hand out, kneels to cup one of the stones. It's still warm. He unslings the rifle from his shoulder and brings the stock to his shoulder. Thumbing the safety off, he surveys the trees over the end of the barrel, listening for anything that isn't the patter of the waterfall or the riffling treetops. The only errant sound is his heart, pounding at twice the speed of each passing second, but slowing as the surrounding stillness remains unbroken.

Minutes pass before Ben flexes his finger away from the trigger. Standing, he sloughs his pack and lets it drop beside the fire pit. The rifle remains ready as he pokes a cellophane wrapper with the toe of his boot, a beer can, a toothpick. Farther away, three narrow depressions are tamped flat in the ferns. A few rocks have been levered from the ground and piled to the side, leaving fresh scars in the dirt. A few shrubs have been pulled up from their roots. Ben frowns at the disturbances.

Three tents were pitched here. Probably three people, unless any of them doubled up. The flattened areas are small, though, so probably just three.

They sat around the fire last night, talking, their voices carried in unexpected directions by the valley walls. They drank beer and ate dinner and picked at their teeth afterward. They told stories and laughed, faces underlit and warmed by the flames. Their backs chilled by the night.

Ben sweeps a foot through the plants, revealing an empty chewing tobacco container.

Maybe the three fell quiet after a while, staring into the flames. Maybe they looked up at the stars and the faint web of the Copernicus colony that had so thrilled Emma. When they grew tired, they went to their tents and fell asleep listening to the dying embers crackle through the constant prattle of the waterfall.

Ben chews his thumbnail, his attention wandering back across the camp for anything he's missed. Even with all they've left behind, he still can't picture them, leaving them as hazy spectres shifting before his eyes.

'Who are you?' Ben wonders aloud.

The rifle rests in the crook of his arm.

'Why're you up here?'

And on the same night as him? Were they heading to higher ground to get a radio signal, too? Were they lost? Or were they following him?

Ben spies a faint trail. The underbrush appears a shade darker than the surrounding foliage, where the branches haven't been bent. Leaves are combed the wrong way, in a line that follows the creek to a gloomy cluster of spruce trees, and then disappears within.

They headed back toward the river.

Ben pulls the walkie-talkie from his pack. The red charge light glows faintly. He digs his logbook and binoculars from a side pouch, then slings his rifle across his back.

The climb back up the escarpment is easy without the loaded pack. At the top, he cups his fingers in front of his mouth and blows some warmth back into them. With the binoculars raised, he scans for movement. Below, stretching down to the river, is a continuous sweep of treetops. The crowns rise again on the far side of the valley, to the distant line on the opposite mountain where everything suddenly becomes bare.

Ben backtracks the glasses and tries to follow the course of the creek from the camp below, but it's impossible to discern through the forest. In the distance, he catches a spark of sunlight off the river, flashing against the dark range beyond.

With a spin of the volume knob, the handheld sputters to life. Ben adjusts the frequency.

'Nordegg Base, this is Ben. Chuck, come back.'

A fading whine replies.

'Useless piece of . . .' he mutters and tunes the frequency back to channel eight.

'Emma, this is Ben. Emma, you there?'

'Go ahead.' Her voice sounds distant, fragile, like it could disappear at any moment.

'Found my ghosts' camp. Looks like there were three of them at the valley head last night.' Ben releases the button.

'Shit, Ben. Have you—' The signal quits.

Ben waits a moment before pressing the transmit button. 'Say again.'

'Have you been able to raise Chuck?'

'Still nothing.'

'I'm up past the Big Horn Dam. I'll try to get him from here. Maybe I—' Her voice echoes metallic and wheezes beneath a wash of noise before flaring back. '—be careful, Ben. I've seen—'

Ben chokes the handset in frustration. He shades the charge light with his free hand. It is still illuminated.

'Emma, repeat that.'

There is no reply.

Ben fights the urge to wind back and throw the handheld off the escarpment.

'Emma, for fuck's sake.' He winces and regains his voice. 'Emma, say again.'

He clicks the button to spell 'Repeat', then listens to the hiss for a reply, but none comes.

The creek slips over the edge, unending. Ben watches the water, unblinking. There is a submerged contour, the bedrock beneath the surface. The smooth, constant motion keeps him transfixed; the rock and gravity will not bend, so the water must.

Ben settles onto a sill beside the falls, with one leg hung over the escarpment edge and the other tucked beneath him. He stares at the camp below, then in the direction his ghosts must have gone. He turns upriver, tracing the course it weaves through the mountain peaks, all the way back to the dam, to his truck, at the end of a skinny mud track leading back out to the highway.

Even if he sets out now and pushes hard, it will take two days to get there.

He pictures himself tossing his pack into the truck bed and clambering into the driver's seat, imagines the squeak and slam of the door, the smell of gasoline burning rich as the engine fires up on the third try, then driving across the dam with the rockslide shrinking in his rearview. Everything is imagined so vividly, except he can't think of where he'd go after that. To Nordegg Base, presumably. To see what's going on with Chuck. To sit in the trailer and tinker with some broken gear, waiting for Emma to come back, like always.

A stitch forms in Ben's brow as he stares through the distortions of the water.

Then again, Chuck might not even be there. Maybe Emma is right, and funding has been cut. Even if it hasn't, it isn't hard to picture Chuck flipping his desk over and storming out of the research trailer. Could be the funding. Could be the power cut out at the wrong time. Could be he ran out of coffee on a morning he really needed it, and last straw, camel's back, he broke. Could be that he was simply done with it all.

Ben's eyes shift again to the receiver clenched in his hand. The tips of his fingernails are white, his nail beds tinged grey from the cold. He twists the knob until it clicks off and places it on the ground beside him. Pulling his logbook and pencil from his pocket, he flips to the last entry and reads.

He had come out of Cougar Canyon, following the tracker's squawks upriver. He'd caught sight of the bear on the following afternoon and watched it from a distant ridge. It stood on a boulder at the base of Quick Fish Rapids, head hung low, searching an eddy for fish. The bear looked healthy enough, but skinny for being so late in the year. It should have been fat to survive the upcoming winter, but its muscles and ribs were visible under its coat.

Ben remembers how he and the bear waited in a shared trance, both of them willing a fish to appear in the eddy. He remembers cursing every dam that had been built along the river. From Big Horn to the ocean, they stand one after the other, like there can never be enough electricity. Each changed the river, causing spawning areas to silt over; each made the perfect still waters for the hookworm to flourish, choking the gills of any survivors.

Ben scans his notes. The bear waited for over four hours for a fish. None came. The bear gave up and went rooting larvae out of stumps in a nearby clearing until dark.

Ben frowns at the date written on the page then glances at his watch. That was five days ago.

On the facing page, he writes the date and his location, cold nights and clear days. No sightings since the last entry. Too long, now. He makes a note of how he hasn't been able to reach Chuck, but he has Emma. With a smirk, he writes how that's preferable anyway. Chuck will get a kick out of that, if he still bothered to review the logs.

Ben writes how his filter broke a few days ago, so he is boiling all his water now, how their gear is old and falling apart, and this job sucks and he isn't even sure of the point anymore. He pauses, the eraser hovering over that last bit before he rubs the line away and blows the eraser dust clean.

In its place, he writes how they should head out and scout around again, to the north, look for a better place, farther away, where they could relocate the bear.

The last time he'd mentioned it, he got a lecture about budget and helicopter costs and logistics and the risk to the bear. He was told there was no better place left than this. Ben still isn't convinced though. Maybe he and Emma should drive north and hike some of the valleys up there on their next break.

Ben's eyes drift back to the creek. The water slips over the escarpment, unending, as it has since the baby mammoth became encased in the glacier. For sixteen thousand years, the water has fallen, stronger in the spring, jagged fangs of ice hanging down in the winter, a mounting trickle again as the thaws returned. The baby mammoth had tundra flowers in its stomach. It was chipped out of the ice to find the same sky overhead, and in sixteen thousand years, the stream has only carved a sliver out of this rock.

Ben blinks and withdraws the battered pack of cigarettes from his pocket. He flips the top and counts nineteen. Pinching one out, he puts the filter to his lips and lights it. He closes his eyes. They remain closed as he inhales, exhales. When he opens them again, his gaze settles on the creek below, running into the dark cluster of spruce trees, and stays locked there.

Whoever camped here is still in the valley, and not far.

When he finishes, he twists the cigarette butt into a crease in the rock and places a slab of limestone over the top. He reopens the logbook and traces his writing with a finger, the pencil lines blurring a little in its wake. Halfway down the page, his finger stops where the words end. He writes about the voices last night, and about finding the remains of the camp. He writes his deductions, three campers, unknown purpose.

It's written, now he will go find them.

Sliding the pencil and logbook back into his jacket pocket, Ben grabs the receiver from the ledge beside him and scrambles back down to the waterfall's pool.

The backpack sags when he pulls out the ballistic vest. It had taken up a third of the main compartment. Emma made him promise to always wear it. Ben told her he would, but he never does. It is too unwieldy for moving through the bush for weeks on end.

Ben sits cross-legged and unfolds the vest, laying the two panels flat beside the fire pit. Wavering lines of salt encrust the neck, the chest plate, the back plate. He fingers two depressions where the fabric has been flayed from the laminate plate underneath, then sits back on his heels and runs his hands slowly through the ferns on either side. Numbing dew soaks them on the first stroke. The sensation of the soft leaves passing under his palms mesmerizes him.

He takes off his parka, jacket, and shirt. The cool air shocks his bare skin. The vest is cold and heavy, but warms quickly against his body. It reeks of someone else's sweat. He pulls the frayed Velcro straps tight, securing the back panel to the front. It takes a few deep breaths to acclimatize to the hug of the chest plate, and the claustrophobia soon passes.

Ben dresses. Under the parka, the vest is barely noticeable. He reconnects the walkie-talkie to the charger and repacks it next to the tracking unit before hoisting the pack onto his shoulders again. The straps need adjusting to accommodate the new bulk.

With rifle in hands, he follows the watercourse to the spruce copse. The only sound is the gurgle of the water slipping over a few of the larger cobbles. The trees grow close together and block out all but the most persistent beams of sunlight. Ben squints between the tight branches. It'll be hard to move through quietly, but at least there is an obvious trail to follow. Many of the branches have been broken. Patches of freshly exposed wood are beacons against the backdrop of grey bark and witch's hair lichens that drape the branches with fine tendrils.

Ben's breath becomes visible again with the first step into the woods. The wind above becomes hushed, the thicket creating an eerily muted world. He weaves through, making slow progress as he twists past branches and steps over deadfall. There is no underbrush, not enough light penetrating for anything but a thick carpet of moss to grow.

He freezes at a noise, his scalp prickling, and eases down into a crouch. It's impossible to tell if it had been close or distant. Minutes pass to the sound of the burbling water. The shock of adrenaline in his veins becomes obvious, the fibres of his muscles humming in the stillness. Minutes more, and Ben stands to stretch the stiffness from his legs. The weight of the rifle in his hands gives him some confidence and he starts downslope again.

The creek makes a sharp bend and the strangers' trail continues through the woods on the far bank, heading away from the watercourse, which means they are shooting a straight line for the river. It also suggests they are navigating with map and compass, working to outwit the watercourse.

Or perhaps they know the area.

Ben finds a perch on the bank and gauges the crossing. The water flows fast and thigh deep, wider than he would be able to jump under the weight of his gear.

With a sigh, Ben steps into the icy water. The current tugs at his ankles and the rocks lining the creek bed make for wobbly footing. He gasps when he stumbles into an unexpectedly deep pocket, the water suddenly swirling around his stomach. Slogging onto the opposite bank, pants clinging, frigid and soaked, he pauses to inspect something glittering in the moss: a candy wrapper.

The grade steepens and the trees grow more widely spaced. At first, a few pine trees are interspersed with the spruce, and then he is in an open pine forest. The confines of the spruce are replaced by an equal discomfort at his exposure. The sunlight shines through the branches with more force here, striking the pine needles and leaves of the understory, casting them radiant.

Ben's pace slows even though the terrain is less demanding. The uneasy awareness that he is more visible has him angling behind clumps of bushy alder and the numerous windthrows, toppled trees with upturned root mats that stand as tall as him.

The slope lessens and then flattens entirely when he reaches the river's broad terrace.

In the distance, the roar of the water is dampened to a constant whisper by the height of the terrace and the nearly sheer ravine it has carved through the outwash and underlying bedrock.

Overlying the whisper, voices.

Ben slips behind a windthrow. He peers around the ragged edge of the root mat, breathing its earthy scent.

Where the trees break at the ravine edge, two silhouetted figures move in the bright light.

3

Ben isn't close enough to hear their conversation. They're men's voices. The deeper one talks more than the other. He erupts in laughter, then there's the sound of a branch cracking. He's breaking sticks from a nearby pine tree and dropping them in a brittle tangle at his feet, talking the while.

The smaller man is on his hands and knees, digging, scooping loose earth and stones into a pile by his side. Occasionally, he pinches something from the soil and brings it closer for inspection. Nearly everything he examines is thrown aside, but a few items are set carefully on the moss.

The larger man watches, talks, rests against the tree with one foot planted on the ground and the other propped back against the trunk. He spits to the side and laughs again.

Ben can't tell if the smaller one joins in on the joke. He looks up briefly, shakes his head, and then goes back to digging.

A rifle leans against a mound of backpacks a short distance away, closer to the ravine edge.

The men are relaxed, not at all wary of their surroundings. Ben worries that means they don't have a reason to be cautious. Then he remembers there are three. He spins and crouches with his back pressed against the windthrow's upturned root mat.

A rock falls from the dirt and lands beside him with a thump. Ben flinches and brings his rifle to the ready. He scans the trees in the direction he came from, lingering on anything big enough to hide a person. The dappled light confuses his eyes.

Ben's finger twitches against the trigger at the sight of movement, but instinct keeps him from firing on a swaying branch or the shadow it casts. Leaves rustle. The quiet rasp of his own breath, in then out. Dry wood snaps. The sound of the men talking ebbs and he is left listening to his own heartbeat once again.

'Come on, Ben.' He sweeps the barrel back, slower this time, scolding himself under his breath, 'Use your fucking head.'

'I'll be damned,' the deeper voice exclaims, followed by clapping.

Ben hazards a glance back, craning around the root mat to see the men huddled, intent on something the smaller one holds. The big man slaps the other on the back.

Ben turns again to face the forest at his flank. No one is there. If anyone had been, they'd likely have shot him. He must look completely unstable, crouched behind the tree throw and flailing around with his rifle.

He pulls in a quick breath and exhales slowly, hoping to ease his nerves.

'Fuck,' he whispers, planting the rifle stock in the dirt between his feet and grasping the barrel in both hands. He presses his forehead against it, trying to distract the tangle of his whirling thoughts. Inverting the rifle so that the barrel is tucked under his armpit and the stock is resting across his forearm, Ben rubs his free hand over his face, repeating, 'Fuck, fuck, fuck.'

With one last look into the woods, one last sharp inhalation, Ben stands and steps out from cover.

'Hello,' he calls.

Both silhouettes turn. The larger man straightens and waves, calling, 'Good morning.'

The smaller one stands and smacks the dirt from his knees. Clouds of dust drift into the sunlight. He takes a step back from the hole he dug and says something.

The big man peers at his wrist and says, 'I guess it is afternoon.'

Ben starts toward them. He tries to mask the caution in his steps, tries to appear casual, but watches the pair for any reason to flip his rifle around and raise it. He struggles to ignore the feeling that the third member of their party is creeping through the trees behind him, closing in with bolder steps than he himself dares take. Every rustle and creak from the woods makes him want to glance back.

Closer now, Ben sees there are two rifles leaning on the pile of packs nearer to the ravine edge, a few strides away from the men. A knife is sunk to the hilt in the earth, beside the pit. The big man's jacket is unzipped, exposing another knife sheathed on his belt.

He taps the brim of his ball cap in greeting, chattering as Ben approaches. 'Haven't seen anyone else out here. Gets a little lonely, but I guess that's the joy of being in the wilds, isn't it? Feeling small again. Learning what alone really feels like.'

When Ben doesn't reply, the man glances uncertainly at his companion. He thrusts his hands into his pockets, then continues, 'Well, not alone when I have my son with me. While it's something to feel the caveman brain stir at the sight of all this wilderness, it's something greater to see it stir in your son.'

He beams at his kid.

Ben guesses the boy is in his late teens, early twenties at most. Strong too: broad like his dad, but still wiry from youth.

The silence draws to a length again, and the man frowns, casting a sidelong glance at Ben.

'Instinct,' he says, raising a finger theatrically, 'our genetic memory from two hundred thousand years of evolution . . . or whatever primordial thing still wriggles around inside our heads, makes me realize that people are more the same than different.'

Ben is close enough now for the man to take a step in his direction and extend his hand with a friendly grin.

'But you haven't said a word,' the man says, 'and I carry on. My wife always said I have such tendencies. Actually, she always just said, "Arnott, shut up," but I know what she meant.'

Ben nods and shakes the man's hand. The grip is firm, and hints that it could become much stronger if needed. The man is shorter than Ben, but more solid, with a broad chest and thick legs. A frost of greying hair peeks from beneath his ball cap.

The big man hooks his thumbs on his pockets and dips his sharp, clean-shaven chin, and spits. A daub of chewing tobacco pillows his lip. 'Name's Arnott . . . in case you missed that.'

Flashing a smile of the whitest, straightest teeth Ben has ever seen, Arnott points at his son. 'And this is my boy, Vito.'

Vito rubs his hand against his pant leg before holding it out for Ben. Ben can see Arnott in the kid, the same grey eyes, but without the brackets of wrinkles, or the ruddy patches on his cheeks from years of wind and sun. Vito's skin is smooth, except for a speckling of acne. They have the same expensive teeth.

Ben steps back and crosses his arms, letting the stock of his rifle point to the ground.

Vito shifts under Ben's gaze, and looks at his dad.

Arnott arches an eyebrow at Ben, then gives him a shallow bow. 'And you are?'

'Ben.' Ben clears his throat. 'Sorry, it's been a while since I've seen anyone out here, too.'

'In that case, I'd say we're lucky to have found each other. And at the moment of Vito's grand discovery, no less.' Arnott rubs his hands together.

Ben cocks his head at what Vito holds cupped. It's a dirt-encrusted stone the shape and size of a thumbnail.

'Go on, Vito,' Arnott encourages. 'Tell Ben what he's looking at.'

'This is a hide-scraping tool.' Vito rubs grit off the stone with his shirt, then holds it up between his thumb and forefinger. It's a round pebble, split in half, and chipped along one arc to sharpen the edge. 'See, once they killed and skinned an animal, they'd scrape this along the hide, to remove the leftover meat and fat and sinew, to get it ready for curing.' Vito's voice becomes animated as he talks. He runs the flat face of the tool over his palm to demonstrate and looks up to see if Ben understands, his eyes bright and excited.

Ben nods.

'Clever Indians,' Arnott says, shaking his head. 'Vito's always been interested in archaeology and history and all that stuff. Always reading books about who was here before us, and not just the white guys either. His head's full of sabre-toothed cats and buffalo hunters. Not sure why . . .'

His son replies, 'We have to learn from the past or we'll repeat its mistakes—'

'Bullshit idioms. That history is what's got us standing here, now.' Arnott points at the wisp of the moon, pale and spectral. 'It's what got us up there. Any mistakes along the way have been the necessary ones.' Arnott waggles a finger at the terrain. 'Our lives are in the future, not the past.'

Vito waits to see if Arnott's finished before turning back to Ben. 'Look.' He gestures up the length of the terrace. 'See them?'

The southern slant of the light casts deep shadows into a cluster of pits. Ben counts five, now largely filled with forest litter and covered with thick moss, but still distinctive.

'Boiling pits and hearths,' Vito says, straightening up and beaming. 'There was a camp here. Thousands of years ago. Picture it, people sitting on this exact spot. Talking and cooking a deer they killed, preparing its skin to make a cloak or something. They looked out over this valley, went down to get water.'

'It's way too steep to go down here.' Arnott cranes over the edge to see the river below. 'Unless you're falling off it.'

Vito continues, 'They sat around a fire, stared up at the moon and told stories about it, legends about spirits and gods.' Vito contemplates the hole he dug. 'I was hoping to find an arrowhead or spearpoint. If I could find one, we could figure out how long ago they were here, by the shape of it. If this is a really old site, maybe the people were hunting mammoths and stuff.'

Ben's gaze settles on the two men. 'What're you guys doing out here?'

'That's quite a relic you got there.' Arnott jerks his chin at Ben's rifle. 'Colt C19?'

Ben nods.

'You're a government man?' Arnott asks. Ben remains silent, so he continues. 'It's in nice shape. Good rifle, that. Reliable. But you should check out these.'

Arnott takes a step toward the weapons propped against their packs.

'Hey,' Ben says and turns his rifle so the barrel points at the ground between them.

Vito steps back, the stone tool grasped tight in his fist.

Arnott freezes. With a glimpse over his shoulder, he extends his hands away from his waist. Slowly, he hooks one of the rifles by the strap. With it hanging, he returns and holds it out for Ben to take.

Ben feels the weight of the weapon, heavier than his own. He turns it over, the blued barrel is an anomaly, absorbing daylight.

'Nice,' Ben says.

'Desert Tech SRS A1.' Arnott beams. 'Five-round .338 cartridge. With the scope I got on there, it can clip a tick from a deer's back, probably two, three times as far as that old Colt. Has night vision, too.'

Ben bites his lower lip and slides the bolt back. The chamber is empty. He leaves it open and passes the weapon back to Arnott. 'You got permits?'

'You *are* a government man, then.'

Ben unzips his jacket and retrieves the wallet that holds his identification from an inside pocket.

Arnott's eyes linger and Ben is certain he's puzzling out the bulk of the ballistic vest under his shirt.

Arnott takes the wallet and flips it open. He squints as he holds it close, then goggles when he holds it farther away. He smiles sheepishly. 'Don't have my reading glasses . . . a Ranger, hey?' He returns the wallet. 'I'll be damned. Ranger Ben, it's a pleasure to meet you. Our paperwork is in the top of my pack. I'll get it.'

Vito shifts from one foot to the other.

Arnott leans his rifle back against the packs, kneels, and opens one of the outer pockets.

Glancing back into the woods, Ben asks, 'Where's your third man?'

Arnott spits to the side. 'Our guide, you mean? He's gone off scouting, south.'

'For what?'

'Here they are.' Sitting back on his heels, Arnott clutches a bundle of documents sealed in a plastic bag. He grunts to stand, and offers the papers to Ben.

Ben pulls them from the bag and leafs through, half his attention still on the pair. 'What's your guide searching for?'

'Animals,' Vito replies.

Ben looks up at the boy from under his brows, then turns his attention back to the pages: permits for the weapons, and back-country permits, too. Chuck's signature crawls across the bottom of those. The inception date is from a few months back, and the expiry is still a few months away. Ben wonders why Chuck hadn't mention them.

'Arnott and Vito Harbron,' Ben reads aloud before folding the papers. He slips them back into the plastic and passes the parcel back to Arnott, repeating the surname, 'Harbron.'

'The same.' Arnott taps the logo stitched into his ball cap. In a swooping font reminiscent of a hundred years ago, it reads, 'Harbron Trucking & Transportation'. 'The face may not be pretty enough to get recognized, but the name always does. Makes it hard to get away.'

'I'm sure.'

'Which is why we're here.' Arnott rolls the documents into a tube and then flattens them again. 'Bringing the boy out for a touch of nature before our shuttle takes us to Copernicus. Want to give him a memory of where he came from, something to hang on to when he goes out deep, what with his interest in our collective, earthborn soul, and all that. With Eurasia a long time done and the Nile skirmishes flaring up again, hell, with the whole damned equatorial world scorched, we couldn't well go visit the spot we crawled out of the Rift, now could we?' He taps the papers against his thigh and shrugs. 'The Nile Valley used to be green, believe that? I've seen the pictures . . . anyway, here we are.'

'You came to see the trees,' Ben says.

'We came to see the trees,' Arnott says.

'And maybe some animals,' Vito adds.

Arnott stops fidgeting and he scowls. 'Sure, it's been a regular fucking safari, so far. Hoping for anything but a crow or magpie, or rat, or racoon. Mosquitoes and black flies, now there are still a few of them around, once the day warms up enough.' He turns to Ben. 'Perhaps you could be a good ranger and point us in the direction of a squirrel or a deer that we could marvel upon?'

'A safari with rifles?' Ben asks.

'Last I checked, it wasn't a crime to carry a firearm.'

'That's right.'

'Got the permits.' Arnott waves the papers.

'You do.'

'Not a crime to shoot a crow or squirrel.'

'That's a lot of firepower for a crow or a squirrel.' Ben juts his chin at the rifles.

'You never know when one of those little fuckers'll come charging out of the bush at you.' Arnott laughs. He sobers quickly when Ben doesn't join in. 'I've heard rumours that there's still a bear in this valley. The last one ever, is what they say. You wouldn't happen to know, would you? I'd love for Vito to see it. Hell, I'd love to see it myself.'

'Rumours,' Ben says, kicking a rock from the ground. With the toe of his boot, he rolls it away and examines the scar left in the moss. 'Ain't no bears left, in this valley or any other. Habitat's too degraded. The best you'll see is a mountain goat. I followed a trail this morning, but doubt you'll see any of them either. Can't remember the last time I even heard of one being spotted. Probably went the same as the bears.'

Arnott casts Ben a slow glare, then kneels again to return the bundle of papers to his pack.

'I hear Australia's nice this time of year,' Ben offers. 'Maybe you should take your safari on over there? Heard there's still a few koalas kicking around, if you're itching to see a bear.'

Without looking back, Arnott says, 'You have been out here a while.'

'What's that?'

'A new variant hit Sydney. Contagious as hell. They've gone full lockdown again, police state with roadblocks all over. Every border's shut, inside and out. Got everyone hunkered down at home, waiting to see where it pops up next.' Arnott sits back, lays his palms on his thighs, and gazes out across the river. His fingers shuffle. 'I wish them the best, of course. Imagine it, in a city of ten million.'

Arnott looks up at Ben. He drums a quick rhythm against his legs before standing. 'Ah, but for rumours and dark dreams, hey? Where would we be without those?'

'I heard there's more people up there than down here now.' Ben flips a thumb at the ashen moon pinned to the blue. 'That true?'

Arnott shrugs. 'Haven't counted how many are left down here, but we've shuttled up enough that I'd believe it. We're moving people and supplies out from Copernicus now too, growth industry, you know.' Arnott smiles. 'The colonies are arks now.'

'Heard your tickets are pricy,' Ben says.

'No more than they need to be.' Arnott grows serious. 'Are you looking for a lift, Ranger Ben?'

'I'm good.'

'Sure, you're good,' Arnott says, his attention drifting into the woods momentarily before coming back to Ben. 'And business is good, yes? Conservation has always been a luxury of the rich. People struggling for survival never had a use for zoos or national parks. Starving people never gave a shit if they were eating some endangered peacock and picking at their teeth with a colourful tail feather after. Never worried about some Pleistocene sloth,' Arnott gestures to the pits along the ridge. 'When it's about survival, you got to outfox, outfight, or out-fuck everyone else. Always been that way, hey boy?'

Vito purses his lips, worrying at the stone tool he holds with his thumb.

Ben tightens his grip on his rifle and glances into the woods behind him, certain he's heard a whisper of movement between all of Arnott's words. There is nothing back there except shifting shadows and bobbing tree boughs.

'We're curious creatures, aren't we?' Arnott asks. 'We can't just be satisfied knowing. We always got to be touching and fucking around with stuff.'

Ben turns back to face Arnott, wishing the man would shut up, even for a moment. He misses the sound of the forest without people.

Arnott grins and raises his eyebrows. It's unsettling, like Arnott is winning at a game that Ben doesn't even know the rules for.

'Before we got fat,' Arnott continues, 'we burned the forests for better hunting grounds, dammed rivers to irrigate our crops, and engineered bigger tits for our chickens. Didn't think anything of it until we were nations full of bored predators looking for a cause.'

Ben takes a step back, trying to widen his view of the surroundings, his distrust seeping deeper as Arnott's words keep muddling any other sounds.

'Ten seems to be the magic number.' Arnott waggles a finger. 'When there were ten white rhinos left, that's when we thought that maybe we should pay attention. It was only then that we asked the question, the only question we should ever ask.'

'And what's that?' Ben asks.

'Of all people, I thought you'd know.' Arnott tuts and shakes his head.

Ben glances over his shoulder again.

'You're an educated man,' Arnott declares. 'Your naturalist's passions have been fanned into a raging fire. Shit, enough to bring you out wandering the wilds by yourself all day, eating dehydrated mashed potatoes for supper, then shivering in your sleeping bag all alone in the night, exposed to the dangers of all these savage squirrels.' Arnott pats his son on the shoulder and turns to Ben. 'There's only one question and it's always the same. What's the point?'

'What's the point?'

'Exactly.' Arnott waves his arm, as if conducting his surroundings. 'Of any of it. Tell me, Ranger Ben, when was the last time a white rhino did anything for you?'

Ben doesn't answer, so Arnott gazes out over the river valley with his hands planted on his hips. 'Magnificent creatures though.'

Vito kicks at the pile of dirt beside the hole he's dug. He stoops to retrieve something, examines it, then throws it aside.

With Arnott's back to him, Ben makes another quick scan of the woods, certain the man's lecture is a distraction.

Arnott squats and strikes a match, sparking the pile of tinder he'd built. Without looking back, he asks, 'Stay for a coffee?'

'I got nowhere else to be,' Ben replies.

Arnott chuckles and turns to his pack, rooting out a blackened pot and a few packets of instant coffee.

The fire crackles and the familiar smell of woodsmoke fills the air. Ben takes a few more steps back and leans against the pine tree, angling for a better spot to watch the pair.

Vito tenses almost imperceptibly, his eyes darting over Ben's shoulder.

There's movement in the forest.

Ben holds his rifle at the ready and twists to see a figure approaching, weapon also raised, and close.

'Ben,' the man says. 'Relax.'

4

Ben's heart trips to rapid-fire. He keeps his rifle trained on Tomos.

Tomos holds the same model rifle as the two others, nearer to Vito and Arnott. The barrel points squarely at Ben's chest.

Both men stand locked.

The world contracts to the twenty paces between them. Each strains to sense the twitch that would predict a shot, and precede the sear of pain. Both struggle to see into the future, even a split second forward, to preempt a bullet. Time slows from adrenaline. Ben's vision blurs but he doesn't blink.

Tomos is broader than Ben remembers. The hollow distance in his eyes wasn't there before, and it makes him a stranger again.

The fire pops.

Arnott breaks a few sticks and adds them to the blaze.

The smell of woodsmoke becomes a constant in the air.

Arnott lifts his rifle from where it leans against the packs. Ben catches the movement in the corner of his vision and begins to turn, an instinct, but he freezes when Tomos inches forward in the distraction.

Rooting through the pack, Arnott says, 'Tomos, you've met Ben?'

Ben remembers to breathe.

After withdrawing a spoon and a few tin cups from the pack, Arnott replaces the rifle and shuffles back to the fire. He stirs the coffee. The side of the pot hisses. Arnott jerks his arm back, wincing and twisting it to examine the underside. He blows across his wrist, his eyes lifting to Ben, and then Tomos, as if just realizing an uncomfortable span of time has passed.

Arnott claps his hands together and rubs them back and forth.

Ben flinches.

An echo bounces back from the far side of the valley.

'Of course, they've met.' Arnott angles to address Vito, who stands rigid near his pit, his face drained of colour. Arnott scowls, as if misinterpreting his boy's tension for confusion. 'These two are old work buddies,' he explains. 'Tomos recruited Ben right out of university, taught him how to track and shoot and live out here like an animal, as I remember the story.' Shaking a finger in the air, Arnott smiles. 'See, Tomos . . . sometimes I listen to your rambling. Hell, like brothers, you two. Makes this kind of like a reunion, no?'

Arnott turns back to the fire and jabs at the embers with a stick before adding it to the flames. 'Tomos, come have a coffee.'

Tomos jerks his chin at Ben, then lowers his rifle. He circles Ben to join Arnott at the fire.

Ben takes a step back and eases his barrel toward the ground.

Vito seems to deflate and moves cautiously to join them.

'Ben,' Arnott fixes him with a pointed stare from under the brim of his ball cap, 'Tomos has agreed to be our guide. I'd appreciate it if you didn't shoot him.'

Arnott waits, as if for an apology. With none forthcoming, his face softens and he returns to tending the flames. 'Being that Tomos used to be one of you guys, I figured he was perfect to lead our safari. And the fact that he used to be on the Ursa Project, I figured he'd be our best chance of meeting The Boss. He knows the area, knows the animal, where it eats, where it shits. He knows where it sleeps.'

'Ursa Project's dead,' Ben says.

'That true?' Arnott asks.

'You didn't check in with Chuck? His name's all over your permits.'

'I'm afraid we neglected to discuss it.' Arnott tongues the lump of chewing tobacco in his lip and spits into the fire. A swirl of ash rises. He points at Ben's hand. 'What'd you do?'

Ben looks down. The bandage is soaked through and a line of blood runs along his finger, tacky and drying.

'Looks raw still, bleeding through.' Arnott puckers his lips in a show of concern. 'You want Vito to patch you up? He's good at that stuff.'

Ben swipes the blood with his thumb. 'I'm okay.'

'Your call.' Arnott shrugs and sighs. 'Anyway, Chuck wasn't in his office. Wasn't in his trailer, neither. I talked to him months ago to line up all the paperwork. Wanted to do it right, not at the last minute. All those extra rush fees and taxes . . . I'm not in the habit of wasting money.' Arnott watches Tomos etch a skinny trench in the dirt with a stick.

'Chuck's gone because the project's dead,' Ben says.

'Project might be dead,' Tomos tosses his stick in the fire and leans back against a stump, 'but the bear ain't.' He gazes down the river valley, propping the rifle between his knees.

'Bear's dead, too,' Ben says.

Vito settles cross-legged near his father, wringing his hands against his knees.

Whistling a single note, long and low, Arnott glares at Tomos. 'It'd be a shame . . . a downright fucking shame, if that was the case. I heard the old brute was as big as a car. Me and my boy were dying to see the last bear.'

'Bullshit,' Tomos mutters. 'The Boss ain't dead.'

'I haven't seen anything to make me believe otherwise,' Arnott says, and he looks around as if waiting for the animal to appear. Turning with a pantomime's subtlety to address his son, he asks, 'Have you seen any sign of the beast?'

'No, sir,' Vito says, his attention locked on his own fingers, clamping and unclamping.

'How about you?' Arnott tosses a twig at Tomos. 'You seen any bears?'

'It ain't dead.' Tomos flicks the twig from his pants.

Arnott contemplates Ben, working to judge him a liar. Ben remains unflinching.

The first bubbles tremble through the coffee.

'Maybe Ranger Ben is right, but I hope not.' Arnott scowls and exhales a sharp blast through his nose. He smacks his thighs. 'Well, shit. Now I'm all broke up. It'd be an awful thing for The Boss to pass on and be rotting away somewhere, unadmired by his fans. I got to see a white rhino, would have loved to see the bear.'

'A shame,' Ben agrees.

Arnott screws his lips to the side as he stares at Ben, the wad of chaw forming a bump in his cheek. A thread of steam curls across the coffee's surface. Then, breaking his trance, Arnott tugs the sleeve of his jacket over his hand and hooks the pot handle. 'The trick with campfire coffee is to get it just before it boils. Otherwise, it burns and becomes all acid and bitter. Kind of like my marriage.' Arnott cackles and elbows Vito.

Vito shifts away.

Arnott raises the pot and asks, 'Care for a cup?'

Ben glances at Tomos.

'Tomos won't bug you,' Arnott says. 'He's on a tight leash.'

'Don't think that was ever the case,' Ben says.

Tomos snorts.

'I know Tomos. Even the dirty bits.' Arnott pours coffee while he speaks. 'It's a special kind of low, a sworn protector of the wilds poaching to sell meat, and getting kicked for it.'

'Never did,' Tomos mutters.

'Had a breeding pair until Tomos's bear disappeared,' Ben says. 'Then pieces of it turned up at some fetish market—'

'Never did,' Tomos repeats, louder this time.

'Powdered gall bladder and rare meat grabs some good coin,' Ben says.

Tomos reaches for his rifle. 'I didn't—'

'Easy there,' Arnott commands, holding a cup out for Tomos. 'Take this.'

Tomos glares unblinkingly at a point on the opposite side of the ravine. His jaw muscle twitches. He takes the coffee and settles back against the tree, resting the cup on the ground next to his rifle.

'You got kicked though,' Arnott says pointedly. 'That's a fact, isn't it? And it weren't for nothing. Whether you poached or not . . . but a man can be redeemed. No, that's not right. A man can redeem himself. A little shame can be a good thing. Ain't a reason to polish up until there's a little tarnish on the finish. It gives a reason to be, gives life a purpose.'

Arnott offers a mug to Ben, 'Anyhow, if he wants to keep his ride, he'll behave.'

Ben takes the mug with a nod of thanks, repeating, 'A special kind of low, indeed.'

'Why do you still bother with the bear?' Tomos sneers. 'It'd kill you if you got close. Meat's not that good. Can't really do anything with it.'

'You used to think it was important.' Ben blows across the surface of his coffee. 'You used to think it was worth more than what you could sell it for. Didn't you, Tomos?'

Tomos stares at the water far below.

Ben shakes his head and takes a sip from his mug. 'Maybe this one's worth enough to buy a ride from Harbron Trucking & Transport? Is that how much it's worth? Did you get a free hat thrown in, too?'

Arnott flicks the bill of his cap and gives Ben a grin and a wink.

Vito keeps his eyes fixed on his coffee. His knuckles are white, clutching the cup.

'The fuck you know?' Tomos threatens to stand again. 'Everyone's gonna do what they need to.'

'Sit,' Arnott barks.

Vito flinches.

Tomos freezes, then settles back down to sullenly staring over the cliff edge. Below, pale grey water slips past, cold and fast.

'The Boss.' Ben takes a sip of coffee. 'I never called him by any name.'

He pauses and gauges the men, all silent, all intent upon him, even Vito.

Ben continues, 'Bears need a big range, lots of food. Not much left of either. That's why the bear stuck to this valley. It's comparatively untouched. He was hungry though. Drought summers and short winters make for hard scrounging.'

He looks from one man to the next. 'Well, it's a story we all know, no rain and no runoff. Seems the bear's fate was linked to ours. With the crop failures again, the rail's been running extra loads, something like a dozen trains a day now to keep the city fed. Trains spill the stuff they carry. The bear was eating grain off the tracks, up near the dam. He got hit by the next train that came along.' Ben contemplates his coffee for a moment. 'And that's how the last bear died.'

Ben purses his lips and nods. 'I mean, how can you not hear a train coming?' Ben shakes his head and stares into the dark swirl of his coffee. 'Poor bastard wasn't meant for this world.'

'Sometimes we can't see danger until it's right on top of us, even when it's as big and loud as a train.' Arnott says with a smile. 'And to think, we walked right over those very rails, right over a spot of history, the place where The Boss died. We didn't even know it.'

'History's got to happen somewhere,' Ben says. 'Then it just disappears.'

Arnott stirs the ashes. 'We parked near you at the dam. Yours is the shitty old truck at the far end?'

'That's mine.'

'Didn't see Emma's truck anywhere,' Tomos interjects.

'Be surprised if you did,' Ben says.

'That so?' Tomos sneers. 'And where's she at?'

'She's far north, doing a fish count. Don't know if you've noticed, but we're a bit short-staffed.'

'Boys, boys.' Arnott swats a plume of smoke away from his face, swivelling from one of them to the other. 'Settle down. All of this leaves one question. I've fronted a lot of money to get us out here to see the bear. Now I hear it's dead. As I mentioned, I'm not in the habit of wasting money. So, what are me and Vito supposed to do?'

'He's lying,' Tomos says.

'If you want, you could go shoot scavenger birds.' Ben tilts his cup in the direction of their rifles. 'Won't be much left of them with that firepower though. I saw four or five crows up the valley this morning . . . if you want.' He takes a sip of coffee and frowns. It's actually pretty good. 'I don't mean to spoil your safari or anything, but I'm telling you what I know.'

A muffled beep sounds from within Ben's backpack.

Tomos's gaze jerks to the pack. His coffee spills. His fingers curl around his rifle's stock.

Vito turns slowly from Tomos to his father, confusion pinching his brow.

Arnott drums his fingers against his thighs. He grunts and cocks his head at Ben.

The embers crackle.

The tracker chirps again.

Tomos rolls to his side, bringing his rifle to bear. A deafening crack is simultaneous with an explosion of earth near his shoulder. Tomos clamps his eyes shut against the pelting dirt.

Ben draws the bolt back and slides it into place again, sprinting away from the fire before the spent casing has even landed on the moss. He staggers under the weight of his pack, his legs leaden when he needs them to be fleet. It feels like he can't run fast enough. In his mind, Tomos's rifle draws a fatal line to a spot between his shoulder blades.

A percussive smack scatters Ben's thoughts further. A tree trunk splinters, showering him in debris. He stumbles behind the massive vertical root mat of a windthrow, cringing as wood fragments strafe him.

Ben lands heavily on his side, knocking the air from his lungs. Scrambling back against the earthen mound, sucking deep breaths, his keening ears struggle for a hint of the three men's whereabouts. He clutches his rifle, spinning left, then right, both wanting and fearing one of them to step around the verge of his cover. Blood trails freely from the cut across his hand, painting his rifle's wooden guard a slick maroon.

A section of the root mat explodes.

Ben falls to the side, blinded, protecting his face with his good arm as gravel and clods of earth shower him.

Shouting materializes from the chaos.

'Tomos. Stop.' It's Arnott. 'Stop.'

Ben lowers his hand. He blinks the grit from his eyelashes and flexes his jaw, trying to work the sound back into the air through the high-pitched whine. Dust drifts through a hole in the root mat the diameter of his fist, particles swirling in a sluggish murmuration. Something flashes past the hole, momentarily blocking the sunlight. Ben clenches his injured palm to his rifle and pulls it tight against his chest.

'Ranger Ben,' Arnott is calling.

Ben remains silent. He doesn't know for how long. He keeps down. His wits returning, he tests his hand. The bandage makes a sticky noise when he unfurls his fingers. Blood streams down his wrist and darkens the cuff of his jacket. Drops fall to the soil and tint it black.

Ben clasps his fingers tight around the rifle again.

He wills his breath slower.

The men are talking somewhere on the other side of his cover.

'. . . fucking idiot. If you've killed Ranger Ben, Tomos,' Arnott shouts, 'I swear, I'll put you in the river and hold you under myself.'

A breeze stirs the high pine boughs; a gentle green sweeps against clear blue.

Ben licks his lips, the chalky feel of dirt, the musty taste of it. His ragged breathing slows and his eyes dart from one side of the berm to the other.

Then, the stillness bullies Ben's thoughts to align. Quiet now, they could be anywhere. He strains to hear them: the shush of their clothes, the snap of a twig, the crackle of dry leaves underfoot.

Ben exhales slowly and rolls onto his stomach. He props himself up enough to peer through the new hole blasted in the root mat. In the distance, past the tree trunks and flickering leaves of the underbrush, shines the expanse of the open river valley. He closes his eyes and pictures the steely water churning below.

Threads of smoke braid up from the lonely fire near the ravine edge. The coffee pot lies on its side. No guns are left propped against the backpacks. Ben shifts and spots a rifle barrel angling from behind one of the thicker tree trunks by the fire. Movement catches his attention in the direction of the ravine. The silhouette of a head pops above the rim and then disappears again.

One is hiding behind the tree and one has found a perch on the cliff edge.

Ben searches for the third man.

'Ranger Ben,' Arnott calls again. The barrel jutting from behind the tree shifts.

Ben pushes off the ground and crouches.

'Ranger Ben, I know you're there,' Arnott says. He sounds amused. 'There's hardly any other place for you to be, really.'

Ben shuffles and peers around his cover, desperate to spot the third man, fearful it is Tomos he has lost track of.

'Fine. Just listen then,' Arnott calls. 'I've been thinking. It's probably apparent that we would like to acquire your tracker.

You see, Tomos was stripped of his when he was . . . retrenched. Keeping them analogue was smart. The range sucks and the encoded signal shifts. It's brilliantly old tech. If it was done through the satellites, we wouldn't be having this chat. But here we are.'

Ben scans his flank, willing Arnott to shut up. It is Tomos he's lost track of. The boy is the one perched over the edge, he's sure. Arnott's chatter camouflages any other sounds. Everything seems to be moving, shadows and light, branches and brush swaying. The sparse understory is a boon and a burden now, nothing for Tomos to hide behind, and nothing to mask his own escape.

And still Arnott talks. 'So, the question is, what do you want? Would you like . . . money? A shiny new truck? A nice cabin in the woods? A seat on a shuttle? I can line up one next to your buddy Tomos, if you'd like. I'll even throw in a hat.'

Ben tries tracing a number of routes away from the ravine. A larger tree trunk here, a low bush there, and then a wide-open space. They all end in the open, a short distance from where he crouches. Additionally, every path leads uphill, which would slow his pace. It will be too easy to put a bullet in him, no matter which direction he goes.

He curses under his breath and turns back to face the river valley. The little fire is dying out.

When Arnott leans out from the tree, Ben hunkers back behind cover.

'Ah,' Arnott says. 'You are still there. Think about it, Ranger Ben. It's a grand offer. Like from a genie in a bottle, whatever you desire.'

Ben scowls in the silence that follows. His pulse throbs tightly in his temples. He peeks around the edge of his shelter and sees Arnott still leaning out from behind his, his outline distinct against the bright daylight behind.

'I was giving you time to consider.' Arnott laughs. 'We could take the tracker from you, but I'm not sure it'd be as easy as us coming to an agreement. I'm familiar with men of your training. Tomos is one, after all. He did train you, didn't he? You never did answer that and the man prattles on, so I tend to tune him out.'

The tracker beeps again and Ben squats, whispering, 'Shit.'

He doesn't want to risk removing his pack to shut it off.

'Sounds like The Boss is alive and well . . . and close,' Arnott says. 'What's the range on those things? Six, seven kilometres? Probably less in this terrain. It's exciting to be so close to him.'

'I'm gonna go now.' Ben struggles into a crouch, fumbling under the weight of the pack to remain below the edge of the windthrow.

'No, you're not,' Arnott says.

Ben draws an unsteady breath and lets it go. 'I want to go.' His voice cracks and he grits his teeth to quell the tremors running through him.

'I imagine that's true,' Arnott says. 'And I want that tracker. You want something. I want something. So, I think we can figure this out.'

Ben grips his rifle closer and looks upslope.

It feels like his teeth might shatter.

'Come on, Ranger Ben.' Arnott's voice loses its friendly tone.

'It seems pretty straightforward to me. You give me the tracker then you head upstream to the dam, get in your shitty truck, and rattle on down the road.'

Ben inches sideways, to the root fringe jutting out like splayed fingers. Through them, he sees Arnott leaning against the tree, picking at the bark with his thumbnail. Ben tries to spot Vito, but there is no more motion along the ledge.

Ben calls, 'Then what?'

Arnott's arm drops to his side. His shoulders slump. The outline of him, spying Ben through the roots, ducks back behind cover. Ben slumps back too, scanning the trees, desperate for a safe path away from the camp.

'I don't care,' Arnott calls. 'Then you do whatever you want.'

'No, I meant, then what do you do?'

A flicker of motion from deeper in the woods catches Ben's attention. Tomos has flanked his hiding spot. Ben drops flat to the ground. The gunshot cracks across the valley and bounces back again.

With the sole drive to put cover between him and Tomos, Ben scrambles to his feet and rounds the windthrow, exposed now to Vito and Arnott, but gambling on them being less keen to shoot him than Tomos is. Another shot, quieter from this side of cover, ends with a thud and the rattle of falling rocks and gravel from the windthrow.

Ben raises his rifle toward Arnott's face, peering from around the tree. Their eyes lock, then Arnott spits and retreats behind the trunk. Ben's finger eases away from the trigger.

The commotion of breaking branches and heavy footfalls

marks Tomos's approach from behind, though Ben can't see how close he is because of the wall of roots and earth between them.

Ben slings his rifle across his shoulders and pushes off the downed tree. He sprints toward Arnott and Vito, toward the ravine edge. His body feels uncoordinated from the shock of being shot at; his legs feel sluggish, stumbling, but his mind remains focused on his only way out.

Arnott's confused expression flashes by as Ben passes the tree he hides behind. Two more steps and Ben leaps, catching sight of Vito lying on a narrow ledge, just below the valley rim. The young man's eyes are wide, his mouth a dark circle.

The report of another shot and Ben folds from the punch of a bullet.

'I got him,' Tomos shouts.

Ben twists in the air, his legs writhing, trying to right himself.

The grey water is overhead.

A shock of sunlight strikes his boots, and beyond them, the sky is the most beautiful shade of blue he can remember seeing.

He imagines the birds, how lucky they are to live in that colour.

The whistle of the wind passes, then everywhere, water so cold it wrenches the breath from his lungs and won't give it back.

5

The gurgling wash of water drowns out all other sound. Ben's hearing is briefly freed to a glittering swell of birdsong, but that can't be, these woods have been quiet for so long, even if for a second it seems real. Liquid confusion regains its hold, punctuated by the muted click of stones colliding on the river bottom, off to one side, then behind him, and then lost to the burble-churn of rapids.

There is no air.

Murky cruciform shapes swim, fish, fighting hard against invisible currents just to remain in place under a river-rock sky. Direction no longer exists, though the sensation of spinning implies that it must still, somehow.

The water runs fresh off a glacier, an ice-age chill released after a hundred-thousand-year entrapment. It had last threaded as a snaking line of snow, hitching a howling wind from the polar midday black and travelling uninterrupted for half a continent, before settling to compress and wait. Centuries pass as seconds. The entire planet shifts and tilts and wobbles before it is freed again. The past becomes present. It remains numbingly cold.

There is no air.

Then a thin gasp.

The scent of soil rises, thick and good and everywhere.

Muted thunder tumbles past. A slab of cloud bumps against a prickly slope of trees, so big it takes up the entire sky. Its underbelly is dark and draped with a tinsel of rainfall, all casting a moody light onto the land below. Speckles of rain tap leaves. Slow and distinct at first, the initial patter grows and melds into a rush. Thunder trails a nova of lightning.

A pixelated blur of colour resolves . . . wildflowers, a meadow full of tiny wildflowers. Yellow, white, red, violet, their vibrancy greyed by mist. Pale green leaves tremble in the downpour.

Sound is cut short by the snort and grunt of a beast. It isn't a threat, simply a clearing of his throat. Even so, the potential for violence sparked by that sound wakes a genetic memory in all creatures within earshot and they become alert.

Remain meek in his presence, the sound warns. Be ready, it says.

The smell of the beast comes, wild and pungent and close. Draped in leaves, only his eyes are visible at first; set wide across a broad muzzle, the feathered brown irises dilating at the sight of another being. He's been alone for so long. He's not scared. With his size, he's never had a use for fear. His adrenaline is meant for hunting, fighting, breeding, never for being prey. His eyes are more curious than cautious. He comes into view, muscle moving under thick fur.

The whine of a mosquito.

The flick of an ear.

Ben looks sideways at Emma, from where they've been watching the bear from across the meadow in awed paralysis. Sensing Ben's attention, Emma smiles but can't take her eyes off the bear. Rain drips from a curl that has escaped the hood of her raincoat. She gently pulls aside a branch to get a better view; a shower of silver droplets tumbles from the leaves.

They watch together and neither talks about it afterwards; neither can put into words what being so close to the creature for the first time has stirred. They don't need to. They both understand how this encounter will stay.

Ben blinks. Something tugs at his thoughts, something important and urgent, but he's too shaken to grab it.

There's sand against his cheek, broken rock with a pink granule of plastic in it. Cold, smooth baubles press under Ben's palms. The taste of earth, the grit of it between his teeth. Delicate water laps against his skin.

The water is farther away, now. An eddy swirls, tethered at the end of his gaze. The space between is filled by a shallow clearing and a ribbon of stony beach, which he vaguely remembers struggling across, to here.

Where is here? Ben scowls.

He sits on a rough-skinned log. The curved finger of a soggy cigarette arcs from between his lips, the end pointed at the ground between his ankles. He raises his lighter, clicks it to hear the butane hiss of the invisible flame. The end of the cigarette blackens and smoulders, but it won't catch. With another click, the flame is off, leaving only the murmur of the eddy behind.

Ben lowers the lighter from the end of his cigarette. He tweezes the filter from between his lips, and rests the cigarette on the log beside him, next to the battered packet. Flipping the top open, he lays the soaked cigarettes out in a line to dry on the log. Those which are pulped, he brushes away. He counts eight left.

Ben's body feels weightless. He vaguely registers that the backpack no longer tugs on his shoulders. It's a relief, to shed that burden of the last thirty-one days, the eternity of a month. Scanning the clearing, he spots the pack lying on its side, halfhidden by a bush.

Resting elbows on his knees, fingers intertwined, he casts a smile at the ground between his feet. A breeze ambles by, heading downriver. It feels colder than it should. Ben examines the branching pattern of orange lichen covering a stone near his boot, a little forest-scape of its own. All is cast in a zebra-light angling through the trees.

He chews his lip, puzzled. His boots are wet; one of his laces is untied. Over the murmur of slow water comes a rhythmic noise, a pat, pat, pat. Movement catches his eye. The orange lichen is turning glossy purple. Ben sits back and holds his hands out before him. For the first time, he registers how they tremble. His nails are pale grey with cold. One of his palms is speckled with bark fragments, the other weeps blood from a jagged gash.

A muted beep emanates from his pack.

The world rushes back with the ghost roar of a gunshot.

Ben wheezes as pain lances his side. He grabs it with his wounded hand. The insulation of his jacket is flayed. He can't breathe. He stands and tears his jacket off. It lands with a soppy noise and Ben claws at the ballistic vest underneath, grappling with the straps, crying out as he tries to lift it over his head. His body can't move like that. He hinges forward and shucks the vest. The air against his skin sears now that the wet clothes have been shed. Numb fingers fumble at the loop of his belt, the buttons of his pants, while he kicks off his boots.

Exposed to the sun, Ben begins to shiver uncontrollably. He holds the pain in his side, feels a massive, solid welt just below his rib cage. A thread of blood strikes a dazzling contrast against his skin. Panting in shallow breaths, Ben doubles over, stars swirling in his vision. He wobbles and falls to the side, the jolt renewing the ache when he thought it couldn't get any worse. Paralyzed, he waits for the wash to fade, which it does, slowly, his body recalibrating to what a tolerable amount of suffering is.

Use your fucking head, Ben scolds himself. Then two thoughts surface through his swirling disbelief. They're trying to kill you. You have to get out.

In a clutch of pain, he figures he's come ashore on the opposite bank from where he'd jumped. He frantically surveys the area for the men, listens for their voices from the riverside, looks for a backlit silhouette in the feathered line of pine trees atop the far ridge, pointing a rifle down at him.

But he's alone.

There aren't even birds circling in the blue.

They're trying to kill you. You have to get out.

The rifle, Ben thinks and arches to the side. He scans the clearing through a film of tears, taking quivering shallow breaths. The rifle is nowhere.

Trying to recall what happened after he hit the water, Ben struggles to stand. His body is made foreign by pain; movements that were thoughtless before now send him into paroxysms. Frantic, he stumbles across the clearing and rights his backpack. The rifle lies pressed into the moss underneath.

Ben kneels and eases his hand from his side. The skin beneath is swollen taut, pulverized black and purple, with a vicious map-work of bruising encircling the middle. He swipes blood away, leaving behind fresh streaks. Confused, there's no broken skin, he swipes again.

The blood is from the reinvigorated wound on his palm. He makes a fist to stem the flow. The fingers of his other hand fumble, dumb with cold, but eventually manage to open his pack. He dumps the contents. With his teeth, he frees a Mylar blanket from its wrapping and drapes it over his shoulders.

The first-aid kit holds a variety of painkillers. He dry-swallows two of the codeine tablets, then eases his injured hand open and pours antiseptic over the ragged wound. The searing sting focuses his mind. He twists the cap off another vial and runs a plastic applicator along the flap of skin. The glue sets quickly and holds. He wraps a new bandage around his wound and flexes his fingers.

A branch snaps nearby.

A spike of adrenaline erases all pain. The emergency blanket hisses as Ben crouches low and waits, desperate to catch movement through the trees. He wraps the fingers of his good hand around the rifle and draws it closer. No one leaps from the bushes.

Foolish, Ben scolds himself. Use your fucking head.

There's no way they'd have caught up yet, he reasons. The closest crossing is at The Pinch, better than a half day back upstream. And only a fool would willingly follow the course he had taken, the river too savage for anyone except the most suicidal pursuer. If they're even coming.

The tracker beeps.

Ben looks at the device. The screen is shattered. He finds a weather-wrapped bundle of clothes in his scattered belongings and pulls the seal strip. His body seizes when he works his arms through the shirt. The ache becomes less acute, the pills creating a floating sensation behind his eyes.

With dry clothes on, warmth ebbs back in by fractions. The shivering eases. He finds he can think more clearly. Occasionally, an unexpected flush passes over him, leaving his skin clammy and his pulse racing. With the pain dulled, his mind is better able to grapple with what happened.

Ben grabs the transmitter and shakes water from the speaker. 'Emma, come back.'

Only a faint hiss of static responds. Ben twists the frequency dial.

'Chuck, you there?'

A shadow has crept over him, the mountain peak behind the clearing blocking the sun. Ben rubs his bare wrist while scanning the pebble shore, resigning his watch to the river when he doesn't spot it.

He looks up the steep valley walls and clicks the transmitter button, three short, three long, three short, and then drops it onto his pack.

The shade has reached the far side of the water. With a skyward glance, Ben figures there is probably a good four or five hours of daylight left. He gathers the cigarettes from the log and returns them to the packet, one by one, while scanning for the hunters.

Eight smokes left; the thought floats through the early currents of the painkillers.

Standing straight is easier than before. Barefoot, he hobbles across the uneven ground to the water's edge, thinking that at least there is feeling in his feet again. The water slips past, entrancing, until the tracker beeps again.

The Boss, they'd called him.

Upstream, behind a frothing heave of rapids, is a sharp bend in the river. The rapids are silent from Ben's vantage. He scowls, trying to place which ones they are. Pale Queen or Quick Fish, he can't tell. The valley widens to the south and the river runs in a shrinking furrow toward a distant purple peak.

They're Quick Fish Rapids, Ben decides, recognizing the eddy the bear had been fishing at almost a week ago. He crouches back into the brush, his eyes darting from the pebble stripe that lines the opposite bank to the ledge of the valley wall rising vertically behind it. No one watches him. He's definitely on the opposite bank from where he jumped, but he figures he hasn't drifted too far from the hunters.

Ben returns to his pack, a plan formulating. His truck is at the dam, a two-day hike upstream. He'll hike through the night. If he makes it to the dam by the following evening, he'll chase his headlights through the twisting maze of logging roads all the way back to the highway, then on through the early morning. He'll contact Emma, tell her to meet him back at the trailer. They will figure out something; they'll be safe with each other.

Ben sighs, knowing it's a panicked plan, a bad one, but it's hard to think straight. They tried to kill him.

The bear will be fine on his own, Ben reasons. Or he won't. The chances of them locating him are slim, even with Tomos as a guide. Without a tracker to sniff out his microchip, they won't find him . . . they probably won't find him.

Take only what is necessary, he thinks. He throws all his spare clothes into a pile and kicks it under a bush. Between glances at the ridge opposite, he reassembles the first-aid kit and zips it closed, placing it back into the pack. Picking six meals from his remaining rations, he tosses the leftover packets onto the discarded pile of clothes. He plugs the transmitter into the solar cells and slides the handset back into its compartment. From the top pouch, he draws a multitool and four clips of ammunition, which he taps against his leg to drain the water. These he places into the thigh pocket of his pants, along with his notebook.

Ben pauses, holding the paperback Poppy had lent him. Its swollen pages are warped, and it feels twice as thick as when he last held it. He carefully stows it in the pack and drags the load back to the log he'd sat upon.

He prods his side gently. The discomfort is still there, but it's different, with softer edges. The effect of the pills will last three or four hours. There are twenty-eight more in the vial, plenty to make it through the hike home.

The vest still lies where it'd been shed. He drapes it inside out over the log. The bullet punched through the laminate plate, a few millimetres of the tip protruding from the underside. With trembling fingers, he wiggles the bullet out of the tufted fabric. The metal slug is dense and distorted. Ben drops it into his pocket and dons the wet vest over his dry shirt. Cold quickly seeps through.

Ben picks up the tracker and frowns at it. It beeps, the cracked display unable to relay distance or direction. He flips the unit over; the broken screen is the only apparent damage. It is the last concrete link to the bear, the thing the hunters are willing to kill him over. The creature will be better off without it. Alone again, with only a tiny piece of hardware under his skin as a souvenir of his brush with humanity.

A few steps away, Ben balances the tracker on a boulder. He picks up a fist-sized rock and raises it. But the bear won't be alone again, he thinks, not with the hunters out here. Ben lowers the rock. The tracker may still be of use. As long as he holds it, the hunters are more likely to follow him, and he could lead them away on his flight back to the dam, give the animal more of a chance to remain alone.

Ben spins the volume dial until it clicks off.

With one last look around the area for any obvious traces that he'd been there, Ben hoists the straps over his shoulders and starts upstream, back in the direction he encountered the hunters, the direction of the dam. Though it would be easier to follow the water's edge, he picks a path through the trees instead, scared of being spotted when he passes Arnott, Vito, and Tomos.

The wild ground is unkind to his progress, and his pain is unpredictable. A misstep sometimes sends a fresh spark through him, other times not. Moving in ways he suspects will hurt often doesn't, and other times a seizure of agony clutches him from out of nowhere.

In the spaces between the trees and the pain, the pills do their work and his mind floats. Tomos's voice murmurs in the distant hum of memory.

'She says you'd be perfect for this,' Tomos said two years ago, after a guest lecture he'd given.

Ben followed his gaze up the sweep of the theatre from the stage. The seats were mostly empty, except for a few students milling about under the fluorescent lights. There weren't many majoring in environmental sciences: most took engineering or physics or mathematics, anything that could help them get a better shot of working the deep colonies.

Ben had enrolled though; people weren't meant to live out there, so here is what needed to be fixed, if it could be.

'She's already on board and suggested I talk to you, too.' Tomos paused, his attention locked elsewhere.

Ben spotted Emma in the small cluster of students, whispering to a classmate, watching Tomos and Ben back, but trying to appear as if she wasn't. Ben gave her a slight nod and returned her smile.

Tomos leaned closer and spoke more quietly, 'You should talk to Chuck.'

In answer to Ben's questioning expression, he held out a business card. 'Chuck's got funding for something he's calling the Ursa Project. He's looking to recruit two students, probably because the funding's weak and he can pay you next to nothing.' Tomos laughed, so did Ben, though he wasn't sure why.

He also wasn't sure why he'd be perfect. Academically, there were better students, but he'd thanked Emma. Jobs were scarce and most of those students on the far side of the hall would be unemployed in a year, saddled with debt that had an unmanageable interest rate tagged on top.

Ben did call Chuck. The employment contract had been a stack of pages coated in a tiny font, which Ben only partially read. It didn't matter. There were no other options and he wanted to meet the bear, protect him. And this way, he and Emma could stay together.

It had only been the two of them in the three weeks of training. They'd followed Tomos on a trip into the wilds, and learned some survival skills, some tracking skills, practiced shooting the Colt until they could do it well enough to hit a decently sized target at mid-range. Tomos taught them through castigation and shame, under the persistent refrain of, 'What are you thinking? Use your fucking head.'

Then, he and Emma were given their paperwork and sent into the bush on their own to enact the vision of Chuck's project: find the bear and follow it, engage poachers, record its activities for posterity, and ensure the lonely creature lived out its natural life with the grace intended by nature.

Tomos's training hadn't really prepared them for combat. The rangers' presence was a well-intentioned whim of a desk jockey, meant more as a deterrent than an active force. Over time, their duties multiplied, fish counts and amphibian surveys, the work became an unending count of waning population numbers, their logbooks filling with notes on a retreating natural world. Chuck had to step in some days, just so Ben and Emma could rest.

By the time Ben reaches Quick Fish Rapids, there is only a sliver of sunlight left on the upper peaks. He stops on the outside curve of the rapids, where the land runs out. There is no river-bank here, just a crumble of massive boulders that has been eroded from the rock face above. The edge is too high to climb, the wall too sheer.

Ben hops to the first boulder and, crouching low, scrambles to the next. Dark water surges and froths through the gaps between. The next boulder is slick and his foot slides out, knocking him to all fours. His fingers scrabble with a sharp ledge to keep him out of the water. He pauses to breathe through the pain. With gritted teeth, he hops to the next two boulders more recklessly, to speed his feet onto firm riverbank again.

Sweat soaks his clothes and he struggles for breath. He wades through a tangle of alder lining the shore and then wipes his brow. As he moves further from the rapids, the river sounds fade enough for him to hear the voices trickling in from underneath.

6

Ben lowers himself onto the moss. The voices are too distant for him to make out words, only sounds. Shadows obscure the surrounding tangle of spruce, agitating his sense of claustrophobia. A thick line of willow and alder borders the river, impenetrable. His gaze is drawn to a nearby rustling, what proves to be an errant twirl of wind.

Ben slips the rifle from his shoulders, ducking under the strap as he repositions himself. The soreness in his side protests.

They've come looking, he thinks. They want the tracker.

Ben crawls into the dense brush lining the river, through to where a gap in the branches affords a view across. He brings the rifle to bear. Moss soaks his jacket sleeves, first through the elbows, then the forearms. The musty smell of damp earth fills his nose. Water burbles in a gentle eddy at land's edge.

Voices come again, with a breeze; a disorienting echo sounds from behind Ben, prompting him to glance over his shoulder to ensure he hasn't been flanked. He holds his breath to hear. For a while, there is only the water, the whisper of swaying trees.

Ben waits long enough to wonder whether the sounds are just from paranoia. His injured hand goes numb from gripping the forestock.

Then the voices, from across the water and drawing nearer.

'See anything?' Arnott shouts.

'Nothing,' comes a reply from above.

Ben cranes and spots movement on the opposite high terrace. Through the scope, he watches the boy, Vito, picking his way between the pines. He pauses at every vantage he finds, peering over the edge, once raising a flat hand over his brow to block the low-angled sun, once wrapping an arm around a tree and leaning out, seeming to stare directly at Ben, but then continuing downriver.

Ben draws back from the scope and releases a breath he'd unknowingly trapped.

Vito disappears for a few moments and reappears farther away.

Ben lowers the barrel, slowly tracking a line back down to the opposite bank, and pivoting it to the sound of someone struggling through the vegetation. The tangle of foliage sways and shakes. Eventually, Arnott steps onto the thin stripe of pebbled riverbank, his weapon slung over his shoulder. Swiping leaves from his hair, Arnott leans to the side and spits into the water. His lip bulges as he tongues a wad of chewing tobacco back into place. He plants his hands on his hips and contemplates the water.

'Current's too fast,' he says with a flick of his wrist. 'Could've carried him kilometres away by now.'

The bushes behind Arnott begin to sway again, the source of the disturbance heading for the narrow clearing.

Arnott arches back to scan the upper ledge, then waves when he spots Vito. Tomos emerges from the verdure, rifle clutched across his chest, barrel angling at the ground. A scowl pinches his features.

'We're wasting our time.' Arnott glares at Tomos, then squats and fingers through a few stones before selecting one. 'Ranger Ben seemed set on being unhelpful . . . and then you had to go and shoot at him. One way or another, the tracker's lost.'

Tomos raises his rifle and adjusts the scope, scanning the bend at the rapids ahead.

'No point.' Arnott shakes his head and stands. 'He's long gone.'

Arnott skips a stone across the water. It rustles into the bushes near Ben.

'Look at that.' Arnott laughs and points. 'Made it all the way across.'

Tomos doesn't take his eye from the scope. 'The river's got to dump him somewhere.'

Arnott kicks at the rocks. They clatter. A few splash into the water.

'You're sure you hit him?'

'I hit him.' Tomos lowers the scope and brushes past Arnott.

Arnott glowers after him, spits again, and follows.

'We'll check around that bend,' Arnott says, 'then we're turning around and heading back upriver to find The Boss. I didn't come out here to dredge some poor fucker's corpse from the water.'

'We find Ben's body and we'll find the tracker. Then we can just walk up to the bear.'

'You think the thing could survive getting shot, falling off a cliff, and being drowned?' The scepticism in Arnott's voice is sharp. He stops, and shaking his head, contemplates the distant frothy rapids. 'We didn't come out here to hunt a ranger. For fuck's sake, Tomos, my kid's here. We came out here to see the bear, to stalk it, own it . . . and now? You really fucked up.'

'Those units are sturdy,' Tomos says, reaching the end of the clearing and elbowing his way back into the thicket. 'It wouldn't survive a bullet, but a fall and a swim, sure.'

'Right,' Arnott calls after him. 'Here's the thing, back there, when we met up, we had been moving upriver with no sign of the bear. Then we find Ranger Ben, and his tracker beeps . . .'

The bushes waver as Tomos moves away.

Arnott leans forward and yells, 'Which means the bear is back the way we came, upriver from here.' He points. 'Behind us.'

Arnott contemplates the vegetation where Tomos disappeared.

'You hear me?' Arnott barks. 'We're going the wrong way.'

Arnott peers at the high terrace again. He waves his arms in broad arcs, waiting for Vito to spot him. The silhouette waves back.

'Wait around the bend,' Arnott hollers with his hands cupped on either side of his mouth. He heaves an exaggerated thumb over his shoulder. 'We'll find a way up to you. Then we're heading back upriver.'

His echo fades and is punctuated with a distant reply, 'Okay.'

Arnott looks up and down the valley again, mutters to himself, before following Tomos's path into the bush.

Ben waits, listening to their voices fade into silence. The eddy laps against the bank. Ben stretches his arm and flexes feeling back into his hand. The sunlight slips from the upper terrace.

Eventually, he pushes back to sit on his heels, his rifle resting across his lap.

They'll be heading this way again before nightfall, Ben thinks.

He doubts they will travel through the night; the ground is too dangerous, and they don't seem to have any urgency. There are a few calmer stretches of the river they could swim across, sure, but with the amount of gear they'd need to keep dry, and the fact they think he's dead, it's unlikely they'd bother. They'll make their way back upstream soon, toward The Pinch, toward the bear.

Ben looks at the fading sky and figures he can still make it to Poppy Freedom's cabin before it gets fully dark. He'll warn her these men are loose in the valley, then push on.

He's never come at the cabin from this side before, but is certain it can't be more than a few hours' walk away. Even if it winds up being more, he'll walk in the dark. It'll be slow, he can't risk a headlamp, but he has to get past the bridge at The Pinch before Tomos leads his group across it in the morning. After that, it'll be less than a day's hard hike to the dam, and his truck.

On the far bank, there's no hint left of the men's passing. With a glance up to check that his path is still clear, Ben struggles out from under his pack. He scoops a mouthful of water and pops two more painkillers, before repacking and clambering back to his feet.

The pack feels heavier than ever. Ben's exhausted muscles resist moving; the brief reprieve has made his body into a stiff, stubborn beast. He sets off once more, determined not to waste the meagre head start he has over the hunters.

The terrain grows easier, a gentle incline rising away from the water. The noise of the river wanes to the silence of the forest. The breeze that travelled the valley throughout the day has abated. The injuries that had settled into Ben's muscles loosen again with the movement.

Dense spruce gives way to more open woods. Most of the pine trees have red needles and mangy patches in their bark, exposing dead blond wood underneath. The beetle has been through this stretch. For decades now, the warmer winters have failed to freeze out the tiny bug, and its spread is unrelenting, burrowing into the wood and sloughing a fungus off its carapace that kills the trees. It doesn't know any better, but it's left a creeping stain across the landscape as it ranges north. Now the forest waits for a fire, and in the meantime, it rains dry needles whenever the wind blows.

The light through the branches drifts away by nearly imperceptible increments. Minutes fade with it.

The pills cast Ben's attention adrift. One foot in front of the other, one after the other, the mesmerism of movement folds an hour into seconds and leaves everything lit by a bluing twilight.

Occasionally, he blinks and comes round. He elbows through a clot of underbrush. Time telescopes away again. He unhooks his thumbs from the pack's shoulder straps so he can balance while crossing a log over a seasonal outwash channel. His legs carry him through the valley, now wide enough that the surrounding mountains become a looming artefact of feeling more than an actual topography.

The tracker drifts to mind as he floats between the trees. It could easily bring any of them to the bear. Ben thinks again and again of pulling it out and smashing it against a rock, better to let The Boss be alone, but he doesn't. As long as he keeps moving, he reasons, it won't matter. The hunters will be far behind him in a day.

Ben stumbles, sending a blunt ripple of soreness through him, a fraction of what it would have been sober. It's a handy reminder that his body still exists. He scowls at his feet; whatever tripped him up gives a hollow metallic tick when he taps it with his boot. A kick at the moss exposes a dented and rusty can. Ben scoops it up and runs a thumb across the maker's stamp on the corrugated bottom. The date '1902' is still legible. This stretch of forest appears no more remarkable than any he's walked through so far, but someone was here, so many years ago.

Ben pictures a mule with bulging panniers, the leather as battered and weather-worn as the grizzled, bearded fellow sitting with his back against a nearby tree. The man digs food out of the can with a fork; gobbets are stuck in his beard. Watery eyes, surrounded by deeply etched crow's feet, squint into the spaces between the trees, like he spots someone, or he's longing to spot someone.

The mule's lead hangs, looped loose and free, but the animal doesn't leave the man's side. It's too old now, sway-backed, with a knee that occasionally buckles. The animal's rasping breaths are the only sound for a long time.

Then the man mutters.

The mule's harness creaks as it looks in his direction.

Squirrels chatter in the trees, barely heard above a layered cacophony of birdsong. Their calls are so varied, it is impossible to tell one song from the next.

The man grunts and waves a hand in front of his face, accidentally swatting the broad brim of his hat. The mule stomps its foot; its tail swishes. Both fight the impossible, trying to dissuade the buzzing mosquitoes and little black flies from landing.

The fork scrapes hollow against the bottom of the can. The man licks it clean, then licks his lips. He wipes a grease-smeared thumb across his oiled canvas pants before reaching for the mule's lead. He stands and tosses the can aside. The animal raises its head.

The can lands silently on the moss near Ben's feet, rusty and dented.

Ben leans to the side, peering into the gloaming. The forest is empty. He closes his eyes and bumps his palm against his swarming forehead.

'Fucking ghost donkey,' he mutters.

Opening his eyes again, Ben chuckles.

A few strides away, a faintly brighter line runs through the moss and underbrush. He blinks to test if it's an illusion, but the subtle trail remains. A series of timeworn blazes in the tree bark become visible along the line.

He follows the old path, a few minutes later coming across a small spring trap with its jaws splayed open. He roots a stick from the forest floor and pokes the trigger. The hinge is rusted solid. Tossing the stick aside, he hikes on. The trail passes through a thicket of blueberry bushes. The leaves have long since turned purple and give up their branches with the slightest touch.

The l[...] the path cutting toward a broad, shallow [...] e hunkers in the trees on the far bank, i[...] a geometric void in the waning light. B[...] oming across this wreck before, so he f[...] on the gully side and observe, marvel[...] l has secrets, even after years of workin[...]

It's a[...] w roof sags with a dramatic swale, seeming to defy gravity. He reckons he would have to stoop to stand inside.

Ben waits. No flickering candlelight comes through the windows. No sounds emanate from inside. The cabin sits alone and forgotten, as it likely has every night for the last hundred years. Ben lets more time lapse before sighing and struggling back to his feet. The pack is a leaden weight and Ben's legs revolt with a spasm. For the first time, he doubts he'll be able to hike through the night. This old cabin is as good a place as any to rest, and if he leaves before sunup he can still beat the hunters past The Pinch.

A dry gravelly channel weaves across the bottom of the gully. Waist-high bushes grow in the trench where water once flowed. On the upslope, Ben grows more cautious, scanning the surrounding woods as he approaches the cabin. The place seems wholly abandoned. No feet have disturbed the tall grasses growing in front of the door, which hangs askew and half open. Shreds of tarpaper hang from the roof like moulting scales. Nobody has maintained the earthen chinking between the logs, the gaps revealing solid darkness within.

Ben runs his fingers lightly over three steel traps hung from spikes hammered into the wood. These are bigger than the one on the trail. The metal parts click together; the chains are rusted stiff.

Ben tugs on the door. The planks flex and creak. It doesn't open any farther, so he hacks earth away from the base with a heel until he's able to pull it wide enough to lean through. The air is musty, warmer than outside still, with the trapped remnants of the sun. His eyes adjust slowly to a shadowy confusion of debris.

Turning back to check the forest, Ben can barely spot the trail he'd been following in the gloom. He spies no glowing headlamps through the trees, hears no distant voices breaking the stillness. He enters the cabin.

His breath, contained by four walls and a ceiling for the first time in weeks, suddenly sounds too loud and too close. Dropping his pack and rifle at the door, he pulls out his own headlamp. The cone of yellow light sweeps the rough walls, scaly patches of bark still dotting many of the logs. The remains of a crudely hewn platform, for a mattress, lie slumped in fragments along one wall. Another construction leans askew against the opposite wall, what might have once functioned as a table.

Ben rummages through a pile of debris immediately inside the door, a few jars, cracked and pearlescent with age, some tobacco cans, and another labelled 'Molasses' in simple script. In the dirt, he finds the rusted saw blade from a bow saw.

Drawing the walkie-talkie from his pack, Ben clicks the receiver on. He keeps the volume low. It is still tuned to the last channel on which he spoke with Emma. Thinking it will be easier to communicate in this wider section of the valley, he holds the mouthpiece close.

'Emma.' He whispers her name without pressing the transmit button. He sets the unit atop his pack and watches the sliver of woods that's visible through the door, listening to the quiet static.

He won't call because he doesn't want the transmission to be picked up by Tomos, even though the chance they are monitoring the right channel is slim, and the chance of the transmission getting through is even slimmer. That isn't the real reason, though, he knows. He doesn't speak to the machine again because he doesn't know what to say if Emma replies.

Nothing moves among the dark trees. Not even a branch stirs in the stillness.

Ben looks at the sodden bandage wrapped around his hand. He picks at a ragged edge of fabric.

The speaker hisses, nearly inaudible, unbroken by voices, just invisible static seeping in from everywhere in the black.

Could he explain to her? Accept her judgement? They tried to kill him. He is leaving. If the hunters find him again, they will shoot him and take the tracker. Then there'll be no more bear. He is abandoning their bear to chance and its own will. No, he thinks, this isn't leaving, this is fleeing, as a coward. He can't face telling Emma that he is giving up, at their first real challenge, and running away.

Ben turns, hunching under the low ceiling. In a few strides, he's at the back of the room. There is a stump in the corner, from a tree that was felled to clear a spot for the cabin. The stump has been squared off as a stool, and a few folded sheets of newspaper are jammed into a crack in the wood. The paper is brittle and yellowed, water-stained, and tattered. Portions of the black ink are still intact, though time-faded.

Ben sits on the stump, draws a cigarette from his breast pocket and lights it. He stares at the walkie-talkie while smoothing the newspaper over his knee, and then angles the headlamp's beam onto the page.

The banner reads 'March 22, 1902', but the paper's name is largely torn off, except for a single bold-fonted word, '—World'. With cigarette smoke clouding the light, he reads the headline. 'Earthquake destroys Tochangri, Turkey'. Ben scans the article. Below it, advertisements for 'Neva & Camille's Biscuits' and 'Map Brand Condensed Milk'. The rest of the page is missing.

Ben takes a drag and flips it over.

A noise from outside causes him to freeze.

He clicks off his headlamp and stares at the glowing ember of his cigarette as he strains to hear anything else. The smell of the smoke will be a certain giveaway, he thinks. It sounded like a branch had snapped.

His vision slowly adjusts to the darkness again. The gap in the door shows nothing but the deepening night and the bent line of a nearby tree.

Ben listens, takes his time with the three remaining draws of his cigarette before stubbing it out on the toe of his boot. The silence persists. He sets the newspaper aside and creeps to the entrance. Kneeling, holding his breath, he peers around the casing.

With a deafening roar, the top half of the door explodes.

Ben falls, pelted by a hail of splinters. He scrambles backward, groping for his rifle. The ringing in his ears and the panicked panting of his own breath shatter the silence. The rifle and his pack have been knocked aside in his retreat. Ben rakes through the debris on the floor, snagging his fingers on something sharp.

'Step on out now,' shouts a voice. 'Slow, with your hands held out.'

Ben's fingers wrap around his rifle.

The click-click of a shotgun being pumped comes from in front of the cabin.

The voice shouts, closer now, 'Do it right and I won't shoot you too much.'

Ben laughs.

7

'Poppy, don't shoot,' Ben hollers, his forearms clasped over his ears and his fingers knit behind his neck. 'It's me. It's Ben.'

Silence follows. Ben lowers his arms. Outside comes a shush of movement through the vegetation. It's impossible to tell from how close.

'Ben?' The voice creaks like it hasn't been used in a while.

'Yes.' Ben laughs. 'Thanks for the warning shot, but you damn near killed me.'

A shape passes the splintered door, darkness moving within itself, then a weathered face in a halo of curly grey hair peers around the casing. 'Warning shot? Bullshit. I was aiming for your chest.'

Ben laughs again, pushing himself upright to sit cross-legged. He looks at the woman. There is a confused expression on her face. Her eyes are tinged with concern, like she is seeing a raving madman.

Ben sobers, brushing splinters and dirt from his clothes.

'Thank Christ you're a terrible shot.' He struggles to his feet, one hand clasped to his injured side.

'Christ's got nothing to do with it,' Poppy mutters. 'I lost my glasses a few days back and now can't see for shit, let alone hit anything I'm shooting at,' she squints at the weapon in her hands, 'even with a shotgun. It's frustrating . . . and you damn well can't find your glasses when you can't see for shit without them, can you?'

Poppy grabs the door and gives it a tug. A shot-riddled plank breaks off and she drops it. 'What are you doing in there? Besides being dumb enough to almost get shot.' Poppy yanks on the door again. It creaks and rattles, but it's wedged firmly in place. 'I'd be so mad at you if I'd killed you. Get out here, Ben.'

Ben gathers his pack and rifle, and squeezes through the opening into the twilit woods, relieved to be out of the confines of the cabin. The bite of gun smoke lingers in the air, and the night seems brighter than it should be, his eyes having adjusted to the darkness inside the cabin.

Poppy stands to one side, the tips of her frizzy hair level with Ben's shoulder. Her jeans have dirty knees and tattered cuffs. A plaid flannel jacket, a few sizes too big, drapes her wiry shoulders. The shotgun's barrel rests comfortably across her forearm, the stock tucked under her armpit.

Ben returns her smile and takes her extended hand. Even though her knuckles are beginning to knot with arthritis, there's nothing frail about her handshake. The skin on her fingers and palms are thick and rough with calluses.

'It's good to see you, Ben.' Poppy releases her grip and takes a step back, screwing up her face at him. 'You look like shit.'

'Thought you couldn't see anything,' Ben says.

'That's how shitty you look.' Poppy snorts. 'Even a blind lady can see you're all raggedy.'

'You're a "lady", now?'

Poppy snorts again and swats his shoulder. Ben winces and hugs his injured side tighter. Poppy doesn't notice; she's already wandered off. After rooting around a nearby shrub for a moment, she straightens and presents a metal bucket.

'Rosehips are ripe,' she says, grinning at her haul. 'Lots of them this year. Big fat ones, too. Be enough jam and tea to last through to next season, easy.'

'It's late to be out picking.'

'No shit, Ben. I found a good patch and picked at it until the sun went. Was on my way home when I see a light on in Grandad's cabin. Was pretty sure the old man wasn't making a comeback after all these years being stuck underground, so I popped over to shoot at whoever was lurking where he shouldn't be. Turns out to be you.' Poppy cocks her head and wiggles the bucket at him. 'It's late to be lurking around Grandad's cabin.'

'I ran into trouble,' Ben says.

'I heard,' Poppy nods and lowers the bucket slowly. 'Overheard you talking to Emma about your ghosts.'

'How'd you get on our frequency?'

'Chuck gave it to me when you all started clambering around out here a few years back.' Poppy shrugs. 'Guess he thought you all could use some adult supervision. Hell, nothing to worry about . . . would have known something was up anyhow. The valley's quiet until you start shooting a bunch of guns in it. Heard you all throwing bullets at each other around lunchtime.' She pats the shotgun. 'That's why I'm lugging this thing around for picking. Wouldn't usually bother.'

Ben glances over his shoulder at the blasted door.

'Yeah, well,' Poppy says, surveying the damage also. 'Nothing can be done about that.' She heaves the shotgun to rest across her shoulder, holds the bucket of rosehips in the other hand. 'Get your shit together and let's get a move on. Light's almost gone. You can tell me about your troubles on the way.'

Poppy heads off along the edge of the gully, not looking back to see if Ben follows. He winces, struggling to pull the backpack straps over his shoulders. The pills are wearing off, the pain returning in force. He grabs his rifle and sets off after Poppy. It takes little time to catch up, the old woman moving slowly through the brush, stepping carefully over deadfall with grunts and groans.

Poppy adjusts her grip on the bucket every few steps. She shunts the shotgun from one shoulder to the next.

'Want help?' Ben asks.

'No,' Poppy replies, sweeping a branch aside with an elbow. She steps past and lets it swing back, thumping Ben in the side. He groans.

'I'm fine,' she continues. 'Just eighty-six years old is all. Arthritis in both feet and my back is killing me. Been out picking all day, bound to be a few aches. What's your excuse?'

'Tomos shot me.'

'That so?' Poppy ventures a glance back, eyebrows raised, before returning her attention to the barely perceptible path they follow. 'I always thought that guy was a little pissant.'

'I was wearing my vest,' Ben adds.

'Obviously,' Poppy says. 'Otherwise you'd be dead, or bleeding out everywhere and making a fuss about that.'

Ben smiles and waits for Poppy to work her way over a fallen tree, then steps over it himself.

'Looks like you did a number on your hand, too,' Poppy says. 'We'll fix you up back at the cabin. Have some stew or something, too.' She pauses for a moment to catch her breath. 'Tell me about your ghosts.'

The bottom of the gully becomes shallower as they walk, until it disappears entirely. Poppy clicks her tongue on the roof of her mouth when Ben tells of his encounter with Tomos and the hunters. She grunts when Ben tells of being shot and washing downriver. When Ben tells of hiding in the brush while they passed, looking for where the current dumped him, she huffs.

When his story is done, they walk in silence. The last of the light leaches from the air, leaving the forest a flat, monochromatic patchwork of greys and blacks. Ben peers up through the silhouetted branches, dead pine limbs wriggling across his vision. There are no stars.

The trail curves through a bramble of wild roses and Poppy slows, peering into the tangle.

Ben waits. 'You say that was your grandad's cabin?'

'Only because it was.' Poppy plucks a few rosehips and adds them to her bucket, then continues along the trail, chattering the while. 'He came up here because someone promised there was gold in the rivers, that it'd be a quick rich. Turned out to be hollow talk, but he stayed around to trap for furs. He never was good at anything civilized society could come up with, didn't do well with math or words. I guess he figured if people didn't have a use for him, he didn't have much use for them. So, he built that cabin and lived in it. Figured nature would have him instead. And it did.'

Poppy pauses, the trail having run out. 'Funny thing is,' she surveys the woods, 'nature's a myth when humans are around.' Poppy chews her lip.

'We lost?' Ben asks.

'Shut up,' Poppy replies, then seemingly sorting out where they are, sets off again through the undergrowth.

'Anyhow, the trapping only lasted a short while,' she continues, 'until the mine came in and all the animals either moved on or were trapped out. They couldn't escape people any more than Grandad could.' She elbows through a thicket. 'So, he worked at the mine, just past The Pinch, trucking coal back and forth all day. Did that until they abandoned it when the dam was built. It powered the local grid easy, and the coal was too hard to get out for export. After that, he plucked what he could from the bush until he died. Lived in that cabin the whole time, in summer and snow drifts, didn't matter. He wouldn't be moved.'

Poppy pauses long enough to point at a sign on a tree. It reads, 'Trespassers will be shot.' She casts Ben a sidelong grin and says, 'Almost home.'

'Should read, "Trespassers, there may be shooting in your general direction", Ben says.

Poppy snorts and fires him a glare without breaking stride. She mumbles a string of words, of which Ben catches only 'smartass'.

Ben smirks, but his expression quickly turns serious. 'If these guys come your way, don't provoke them. Arnott and his kid, they want to shoot the bear, but Tomos has had a screw or two rattled loose.'

'Your concern is cute, Ben. You were always my second favourite. But I can handle myself.'

'I know it,' Ben says. 'Wait, second favourite?'

'Yeah.' Poppy laughs. 'Emma's so much better than any of you.'

Ben chuckles, too. 'I know it.'

'And she's a way better crib player.' Poppy sighs. 'If your ghosts come my way, I'll manage. Who would harass a harmless little old lady? As for Tomos, that poacher had a screw loose even before Chuck gave him the boot. The pissant was always more about the money, always working angles.'

'Just don't get him riled. He's not the same guy, seems more . . . unhinged.'

Poppy huffs and waggles her bucket in the darkness ahead of her. 'We've made it.'

They arrive at the cabin from the back. Down a trail to one side is the outhouse, a slender, tilting closet. The cabin itself is a low building with a steeply angled roof. A window at the back looks out from the tiny bedroom.

They circle to the front and Ben smiles. It is like a fairy tale house, with a plank porch, sheltered by a corrugated metal awning that seems to have been tacked on as an afterthought. The door is set in the middle, a window on either side. A few crates are stacked to one end, and in the shadows at the opposite side are a low table and a chair. An old transmitter rests on the table, a bulky box draped in a plastic sheet.

Poppy steps onto the porch, saying, 'Take your boots off. I don't need you tracking mud all over.' She points at the weathered chairs. 'Sit. Let me see your hand.'

'It's fine.'

'Sit,' Poppy repeats and kicks off her boots. She ducks inside for a moment, to return with a first-aid kit and a glowing oil lantern.

Poppy tugs the second chair closer to Ben and unwraps the bandage. She clicks her tongue against the roof of her mouth. 'That ain't something I can kiss better. You need a stitch or two.'

Poppy pulls a vial from the kit and upends it over a rectangle of gauze.

'Your glue's holding up pretty good, but it's let go at the ends. Won't be another day until you're bleeding again, or infected.' She swipes the gauze across the cut and grimaces along with Ben at the sting of the antiseptic. 'Quit being a baby.'

She finds a fine curved needle and a length of nylon thread in the kit, and flinches at the first puncture of the needle through Ben's palm. The thread pulls taut. The needle goes back through his skin.

'Your bedside manner needs work.' Ben looks away.

'Shut up,' Poppy says. 'Don't distract me.'

After the last stitch, she fiddles with the knot, then snips the nylon with a small pair of scissors. The door creaks open and bangs shut, and Ben is left on his own, examining the tidy row of stitches sealing his skin shut.

'Thanks,' he says ⟨…⟩ ck out onto the porch.

She waves dism⟨…⟩ g her chair back and leaning to the side. ⟨…⟩ rom under the window, the metal bumping ⟨…⟩ en wooden planks.

'What does tha⟨…⟩ sks, jutting her chin toward his rifle. 'S⟨…⟩

Ben nods and fl⟨…⟩ he pull of the stitches across his palm.

Poppy screws he⟨…⟩ en the other, her eyes locked on him. With a wrinkle knitting her brow, she says, 'Don't think I have any.'

She sets the weatherbox between her ankles. The clasps click free and she peels the lid off. It makes a quiet sigh as the seal is breached. Poppy hovers, rooting through the smaller cardboard boxes inside. A few ring metallic as she shifts them aside; others are still full of ammunition and don't make any noise.

Poppy angles a label toward the lamplight and reads, 'Five fifty-six.'

Ben shakes his head and looks out into the night as Poppy continues to rummage.

At the bottom of the weatherbox, Poppy exclaims, 'Ah, here we are.' She lifts a small, tattered carton and shakes it back and forth. Bullets chime within. She grins. 'Peter had a love affair with an old Russian rifle once. I pretended not to notice.'

Poppy passes Ben the container, and while he flips the lid and dumps four cartridges into his palm, she says, 'Wouldn't trust them much. Peter died fifteen years ago. Probably didn't shoot that calibre for twenty years before that.'

Ben makes a fist around the bullets, then funnels them back into the box. He stares into the night again, fidgeting with the container held in his lap. He tries to ignore Poppy, who, at the edge of his vision, is inspecting him.

'You want my shotgun?' she asks. 'Got plenty of ammo for that.'

Ben glances at her and shakes his head.

Poppy contemplates him a moment longer, then busies herself repacking the weatherbox. She clamps the seal back into place and pumps the air out with the plunger built into the side. When the rhythmic hissing stops, she pushes the box back under the window.

They both stare into the darkness. It is suffocating and close, absolute.

'Are they coming this way?' Poppy eventually asks.

'Don't know.'

'They think you're dead?'

'They do.'

'That's good.'

'They're on the other side of the river. I left them down by Quick Fish Rapids.'

'Well, they'd have to backtrack all the way up to The Pinch to cross without getting their gear soaked and themselves swept away in the process. River's cold and savage from here to there.'

'How far's The Pinch from here?' Ben asks.

'About three clicks up.' Poppy points. 'Soonest they'd get to my porch, if they are coming at all, is tomorrow afternoon.'

'Unless they push through the night,' Ben says. 'Maybe your shot brings them running.'

'Maybe that,' Poppy shrugs, then shakes her head. 'They'd be nutty to push that far in this terrain at night, nuttier still to cross The Pinch in the black. And they'd have no drive to do it, if they're really thinking you're dead.'

A blast of wind soughs through the trees, swirling in one direction before rustling back upon itself. Pine needles rain from the dead trees, pattering against the metal awning like heavy rain.

'Weather's shifting,' Poppy says.

'Maybe it is.' Ben shrugs. 'You'd know best.'

'I would,' Poppy agrees. 'New system's coming in from the north. It's going to be cold.'

She crosses her arms and shifts in her chair, working a kink from her lower back.

They listen to the wind, the rhythm of pine needles falling on the roof.

'Where are you going?' Poppy asks.

Ben frowns and picks at a stitch in his palm, pulling the skin up with it. 'To the dam. To my truck.'

'Picking up supplies from Cache Cave?'

'Nope.'

Poppy's chair creaks as she leans forward and rests her elbows on her knees. She stares at the splintered plank between her feet. 'You're leaving then.'

'Yes.'

'Well, you can't.'

Ben stares into the night.

'They'll kill the bear,' Poppy says.

'If they find him.'

'They'll find him.'

Ben draws his rifle from where it leans against the wall and lays it across his lap. He takes three bullets from the box, pulls the clip from the rifle and reloads it with two. Easing the clip back home, he pulls the bolt back and chambers the third. He slips the remaining bullet from the box into his pocket. It ticks against the slug he had pulled from the vest. His side twinges, as if the pain and the slug are still linked, the memory now embedded in his bruise. Ben props the rifle back against the wall.

'I can't stay,' he says quietly.

'You should fight.'

'They got guns, better than mine.' Ben looks at Poppy. Her expression is unyielding, so he turns away again. 'They're three. I'm one.'

'You made a choice to be out here. You made a promise.'

'I'll make a choice to leave.'

Poppy shakes her head. 'Then you'll have lost something vital.'

'What's the point?' Ben snaps, instantly regretting his tone.

The lamp hisses and sputters, then the wavering light settles again.

Poppy mutters. Ben waits, expecting a tirade, but when Poppy speaks, her tone is even and firm.

'Don't run now. You knew what this was. You know what your job is, that it's serious, not just boys playing at war. It's real. What's the point, you ask . . . shame on you, Ben.' Poppy draws a breath to continue, but pauses, reassessing her words. 'If the answer's not in your brain, then what's the point of anything, of us talking, of us acting, of us doing anything, of living. If you don't do this, you'll have lost purpose.'

Ben stares into the woods.

Poppy leans closer. 'The world's old. It don't care much about you, or a bear. One way or another it'll keep going.' Poppy looks at Ben, her jaw set firm. 'The only reason anything is important is because we make it so. You go back. Do your job. The point is just that, you will protect The Boss.'

Ben brushes rust-coloured pine needles from his pants. 'I can't do it.'

'Bullshit,' Poppy says and flicks her hand into the darkness. 'You won't do it.'

'I can't.'

'You don't know that. You haven't even tried yet.'

'They'll kill me.'

'Maybe. And if they do, you can come back here and tell me with a straight face that you tried. Then you'll at least know you couldn't do any better.' Poppy's tone softens. 'You only get this once. Be brave. Never stop until you're stopped.'

Neither says anything for some time. Poppy mutters to herself again and Ben waits until she's sorted.

'What you do next is important.' Poppy rubs her thumb and index finger together. 'Don't doubt that. You will be judged, by me for sure, but more importantly by your own damn self. If you leave, you will be found lacking, and I hope it torments you every waking minute. I hope it never lets you sleep another night in your life.'

The chill creeps deeper into the air, pushing into the space between them. Ben finds his thoughts drifting, finds himself staring into nothing, not knowing how long has passed before blinking back into consciousness, such is the depth of his exhaustion.

'I've got to talk to Emma,' he says.

'Yeah, you talk to Emma.' Poppy's chair bumps backwards across the boards as she stands, quick like she's been waiting for him to say those words. 'You're welcome to try that thing,' Poppy says, pointing at the transmitter next to Ben. 'The solar panels still work fine, but the battery's almost shot. It charged all day though, should give you a few minutes.'

Ben nods his thanks and slides his chair closer to the machine. He pulls the plastic cover off and folds it to the side, while Poppy shuffles about behind him.

'I'll make us some supper,' she says. She drapes a wool blanket across his shoulders. 'Come in when you're done. It's getting cold.'

The hinges groan and the door bangs shut. Ben pulls the blanket around his neck and glances back to see Poppy's outline moving about inside the cabin. A moment later a soft amber glow wavers through the window. Ben shivers and turns back to the machine. The button sticks, but the circuits hum to life on the second try. He spins the frequency dial to their last contact.

'Emma, you there?'

The speaker pops like gunfire; the echo is lost among the trees hidden in the surrounding night. Ben grimaces and tunes the volume and frequency dials.

The hiss vibrates and then, as clear as if she were sitting across from him, 'Ben, are you okay? Where are you?'

The tension flees Ben's chest at the sound of her voice, and only in its absence does he realize how tightly he's been wound. The heat of tears grows in his eyes and he has to draw a steadying breath. He wishes she was sitting here in front of him, that he could see her face, that she was more than a voice in a speaker.

'Emma, God it's good to hear you. I'm okay. I'm at Poppy's.'

'What the hell is going on there. I thought I heard shots. I tried to raise you, but couldn't.'

'Listen, we don't have much time before this thing dies. There's three of them. They're coming for the bear. Tomos is guiding them. They attacked me for the tracker.' Ben releases the transmit button and stares at the glowing red light near the volume knob.

'Are you okay? Get out of there.'

'I'm okay. Listen, I don't know if I can get out . . .' Ben holds the button down as he thinks about his words.

He releases the button.

A squabble of interference whines through the speaker.

'Repeat,' Ben begs and clicks the transmit button a few times.

Fragments of Emma's voice break through.

'—anything stupid. Just leave, I'll—'

Ben leans closer to the speaker, struggling to parse words out of the scramble.

'—coming down to you, Ben. Repeat. I'm coming your way.'

Ben presses the button. 'No. Stay away. Emma, you stay away. Get Chuck on the horn, tell him what's going on here.' Ben releases the button. The speaker wheezes and the red light near the volume dial fades.

Wind murmurs high in the trees, stronger and more persistent than it was earlier.

He says, 'Don't you come. Emma, are you there?'

He knows she isn't.

Ben stares out into the churning black, the wind steady now. Falling pine needles click constantly against the awning.

Something clangs in the kitchen and Poppy cusses.

Ben presses the button.

'Don't come,' he says. 'I wouldn't know what to do if something happened to you.'

Ben places the handpiece on the table, unfolds the plastic and covers the transmitter. Something scrapes across the table beside the machine, Poppy's glasses. He pulls the blanket tighter over his shoulders and picks up the glasses. He blows out the lantern. The hinges groan and the door slams behind him.

8

Ben lets the tracker's cracked display clink against the scarred wood tabletop. He looks up from the wires and mess of the unit's innards.

In the kitchen nook, a pot of stew bubbles over a burner; yellow sprites flick through blue flames. Poppy stirs slowly with a wooden spoon. She sets it against the pot's rim and swipes her palm across the film of condensation coating the window above the burner. She runs her thumb across her wet fingertips and leans forward, adjusting her glasses, and searching the night for the white light of men.

Ben watches, too. The woods crowd close. Branches writhe, shadows upon shadows, gathered at the boundary of the glow seeping out from the cabin windows. Figures drift between the trees, their movements a function of imagination. Poppy and Ben remain fixated as the stew bubbles. It's fear skulking around out there.

The tracker chirps. Poppy turns slowly, her face composing

bravery from worry when she notices Ben watching. He turns his attention back to the machine.

The chair creaks as he leans back with a grunt, his body seized by pain. He pinches the bridge of his nose, closes his eyes. He breathes his muscles loose again.

'No luck?' Poppy stirs the stew.

Ben lowers his hand and starts to reassemble the unit. He pins a circuit board in place with his thumb, and manoeuvres a tiny screw into place. Twirling a jeweller's screwdriver, he mutters, 'Some things can't be fixed.'

The hiss of the burner's flame dies with the spin of a knob. It sounds like rain pattering on the cabin's metal roof, but it's pine needles falling in the wind. Poppy inches the curtain farther aside and peers at the night once more.

The woods remain a void.

'It still beeps fine,' she offers.

'It does that.'

Ben fumbles another screw. It ticks off the table and onto the plywood floor, then rolls into the closest gap between planks. Ben frowns at it. The oil lamp hanging over the table gutters. He tweaks the dial to lengthen the wick.

In the kitchen nook, Poppy ladles stew into bowls. Ben tries to rise to help, but finds himself shackled to the chair by pain. He leans back, straightens, shifts to one side, working to find a position that will ease his discomfort.

'Beeper's not the only thing that's fucked.' Poppy crosses the three strides from the nook to the table and plunks the bowl down in front of Ben. The spoon rattles against the rim. She sets a scratched plastic cup of water beside it. 'You're a mess. Even in your eyes, you look in agony.'

Ben takes the bowl and holds it under his chin as he shovels spoonful after spoonful into his mouth, realizing that the last food he ate was the protein bar at his camp on Mallard Peak at sunup.

Halfway through, he realizes Poppy has settled across from him, entranced. A flush rises in his cheeks. He wipes a glistening smear of stew from the corner of his mouth with the back of his hand.

'Peter used to eat like a hyena, too.' Poppy smiles. 'What're you going to do, Ben?'

Ben chews briefly and swallows, chasing the mouthful with half of the cup of water. 'Stew's good,' he says around another mouthful.

'It's from a can.' Poppy keeps her eyes on him as she lifts a spoonful and blows the steam off it.

Ben nods, scraping his bowl clean. 'Hey, I got your book.' He fishes the paperback from his pack beside the table. The pages are still damp and the spine is swollen. He pushes it toward Poppy, who eyes it askance.

'Don't speak with your mouth full,' Poppy chides. She picks up the battered book and flips it over, then slides it back toward him. 'Keep it.' She jabs her spoon in his direction. 'You wrecked my book. You're kicked out of my book club.'

He chuckles, the movement prompting an involuntary moan.

Poppy sets her spoon on the table. 'Let me get you something.' She disappears to the bedroom at the back of the cabin, a room hardly bigger than the cot and cabinet housed within.

'I'm fine,' Ben calls.

The oil lamp shines, soft, the flame steady now. Pine needles tick against the roof. Each new rush of wind sounds stronger, closer. Ben listens for voices it might carry from far away, though he knows the effort is foolish.

Poppy grumbles in the bedroom. A drawer opens and slams closed again. She shuffles back with two glasses pinched by the rims in one hand and a bottle of whiskey choked by the other.

'Sure, you're fine,' she says, setting the glasses on the table. She shoves one his way. The whiskey sloshes as she holds the bottle up between them. 'This is more for my discomfort. I can't stand your suffering. It's annoying.'

She jerks her chin at the glass. Ben leans forward, his smile turning into a grimace. Two pills rest in the bottom. He tilts them into his mouth then holds out the glass. Poppy fills it to half and he chases the pills down, sputtering and coughing. Clutching his side, his eyes turn bloodshot and glisten.

'My finest vintage.' Poppy pours her own glass full. She beams at it. Her smile ebbs. 'What're you going to do?' she asks again.

Ben looks at the tracker on the table. He takes another sip of whiskey. 'I'm going back to my truck.'

'All out of cigarettes?'

Ben grins and fishes the battered packet out of his breast pocket. He tosses it onto the table. The top flops open.

Poppy's eyes dance as she counts the filters. 'You're either cutting back or cutting out.'

No judgement tarnishes her tone. Ben shuffles his bowl back and forth between his palms, grating it across the wood. Poppy drinks.

The tracker beeps.

The bowl falls silent.

They both look at it.

Poppy sighs. 'Checking out's easy.'

Ben's ears flush red. 'Is that how you wound up here?' he snaps. Then quickly, 'Sorry.'

Poppy swirls her glass, concentrating on the amber whirlpool within.

Ben picks at the crack in the tracker's screen, his fingernail catching on the ridge.

'More stew?' Poppy reaches for his bowl and when Ben shakes his head, she takes their dishes to the kitchen. The sound of water splashing is followed by the clank of cutlery landing in the drying rack.

Ben slips the screen back into place and sets the last tiny screw.

He fumes. Poppy doesn't know . . . there are three of them, better armed, and better equipped. He is cutting out. He is scared. Anyone would be. He loses his grip on the screwdriver with the final torque and it rattles to the table.

'Fuck.' He clenches his trembling fingers into fists and glares at the seam in the plywood where the other screw disappeared. He feels like throwing up. He wants to blame the pills, the stew, the whiskey, but he knows the cause is deeper.

Poppy carries the washbasin to the door. She wiggles the handle and backs through into the darkness. Night air slips in and Ben shivers. It smells sweet with leaf rot and pine. At the edge of the porch, Poppy tosses the greywater, making shards of the light's edge. A whisper runs through the tree boughs and doubles back again, louder on the return, strong enough to fling the door back against the wall with a bang.

Poppy tenses and stares into the darkness with an intensity that makes Ben's heart pound instantly. His eyes are locked on her for a sign they've come; he gropes for his rifle, but his fingers remain empty. He thought he'd leaned it against the wall behind him, but it's not there. Poppy tilts her head at a noise, then shakes the last drops from the washbasin. She turns back to the cabin.

The muscles between Ben's shoulders unknot a little. It was a mistake to come here. Ben stares at the seam in the plywood flooring, absentmindedly pushing the tip of the screwdriver against the pad of his index finger. His selfish need for consolation has endangered her. He should have declined her offer to stay and carried on toward the dam. The skin turns white and then pricks with a tidy bead of blood. Ben flinches and brings his finger to his mouth.

'The nights are getting cold,' Poppy says. The door slams shut behind her.

'What am I supposed to do?' Ben asks, unable to make eye contact.

Poppy settles back at the table and sets the washbasin on the floor.

'The bear will be fine on his own,' Ben reasons.

Poppy snorts. 'Will he?'

Ben sucks his fingertip and places the screwdriver on the table.

'Him alone against three poachers?' Poppy shakes her head and reaches for her whiskey. 'Doubt it.'

The tracker beeps. She raises her glass to it and takes a sip. 'I didn't run.'

'I didn't mean—'

'I was young and dumb, like you. Watched the water tables drop, the dirt turn sour, the plastics pile up, and on and on. It was all in tiny increments, each seemingly manageable, but together . . . ecological exhaustion, they called it later. So, I figured if humanity was the problem, the problem could be fixed by losing humanity. I thought it would be best if I removed myself from the equation.' She sighs and looks around the cosy glow of her cabin.

Books are stacked haphazardly on a shelf in the corner, in a pile on the coffee table. A crocheted blanket is crumpled on the couch. A paperback sits facedown, marking a page on the couch's arm. She turns back and Ben meets her gaze.

'Turns out, the very fact of existence alters the equation. One person can't balance it, can't negate the very being of us.' Poppy taps her finger on the table and squashes a crumb. She muddles it into the washbasin. 'Stepping out was never a choice.'

Ben digs gunk out of a scar in the table with the screwdriver, while Poppy takes the washbasin back to the kitchen nook. When she returns, she has a grin on her face, a cribbage board and a deck of cards in her hands.

'No way.' Ben smirks and shakes his head. His eyelids droop. Waves from the pills start to whittle the ache from his side.

Poppy cackles to the applause of shuffling cards. A gust pushes against the cabin. It creaks and a loose panel of tin sheeting taps on the roof. Ben tenses at the sound.

'Relax, they're not coming tonight,' Poppy says. 'Let's have a game. Maybe you'll win for once.'

Ben lazes against the chairback and peers at her. 'I swear, you drugged me just so you can win.'

'I don't need to drug you for that. I drugged you 'coz you were thick-headed enough to get shot and your body needs a break from the pain.' She thumps the cards onto the table and slaps the top of the stack. 'Now cut.'

Ben cuts a five. Poppy smirks. She cuts a three and cusses under her breath. Ben shuffles and deals. They fan their cards. Poppy's lips move as she counts combinations.

The tracker beeps twice.

Ben lowers his cards a fraction. Poppy lays her cards facedown and takes a sip of whiskey. Both stare at the receiver.

'Is that just it being broke?' Poppy asks. 'Two beeps?'

Ben drags the machine closer by the antenna. He sets his cards down and picks up the screwdriver. Poking at the screen, he twists his mouth to one side, then the other.

Poppy leans her chin on tented fingers and watches.

'Two beeps means the transmitter and receiver are less than five kilometres apart,' Ben says.

'And three beeps?'

'One kilometre.'

'Four beeps?'

Ben's chin puckers as he works. He shakes his head. 'Three's the most.'

Poppy retrieves her cards and scrapes them against her chin in thought. 'Bear's getting closer.'

'I know it.' Ben nudges a thatch of wires aside and pokes deeper with the screwdriver. It isn't going to work, Ben thinks. The bear is upstream somewhere. One beep at Quick Fish Rapids. One beep where he'd run into the hunters. Now, two here.

'I don't need to see him,' Poppy sighs, 'but it is nice to know he's still out there.'

'I remember the first time I saw him,' Ben says. 'Early in the program, me and Emma took a tracker and sneaked out without Chuck or Tomos knowing.'

Ben squints into the wires; in the yellow lamplight, it is hard to tell the green ones from the blue. He puts the screwdriver down and rubs his eyes. 'It was summer, that one week when all the alpine flowers bloom. We followed the tracker's signal for two days. In our minds, we saw the bear everywhere, through every gap in the trees, sitting in every berry patch. We both wanted so badly to see him. When we finally did, it became everything.'

Ben wants to live up to the naive optimism that he and Emma used to share, the bravado of being out here, but now everything's become real and he's terrified. He wants to protect what he'd felt that first time they saw the bear in the meadow, in the rain, surrounded by mountain flowers.

'You don't smile much,' Poppy says. 'Looks good on you.'

Ben sobers, then asks, 'You said it's what, three kilometres to The Pinch from here?'

'About that,' Poppy replies. Her expression sours with the realization. If the poachers were making their way to cross The Pinch, they'd be heading right for the bear.

Poppy draws a breath. 'They'd be nuts to cross in the dark.

The canyon's deep and the bridge is all but fallen over. And in this wind . . .' She taps her cards against the table. 'The Boss is probably settling in for the night, which means he's just at the five-kilometre mark. By my math, that means he's still two clicks farther than the bridge.'

'It's too close.' Ben tries to blink away the fuzz that blurs his vision. The painkillers set his mind to float. If he doesn't get past The Pinch, Arnott will be between him and the bear. He'll have to leave as soon as there is light. He mumbles, 'How'd the world get so small?'

Poppy fans out her cards again. 'Nothing we can do until dawn,' she says, but a peek at the door betrays her lack of confidence.

Poppy plucks a card from the middle of her hand and slots it to the outside. 'Wasn't that long ago that the world was still big. Imagine never leaving the valley you were born in. A grass roof on a mud house, and the farthest horizon you knew was the one you could see from the pasture you'd work in your whole life. Beyond that was the land of monsters.'

There is a red six in Ben's hand. He squints, turning it into an eight. Tomorrow, he thinks, is going to hurt. He will have to be clear-minded; the pain will have to be endured, not medicated.

Poppy tilts her whiskey back. 'Your crib, right?'

Ben nods.

She scowls at her cards and refills her glass, pours a splash in his, but cuts it short when he shakes his head.

'I don't want to give you any of these,' Poppy says and jerks her chin at her cards.

'Tough,' Ben says.

Poppy smiles, gap toothed, and flicks two cards atop the ones Ben has laid. She cuts the deck. 'Then, over time, your valley fills up. There gets to be too many who ask too much of the soil, and it gets tired, turns fussy and uncooperative. All your aunts and uncles and sisters and cousins, they spill over into the next valley, and the next—' Poppy glares at the black seven Ben turns. 'That don't help me for shit.'

'It's all right.' Ben shrugs.

She peers at him, her eyes magnified by her glasses. She reunites the deck, leaving the seven showing on top.

'Imagine it,' she continues, 'living on a continent you don't know the shape of. Its mountains and plains, all a mystery. You don't know where the rivers come from, or where they go. They're infinite, as far as you know anyway. Then the cartographers figure out that it does end.' Poppy lays a card. 'Nine.'

Ben lays a six, counts, 'Fifteen for two.'

'Son of a bitch.' Poppy chews her lip and glowers at her cards, scrutinizing Ben like she can read his mind. 'Then, we start exploring and naming all the bumps and divots, tallying up the bounties, the flowers, the animals, the rocks, all for king and empire.' She takes a sip.

'Are we playing?'

Poppy's glass thunks on the table. 'Twenty-one, and a pair for two.' She cackles and pegs herself forward.

'Twenty-seven, for six.'

'Fuck off,' Poppy mutters, causing Ben's grin to broaden. She waves a hand. 'Pass.'

The tracker beeps twice.

Go the other way, Ben thinks.

'One for last card,' he says. His tongue feels thick.

Poppy waves that it's okay for Ben to light a cigarette when he shoots her a questioning look. She stretches. 'Pretty quick, we knew the whole world.'

Ben inhales and rests a hand on the welt Tomos had shot into him. He exhales.

Poppy teases a tattered cigarette from the packet and lights it.

'These are all I got,' Ben says.

Poppy shoots her remaining whiskey, then ashes into the glass with a hiss. 'Thanks.'

Ben shrugs, floating on the pills. 'No . . . thank you.'

'Yeah, you thank me,' Poppy agrees. She waggles the cigarette around the room. 'Thank the whole goddamned world, right? The small world, too small for us, so next we found the solar system, fired our robots out to have a peek, popped off the planet ourselves, to hang around upside down for a while, and see how ants build their nests in the weightlessness of space. Did a quick jaunt to the next closest rock, didn't we?'

'We did.' Ben's head bobs in agreement and he closes his eyes. They are hard to get open again.

'You're stoned.'

'A little bit.'

'Go,' Poppy says.

'It's your card.'

Poppy pauses to recount the last round; it is her card. 'Six.'

Ben places a nine on top and pegs two points. Poppy throws

down her last card and pegs one. She examines Ben, then takes his whiskey. 'When the solar system becomes too small, then what?'

Ben shrugs and stares at her with groggy eyes.

'The next bit,' Poppy swirls the whiskey, 'it's ever expanding. The universe, red-shifting away from us and gaining speed. And that's how we know we belong, we're ever expanding too.'

Ben closes his eyes and nods.

'But we're reckless explorers,' Poppy continues. 'Our conquest is bumbling. The good scientists, the good captain of our boat, the good astronauts in their rockets, they've grown scared because they just figured out that existence isn't free. Existence has impact.'

'But we go too far,' Ben mumbles. 'We're too many.'

'Yeah, I expect that talk from you. Emma would never say that. She's the dreamer. You have no dreams.'

'I got dreams.'

'In your state, you've only got hallucinations.' Poppy's expression is softer than her words. 'And getting shot up, that's probably preferable. Your conservation is a hallucination, like we can somehow bully change from happening, freeze in place what's always been in motion, billions of years of motion. Can't stop that. Constant motion's what got us here.'

'Count.' Ben points at the cards.

Poppy gathers hers and tallies them. There's mischief in her eyes that makes him suspicious that her score is generous. Ben looks down at his swimming cards.

'Now, count mine,' he mumbles.

'Poor bugger,' Poppy says, but she does as he asks, then scores his crib.

'Our greatest leap wasn't getting off the planet,' Poppy says, straightening one of her fingers from the whiskey glass and pointing across the cramped cabin. 'It was the one across the Indian Ocean. Picture the yellow savannah sun, you or me, the first human to hunt down an ibex, or whatever. We were slow for a hundred and fifty thousand years. Shit, sometimes we might have even teetered on the edge of disappearing, a bad flu here, a tribal spat there, and we're done.' She snaps her fingers.

Ben raises an eyebrow, but not an eyelid. He can't.

'We crept east. We hit a bunch of islands. And we crawled across those, too. We went until we couldn't see the next spot of land. Theory is, one black night, there was a glow out on the ocean. Bushfires in Australia. Then we built a boat and crossed. Maybe it was that, maybe currents took a fishing boat or maybe it was following the gods or the stars, but it was inevitable. Quick as a blink, we changed that land and ate all the plants and animals on it. That was our greatest leap. That was the first time we stepped out of our valley, and we've made everything ours ever since.'

Ben slumps in his chair.

Poppy finishes his whiskey and chases it with the final pull of her cigarette. The butt hisses in the bottom of the glass.

She watches the rise and fall of Ben's chest, her vision swimming at the sight of him. She blinks back tears, draws a firming breath, and turns the dial on the tracker until it clicks off.

She moves her peg one hole past his and mutters, 'I win.'

9

Hands scrabble through hard, red dirt and across friable rock, softer than fingernails. Muscles tense, pulling toward the ragged-edged bar of sky above. The canyon walls are close, the footholds unreliable, the bedrock ancient, weathered, and rotten. His breath echoes unevenly, sounding panicked. A handhold fails. Debris rains into the darkness below, a hollow applause that doesn't seem to find the bottom before it is out of earshot.

The next purchase holds, packed dirt brown under his fingernails. He scrambles over the lip and out of the rift in the earth.

Hard sunlight blanches everything white, the rays so strong they carry actual weight, pushing against his skin. Tufts of straw-coloured brush dot the flat plain, outward to forever. The sprig of a tree bends gnarly between him and the pale blue horizon, a distant, brittle silhouette. A box-shaped rhino and her calf stare, close enough for him to see their wary eyes on him.

The moon is a washed-out circle pinned in the daytime sky. The air is uncluttered by radio waves and feels different in their absence, less charged, less rattled, less used. It's an impossible and forgotten sensation, as if from far in the past, or from some distant future.

Talc dust slips under his bare feet, sucking the sweat away instantly as he walks. It rolls, soft between his toes; a hidden stone presses smooth against his sole.

Animals, four-legged and sprite, bound from behind tufts of blond scrub as he approaches the tree. Their glistening horns are pure black, a failure of light. A line twists up the corkscrew curve of them, a ridge in the bone, giving them form. The creatures are silent as they flee, liquid muscles under the tawny coats. He thinks of water. His mouth is so dry.

Sitting back against the tree for shade, fine sediment billows up between his fingers. Ants stutter across the rough bark, across his legs, across his chest. A trickle of sweat rolls from his armpit, a cool line unfurling down his side. A breeze swipes low across the ground and swirls around him. He closes his eyes to the heat and grit; it smells of iron and carbon and something like life.

Under the tree, two burly hyenas have appeared at the threshold of the shadow and sunlight. They're threatening, wedge-shaped beasts, panting and huffing, teeth and claws.

One chuckles.

The other grunts.

Colourful birds perch overhead. Luminous yellows, iridescent greens and reds. A few are jet black and glossy-winged. They chatter in waves, a shrill rise and fall. In the in-between, the branches click like bones.

He watches the birds flit, fast and weightless through the

deadwood fingers, squints against the bright backdrop of a sky, so blue that his eyes water. He lowers his gaze. The hyenas have crept closer, but freeze under his scrutiny.

One clicks his teeth, rapid-fire.

The other huffs, then sneezes.

Something dark shimmers, distant in the heat, a shadow without a source. The hyenas sense it. They turn to watch. They cackle warnings to each other. Taut minutes pass until the time snaps and muscles tense. One bolts. The other follows. Moving as one, they disappear, though there is so little to hide them.

Three figures materialize from the wavering thermals, these moving on two legs.

Ants and sand fall as he rubs his hands together, then holds one up to shade his eyes, watching the approaching trio. Something in his stomach tightens, not a muscle, a feeling, a sensation of chemicals and electricity.

The figures carry spears angled across their shoulders, long and wavering skyward lines that flex with the rhythm of their stride. The sight trips his heart to pump faster, begging to flee, but he finds he can't stand. His legs have gone numb. The ants bite, but their pincers don't hurt.

A shock of colours screeches into the sky from the branches overhead and what's left behind is pure silence.

The three figures draw closer and he hears something for the first time, voices. The peace in his mind clouds, instantly and irretrievably lost with the noise of their ideas and thoughts and opinions and squabbles.

* * *

Ben blinks. He lies in a bed, under a window. Early sunlight slants beneath red-and-white chequer curtains. The fabric ripples in a draft seeping through a gap in the casing, causing the light to swell. The windowsill is grey wood under peeling white paint.

He swipes the covers aside, soaked by sweat, panting, too hot to breathe. There's pressure, like there's too much blood in his veins, like a hand is holding him down. Overhead, a ceiling with wooden beams and cross-slats. The glimmer of corrugated metal is visible between the planks. His mind stumbles, disoriented. Accustomed to waking under the sky, the roof feels too low, claustrophobic, a coffin.

Ben clamps his eyelids shut and forces his lungs to pull air.

Something is still out of place.

He scowls, trying to chase away the confusion.

Something has followed him back.

The voices.

The distant voices, they remain.

Ben tries to sit up and he's punished for the effort with a stab in his side. The shock is less severe than yesterday, but still causes his muscles to seize. He holds his breath, trying to parse words from the pulsing in his ears. They're muffled and distant. He recognizes one of the voices. It's Poppy. She's talking on the front porch. Someone responds, a deeper timbre, a man.

Arnott.

The ache flees in a rush of adrenaline. Ben kicks and struggles upright. He's in the bedroom of Poppy's cabin and he tries to work through the fog of memory to discern how he wound up there. He swings his legs over and stumbles on his boots, trying to swallow back the swell of nausea. The grogginess fades. His muscles aren't as fatigued; his legs feel less leaden. There's stiffness from an unmoving sleep that's easily chased away as he crosses the tiny bedroom.

Daylight slices through a gap in the bedroom door. Ben pivots, panning to see the couch with the paperback splayed facedown on the armrest, a colourful afghan piled to the side. A cup of coffee sits on the side table. Steam rises above the rim.

A shape passes the front window. Footsteps thump across the porch planks. At the edge of his vision, the cabin door is hinged slightly ajar.

'We'd like that, ma'am,' Arnott says. 'A hot cup of Joe on a cold morning? I can't think of anything better.'

'All three of you?' Poppy asks. The replies must be in gestures, because Poppy continues, 'All right. You boys can stay out on the porch though. Don't mean to be rude, but I don't need you all tracking mud through my house.'

The light is blotted out at the door and it squeaks further open. Poppy spies Ben and looks back over her shoulder. She scolds, 'Tomos, the outhouse is down that trail. You know damn well it is. No pissing around my house like an animal.'

Tomos says something that Ben can't hear, and Arnott laughs.

Poppy steps into the cabin and stares straight at Ben. The door bangs shut. She jerks her chin, sweeps a subtle hand at him to go, and disappears into the kitchen. Moments later, she returns with three mugs looped over the fingers of one hand and a battered coffee pot in the other. She steps out and closes the door.

The rise and fall of their conversation murmurs through from outside. Ben eases back from the gap in the bedroom door when Arnott steps up to the window, cups both hands against the glass, and peers through.

'You going to clean my windows?' Poppy asks. 'Move your greasy mitts.'

A coffee cup is thrust Arnott's way and he smiles and nods thanks before stepping away again.

Ben scans the bedroom for his rifle and pack, but they're not there. He grabs his jacket from a chair at the end of the bed. It's dry now. It smells thick with sweat. He pats his pants pockets and the clips click metallic together; he feels the spent slug in another.

Back at the gap in the door, Ben cranes to one side and catches a glimpse of his pack against the wall, hidden from view at the nearer end of the couch. His rifle is propped against it.

'Nice set up you got here,' Arnott says. The boards on the porch squeak as boots clump from one side to the other, to the radio. 'This contraption still work?'

'Still does,' Poppy replies, 'but the batteries don't store much a charge anymore.'

Ben inches the bedroom door open, wide enough to slip into the room.

Outside, the radio squeals and is quickly cut silent.

Arnott says, 'Hello. Hello. Is anyone out there?'

Ben crawls toward the couch, terrified that Emma will reply to Arnott's call. The response remains static.

'Still makes plenty of noise,' Arnott says.

'Told you that.' Poppy's words are clipped, her tone stern. 'Also told you not to waste my charge.'

'Sorry, ma'am,' Arnott says, and the static is silenced with a click.

'You can call me Poppy. "Ma'am" makes me feel old.'

Arnott laughs. 'I will then, Poppy.'

A floorboard groans under Ben's knee and he freezes, arm outstretched toward his pack. His eyes dart from the door to the window and back again. A bang sounds from outside and footfalls thump across the deck. A figure passes the streaked glass.

The door hinges creak.

Ben lunges for his rifle and spins, the stock pulled tight against his shoulder. The trigger is cold under the curve of his finger.

Poppy glares at him, anger more than fear crosses her face in the low-angled morning light. She says, aside to one of the men on the porch, 'Only be a second.'

'We're in no hurry,' Arnott replies. 'It's a lovely morning.'

Poppy smiles and nods. The cool rush of fresh air is cut short when she closes the door. Ben hunches, hidden behind the arm of the couch, and hoists his pack over a shoulder. His eyes remain locked on a shadow cast across the windowpane by one of the men outside. It shifts and Ben crouches lower.

'Get gone,' Poppy hisses as she crosses to the kitchen. She slides the curtain aside and scans the woods. Dishes rattle. 'Out the bedroom window.'

'I'm not leaving you,' Ben whispers.

'You are,' Poppy says. 'I came in here to tell you that. They'll have their coffee and go. Tomos is a pissant, sure, but he won't do worse than harass an old lady with words.'

Ben peers over couch and spots Vito in profile, talking quietly to whoever's on the other side of the porch. Ben concentrates on the sound, but Vito's words keep their secrets, which makes him nervous.

'You don't know him anymore,' Ben hisses. 'He shot me.'

Poppy rummages through a kitchen cabinet and pulls out a pack of biscuits and a pot of sugar. She glances at him, then stares out again. Her shoulders fall a fraction.

'I can handle myself,' she mutters as she dumps the biscuits into a bowl and grabs a few spoons from the drying rack.

'You don't know—'

'Go. Do your job.' Poppy starts back toward the door, the bowl in one hand and the sugar tucked between her hip and elbow. 'I'll keep them here as long as I can. Go. I'm out of excuses to keep coming in here.'

She fumbles the door open, then kicks it closed with a bang once she is through.

Muffled, Arnott says, 'You didn't need to do that. Thank you, though.'

'Young men need to eat,' Poppy replies. 'Your boy is too skinny. He looks hungry.'

Arnott laughs. 'He always looks that.'

Ben lifts his bag and rifle, and backtracks toward the bedroom.

'Tell me,' Poppy's voice, 'what brings you all the way out here?'

'Wanted to get the boy a bit of nature,' Arnott replies. 'It was different when I was his age, the wilds were wilder, but everyone should get out here at some point, make a memory, feel the wilderness stir in their genes, in their genetic memory. The boy—'

Easing the bedroom door shut, Arnott's words click into

obscurity. Ben slips his boots on and laces them. Every move-ment sounds too loud with Arnott so close. The curtains ripple and the trees are bright, the morning casting long shadows through the bedroom window. The draft dies and the curtains become still.

Ben pulls the clip from the rifle and checks it before sliding it back home. He eases the window open and pulls the screen from its frame. The backpack drops quietly into the bushes behind Poppy's cabin. Ben follows it out, slinging the straps over his shoulders before starting away.

Pushing through the thorny branches of a wild rose bush, a distant snap brings Ben to a halt, his pulse firing tight through his body. The noise repeats and Ben catches move-ment in the woods. Tomos slouches back along the trail Poppy cleared decades ago to her outhouse. His thumb is looped through the rifle strap slung across his shoulder. His focus is locked on the path.

Ben sinks to one knee and brings his rifle up, wrestling with his nerves to steady Tomos's image in the scope.

Poppy won't have me stay, Ben thinks, but maybe I can draw away the trouble I brought to her door.

Tomos carries on along the path, talking quietly to himself, and shaking one hand out to the side as if dealing cards. Ben's finger hooks over the smooth metal of the trigger. Tomos continues, unknowingly walking along the tip of a rifle barrel.

With a squeeze, Ben thinks, Tomos would cease. He would stop walking. He would stop talking, stop breathing. His eyes would no longer register colour or light or darkness. The chemicals in his muscles would settle; their contractions would stop. Movement would stop. Breathing would stop. He would just stop. The electricity in his brain would disperse . . . into what?

Ben bites his lip.

Into nothing.

Tomos would simply cease.

As if sensing something awry, Tomos's footsteps slow and then stop. He scans the forest, his features screwed up in confusion.

Ben can't bring himself to shoot and knows he is exposed, kneeling in the sparse undergrowth. If he sinks lower to the ground, Tomos will certainly spot the movement.

A volley of Arnott's laughter fills the air and then goes silent.

Tomos scowls at the back of Poppy's cabin. The bedroom window is still open. The chequered curtains bloom outward.

Tomos shrugs his rifle into his hands, crouches, and pans the woods again, slower this time.

When their eyes meet, Ben still can't shoot. Even as a snarl curls Tomos's lips, even when he brings his own rifle to bear, Ben can't squeeze the trigger.

Tomos shouts something.

Ben shifts his aim a fraction and fires. All sound is battered from the air. The tree over Tomos's shoulder splinters. Tomos flinches and falls to the side. Ben drops into the foliage. Only then sound returns, the crackle of forest litter under his own deafening breathing as he scrambles away.

'He's here,' Tomos hollers. Then, in answer to a question that doesn't reach Ben's ears, 'Who the fuck you think? Ben. Sneaking out the back window.'

On his forearms and knees, Ben clambers away through the undergrowth. Shouting fills the air from the front of the cabin, the clamour of movement, feet thumping across the porch boards and then quieter when they hit the ground.

Ben slithers down a shallow embankment, into a narrow swale, deep enough for him to remain hidden if he crouches.

'I don't know,' Tomos shouts. 'He took his shot . . . then gone.'

Ben pushes through the elastic alders lining his path, following the slope of the swale toward the cabin, whipped and scratched by the skinny branches. Eyes half-closed for protection, he struggles until the creek bed brings him broadside to the cabin. Easing onto his stomach against the incline, he peers over the lip of earth, through the hash of undergrowth, and onto a side view of the porch.

Arnott holds Poppy by the elbow. Pulling her closer, he leans in and hisses something. Poppy tries to jerk her arm free but can't. Her expression remains stoic, though she doesn't meet Arnott's glare.

Vito takes a step closer and rests a hand on his dad's shoulder. He whispers and Arnott looks out to the forest. His face is hard, his eyes shadowed.

Tomos rounds the corner of the cabin, rifle still raised as he scans the underbrush. 'She was hiding him,' he says. 'He crept out the back and ran off into the forest.'

'Come on.' Arnott shoves Poppy backwards toward the cabin door. Poppy stumbles and Vito reaches out to steady her.

'Easy y'asshole.' Poppy glares at Arnott before spinning on Vito. 'Get your hand off me, boy.'

Vito draws back, as if burned.

'Both of you,' Poppy continues, 'I can manage on my own.'

Vito ushers Poppy inside, visibly blanched and uncertain under her ongoing tirade.

'I'm going after him,' Tomos says. He thumps across the porch and down onto the ground.

'You won't,' Arnott states. 'Come back here and sit.'

Tomos doesn't move.

Arnott continues, 'This old lady, is she going to be trouble for us?'

Tomos looks over his shoulder at Arnott, then to the cabin door. 'No,' he says. 'You saw her, bluster, but all crippled up with arthritis. She couldn't follow us if she tried.'

'Okay,' Arnott says. 'You take a seat out here. I'll go in and talk to her, see what she'll tell us, and then we go.'

Tomos turns back to the woods and Ben shrinks below the edge of the channel to avoid being spotted. When he peers over the rim again, Tomos is seated near the old radio. Through the window, Arnott paces back and forth, talking. The back of Poppy's head is visible where she sits on the couch. Tomos stands and steps off the porch, staring in Ben's direction. Ben eases himself below the gully rim.

They won't hurt Poppy, Ben reasons. At worst, they'll bruise her pride before they go. But they will chase me, or the bear. And, one certain thing, Poppy could handle herself.

Ben scuttles down the drainage, away from the cabin.

As he gains distance, his movements become more reckless

for the benefit of speed, a renewed urgency driving his legs. He has to lead them away.

Ben comes across an old trail, a gap cut through the woods, cleared to the width of his shoulders and the ground packed firm by years of travel. The trail eventually meets the river and will lead him north, toward the dam.

He glances over his shoulder every twenty steps or so. They will come this way. The bear is this way. He picks up his pace, hoping Poppy won't be so proud as to provoke the men, or to follow them once they leave her.

A breeze kicks up and Ben realizes something is off. He presses a palm against his chest and feels his heart hammering doubly hard. He's missing the weight of the bullet-proof vest on his shoulders, its constriction of his chest replaced by the squeeze of panic.

'Fuck,' he whispers. A flush prickles across his scalp.

Ben rips the backpack from his shoulders and throws it to the trail in front of him. Dropping down beside it, he claws through the contents and comes up empty. In the fading haze from last night, in the panic of being found this morning, he has left the tracker on Poppy's kitchen table.

Ben stares at his hands, and through his trance, hears movement. He crouches, pulse pounding loud in his ears.

Motion catches his eye, a flash through the undergrowth, close enough for him to recognize the colour of Tomos's coat.

10

Ben holds his breath and watches Tomos slink through the undergrowth, drawing closer, reported only in ragged fragments seen between tree trunks and drooping fall leaves. Tomos pauses mid-stride and crouches lower, scanning. Ben remains still; instinct dictates to stay motionless, as prey ought to, unless the predator comes too close and nerves fail.

There's still space between us, Ben thinks, there's still time.

Tomos starts forward again, slowly, pushing silently through the undergrowth. Leaves tremble; one falls against his rifle that is held ready.

Ben wonders what deficiency in his own movements has allowed Tomos to get so close before he sensed him. Ben can't remember; it still all strikes him as surreal, waking to hear their voices so close, fleeing Poppy's cabin under threat of violence. Violence always happens to someone else, in someplace else, not here, not in this valley.

His mind has been so addled with shock and the painkillers' contrail, he can't remember much of his flight. There had been Tomos in his sights behind the cabin. There was Arnott pulling Poppy into her cabin by the arm. Their shapes flashed past the window, seen from outside. There were shouts and the hammering piston of his own breath dominating his ears, filling his memory. He recalls leaves brushing under his palms, the sting of branches whipping his hands, his face, and he remembers stumbling along the swale. The ground became rockier as he went.

With thoughts of Poppy, his mind seizes in fear of her being alone with the men. Seeing Tomos here, a blot of movement stalking him through the gaps in the foliage, the most unpredictable of the bunch, he's glad for the reprieve it affords her.

My escape was quiet, he thinks, sinking lower in the foliage as Tomos's gaze passes. And he hasn't spotted me yet. It's more likely it was the terrain that brought him so close. He doesn't have my trail, just thinks I've come this way because that's what the land dictates.

I have to lead Tomos as far from Poppy's cabin as I can, he thinks.

The terrain north of the cabin is more rugged. The mountains creep closer together again, pinching the river valley tighter and gaining elevation. Jagged outcrops of bare stone jut up. The moss cover thins, and the trees twist and become stunted. Their roots scrabble through the thin soil that centuries have deposited into shallow pockets, before arcing out again, clawing across the bedrock and callused by their exposure. There is less ground to hide his trail, but more topography for him to shelter behind. The rock forms choppy swells as tall as a man, like the curved backs of stone whales, breaching the surface for millions of years, until the wind and rain push them under again. The spaces between these outcrops becomes a maze of narrow fissures.

Ben slips behind a ragged outcrop and edges toward the distant end.

'Use your fucking head,' Tomos growled from behind his rifle. Having crept up behind Emma and Ben, his voice was the first hint that they had been found. 'There're two of you and one of me. I shouldn't stand a chance . . . but here we are.'

Tomos had his rifle trained on their backs, aimed at them where they hunkered in a depression in the landscape, peering stupidly the wrong way. He'd perched on the edge, like a gargoyle scowling down upon them. The weapon seemed unnecessary, it was a training exercise, yet Tomos kept it on them until Emma told him to stop. Even then, he hesitated in turning the barrel away.

Tomos had dropped them off the day before. The truck doors slammed and he draped a wrist over the steering wheel, his other arm hanging out of the window. He appraised them both, up and down once, where they stood on the side of the dirt track before a wall of trees.

'Part of you two surviving may well hinge on being able to hide as well as you can track. This scenario is easy. Try to catch me, before I can catch you.' With a sneer he said, 'Believe this is real. You got a day's head start. I'll be back to hunt you down in the morning.'

The engine revved and the truck lurched forward.

'He's a little intense,' Emma said, squinting and waving away the dust the truck kicked up.

Ben watched it bump and hop along the track that cut through the forest.

'Chuck says Tomos is a vet,' Emma said. 'Part of the reason he hired him. His service wasn't on his CV, just his record when Chuck did the background check. From the years he was stationed in Ethiopia, Chuck figures it was during the first Nile River Conflict.'

Ben glanced at Emma, standing beside him, also staring after the truck as it rounded a curve, leaving a curtain of dust drifting through the long morning sunlight. Ben and Emma gathered their supplies from the trackside pile and stepped into the trees, grateful for the shade in the mounting heat.

They had followed a ridge until it broke from the tree line. The valley swooped out below them. The track Tomos had driven was invisible in the trees, obscured by the forest in the late daylight, but out there on the horizon somewhere.

Emma scrambled up a steep incline, her rifle slung across her shoulders so she could use both hands for balance. She stood when she reached the top and turned to face Ben. She smiled. 'You staring at my ass?'

Ben felt heat rise in his face and he looked at the ground. 'I wasn't,' he said, turning away, as if to spot the source of a sound that only he had heard.

'Come on.' Emma crouched and reached down. Ben took her hand and scrambled up after her. Emma grunted. 'Tomos thinks we're some branch of the military or something. I wonder if Chuck knows about these "scenarios" he's running on us?'

Ben looked back again, scowling down at the tree line. This time he had heard an errant noise, he was certain. But they still had until morning before Tomos would put the chase on them, or so he had said. Ben didn't trust him. If they were being trained for the unexpected, he thought, then Tomos might have started after them at any time.

'He's got a screw loose,' Ben said, leaning to the side to try and see deeper into the trees. 'The sooner we're done with him, the sooner we're on our own.'

Emma stared in the same direction as Ben, unsettled by his focus. A draft brought a swirl of dust up the rock, and they both interrogated the silence that followed for any whisper of movement, the click of a rock knocked loose, the snap of a branch. There were no more sounds.

'Let's go,' Emma said, giving his arm a gentle squeeze. 'We can spend the night out on Posie Point. Tomorrow, we'll circle back on Loggerarm Ridge and try to pick him up there. Outflank him, yeah?'

Their plan had been predictable, or so Tomos had said after he had pinned them down within a few hours of stepping out of his truck. They hadn't been thinking like Tomos; they hadn't been taking it seriously. The ride back had been tense, Tomos gripping the wheel, his knuckles white. Emma sat in the passenger seat, her eyes locked on the trees blurring by outside, the window rolled down and the airstream riffling her hair. Ben caught Tomos's eyes in the rearview once, the stitch in his brow told him all he needed to know. Tomos thought they were a disappointment, a mistake.

Or, Ben now thought, placing a hand flat on the cold rock for support and leaning forward, maybe he thought we were an inconvenience. How long has Tomos been planning to trade the bear for a seat on one of Arnott's shuttles? Had he and Emma been a wrench in Tomos's scheme from the start?

Be unpredictable, Ben thinks as he peers around the outcrop, in the direction he'd last seen movement through the trees. A moment later, a flicker fills a gap in the branches and leaves, much closer this time. Ben cranes, surveying the top of the outcrop he's tucked behind. It rises a good distance overhead.

High ground is predictable, Ben thinks, hiding is predictable, being hunted is predictable . . . not being able to pull the trigger on Tomos is predictable. Ben's stomach knots with frustration.

Silently, he makes his way back to the far side of the outcrop. Losing sight of Tomos torques the knot of anxiety in his gut and a nauseous wave passes over him. He hates not knowing where Tomos is, hates having to keep checking his own footing on the uneven terrain instead of watching for him. Silent movement is intolerably slow. Ben looks back often at the retreating edge of the outcrop, not knowing which second Tomos will step around it, spot him, and shoot him.

Be unpredictable. Tomos will expect Ben to keep moving

forward, but won't expect him to head back to the cabin, back to Poppy. He can't leave her behind, not when he doesn't know what these men might do. He doesn't suspect Arnott will do much more than talk, but they are alone out here. He can't know what the man will do when there's no threat of retribution or justice.

Vito isn't a threat, Ben's pretty sure.

It's Tomos who has become something different, something unpredictable. Ben saw it on the river terrace where they first met, and again on Tomos's face behind the cabin. Tomos is leaving and he isn't bound to the rules here anymore. It's like he's already gone.

Ben reaches the end of the outcrop and places a hand on the rock to steady himself. He leans out from around the corner, then quickly draws back, rifle pulled tight to his chest. Tomos had stepped from the trees into the space where none grew along the base of the outcrop, much closer than Ben expected. Tomos was facing the other way, but close enough that Ben's breath catches for fear of being heard.

Ben strains to remain still, where every instinct screams for him to run. His pulse fires viciously in his ears, drowning out the tiny noises that could tell him where Tomos is. Electricity cinches his muscles tight, ready.

Has Tomos heard him? Sensed him somehow?

Is he now inching silently toward this hiding spot?

Please don't let him have seen me; Ben releases a quivering breath that his lungs can't hold any longer.

Poppy told him to fight, convinced him that he chose this,

that it was the only thing that mattered because he chose for it to be the only thing that mattered. Now, the resolve he felt the night before has fled.

The stock of his rifle ticks as his grip tightens, his skin creaking across the smooth wood and his joints aching from the death grip they hold. Ben is less certain he can fight Tomos, isn't sure he can even punch him, let alone shoot him. The ease with which such violence came to Tomos makes Ben question how someone could disregard the value of a life. But Tomos is leaving if they succeed, Ben thinks, and maybe there's no worth in anything but that for him.

Ben seats the rifle butt to the crook of his shoulder. He grips the forestock and arcs a finger over the trigger.

A pebble rattles down the outcrop.

Ben takes an involuntary sip of air.

The noise is farther away than the place he last saw Tomos.

Ben eases down on one knee and leans out again, slower this time. Not more than twenty strides, away creeps Tomos, his body angled so his back arches slightly against the contour of the outcrop. His shoulder must have brushed a stone loose. His rifle is held at the ready, his finger resting against the trigger guard. Tomos's attention is locked on the far end of the outcrop, where Ben was just moments ago.

Ben raises his rifle and leans against the rock face to steady his aim. Through the sight, the fabric of Tomos's shirt sags, then tightens across his shoulder blades as he twists around a bush. The sweat stain creeping from the collar down is a shade darker, ending in a point in the middle of his back, making an arrow, a target. Put a bullet here. Tomos's heartbeat is visible as a vibration running through the fabric. A bead of sweat runs down Tomos's neck and disappears at the collar.

'You two are really something else.' Tomos had swiped a fly from the back of his neck. The insect disappeared in the wind lashing through the cab.

Ben, sitting in the back seat, raised an eyebrow. Those were the first words Tomos had said since he'd pinned them down at the end of Loggerarm Ridge.

The truck jolted over a pothole. Tomos jerked the wheel so they didn't leave the narrow track winding through the trees. Emma grabbed the doorframe to steady herself. She glared over at him.

Tomos smirked when he glimpsed her expression. Emma didn't need words to tell him what she thought of him. She couldn't hide it. She looked out again at the blur of trees.

'You spend a cosy night together in the woods,' Tomos laughed, 'and you think you can just round back and outflank me?'

Tomos grinned. He reached over and patted Emma's knee. She pulled away and looked outside. She hooked a writhing loop of hair behind her ear.

Tomos raised his offending hand between them before placing it back on the steering wheel. Shaking his head, he pushed back in the driver's seat and flexed his knees out. Tomos slung an elbow onto the window frame and brought his fingers to his mouth.

'It's like you guys aren't even thinking,' he said while chewing a nail. He glanced in the rearview, then over at Emma.

Ben touched Emma's shoulder secretly. She didn't respond, just stared out the passenger window. A twitch hammered in her jaw.

The truck hit another rut. The chassis thumped against the bottom of the suspension. Tomos didn't slow the vehicle and it jolted again.

The truck rattled and bounced for another half hour. Wind buffeting the cab was the only noise the whole while, and then the wheels bumped one last time. The tires squeaked and shimmied against the pavement; the ride became instantly smooth. Tomos hooked a sharp turn onto the highway, not slowing, not checking for traffic when they broke from the edge of the woods. He tweaked a knob on the dash-mounted radio, unclipped the transmitter from the visor, and brought it to his mouth.

'Nordegg Base, this is Tomos,' he said, flicking his wrist to get the coiled cable under control.

'That was fast.' Chuck's voice crackled.

The engine rumbled as Tomos accelerated, drifting over the yellow centreline.

'Yeah, well . . . we hired a couple of geniuses here.'

The response was static.

The radio on Tomos's belt hisses with Arnott's voice.

'Where the hell are you?'

Ben flinches at the words, thinking his vantage has been discovered.

Tomos drops low and rips the transmitter from his waist. Only the bill of his baseball cap is visible through the leaves, swivelling back and forth.

'For fuck's sake,' he hisses.

Ben pulls back behind cover. He leans as close to the edge as he dares, listening to Tomos reply in hushed tones.

Arnott is speaking, '—get your ass back here. We have the tracker. The bear's to the north.'

'What about Ben?' Tomos's voice is louder now, more confident, figuring he's alone.

'What about him? We came out here for one reason, and it weren't to hunt a ranger. Let him be. The old woman said he's running for his truck, anyway. Going to get the hell out of here. I believe her. The guy's done here.' There's a pause and when Tomos doesn't answer, Arnott continues, 'Get back here and get the rest of your shit. We're heading out.'

Ben waits in a silence that stretches out so long he wonders if Tomos is going to reply.

'On my way,' Tomos says.

Ben settles back against the outcrop, sitting on his heels with the rifle gripped between his knees. He rests his cheek against the barrel, listening to the noises of Tomos departing grow fainter until everything falls to silence once again.

Still Ben does not move. He closes his eyes. The image of Tomos at the end of his rifle barrel is etched in the darkness. He imagines squeezing the trigger, throwing a jolt through Tomos's body the instant before he falls dead on the ground. The crack of the rifle numbs all other noises, leaving a whine in its wake that takes time to fade.

Ben opens his eyes and looks back in the direction of Poppy's cabin. The trees to the south are woven tight and he can't see very deeply into them, but everything that he can see is calm. Ben sits, his legs stretched out before him.

The brief conversation he had with Emma last night, sitting in the dark of Poppy's porch, echoes back. He misses her voice, and even the memory of that brief contact, disembodied but familiar in the night, nudges the loneliness away. In the last fragment of their conversation, he remembers her voice as static saying, 'I'm coming your way.' A cold wave prickles across his scalp.

Ben struggles out of his pack and slings it to the ground. Panic spikes his heart as he fumbles through the pouch for the transmitter. He upends the bag and shakes it. The heavy unit is the last item to tumble out. Ben clicks it on, wincing and adjusting the volume down as a squeal rips through the silence. He surveys the bush in the direction Tomos had retreated and waits, fully expecting bullets to come tearing through the leaves and lodge into his body. The quiet tide of static remains undisturbed.

Ben presses the button. 'Emma, do not come this way.'

He waits, begging the device for her voice. If he knew where she was last night, he would be able to judge how close she is now. If he hadn't been drifting in a haze of painkillers then, he might have been able to convince her.

'Emma, stay away,' he repeats.

He jabs the button, four quick then two quick.

He waits, then presses it again. 'If you can hear me, stay away.'

Silence follows. He shakes the handheld in frustration, groaning, 'Emma, please . . .'

'Ben,' the speaker crackles.

'Emma, thank God,' Ben replies. 'Stay away. Don't come my way. You hear me?'

'Jesus, Ben. Settle down.'

Ben scowls in confusion.

'It's Poppy,' the voice says.

'Are you okay? Poppy? I'm sorry for bringing this to your door,' Ben says.

'Shut up and listen,' Poppy says. 'Battery's gonna die, right quick. That pissant Tomos came back. They all packed up and left, heading north, back to The Pinch, following the tracker. I'm fine, but I can't help you much. I can't move around like I used to. If they come back, my shotgun will be waiting for them. Head to The Pinch. Be quick and you can beat them there. The bridge will be the perfect place to—'

Ben stares at the handheld.

The Pinch would be the perfect place to pin them down. The bridge is exposed and their numbers wouldn't matter if he is on one side of the ravine and they are on the other. Ben feels the metal rectangles of the clips in his thigh pocket. He could hold out as long as his ammunition does.

Frantically stuffing everything back into his pack, Ben keeps an eye on the woods to the south. They are coming back this way. He stands and slings the pack on, grimacing at the ache in his side. The pain wakes his mind though, drives him to focus.

His first few steps are stumbling, then, reacquainting himself with the uneven ground, Ben runs. With distance from the outcrop, he grows more reckless; he must be quick. He shoulders through bushes and grunts over logs. He shoves his way through thickets, not caring if he leaves a clear trail; they know he is out here anyway. The better for it, he will give them something to follow, away from Poppy. All he knows is that he has to get across the bridge at The Pinch before they do.

He bursts from the tree line and stumbles up a gravel incline onto the mine's old rail line.

He looks down the corridor cleared through the trees in one direction, then the other. The raised ballast is covered with decaying leaf litter. The track is fully shaded in the late morning, but it will soon have a brief period of direct light when the sun hit its zenith.

I'll be across the bridge by then, Ben guesses.

The derelict rails stretch out before him, uneven, and in places the wooden ties pop up at steep angles from the gravel. Ben moves slowly at first, conscious of how exposed he will be if Tomos or the others step out of the woods.

He starts to jog; he has a good head start over them.

His jog turns into a sprint. They are already on their way.

He needs to make The Pinch before they do.

The muscles in his legs start to burn.

11

Ben hits a rhythm and surrenders to it. His breathing, his heartbeat, the one-two crackle of gravel under his feet tick off the time that he quickly loses track of. His eyes stay locked on the rail ties; his gait is short-step, awkward from trying to land on the ties and not twist an ankle between them. He tries running along the ballast slope for a while, but the footing is uncertain. The gravel rolls away without warning and there are too many deep ruts and gullies.

Running becomes animal movement; the repetitive motion, the meter of his breathing, his muscles working on automatic, all driven by purpose and not thought. He feels he could move like this forever.

Ben thinks of the bear. There were two beeps at Poppy's cabin, and it was somewhere to the north, somewhere around where he is right now. His focus becomes unsettled, glancing over his shoulder at intervals, constantly scanning the trees for the beast, his charge.

In tracking the bear, Ben always tries to remain in proximity but out of sight. He likes to think the bear prefers that as well. Surely, it is aware of him in the area, the bear's nose filling in for the deficiencies of his vision. They smell each other. They hear each other moving through the bush. They spot each other periodically, and on those instances, they travel in parallel lines with a wary eye kept on one another.

It makes sense that t[...]d mine; Ben chastises himself for not th[...] tracker has been telling him what he sh[...]n. It's fall and the bear is preparing to hil[...]und the old mine is riffled and wrecked. [...] and the disturbed earth. The old buildin[...]pment are perfect for rats and cockroach[...]there in the past, moving between the ab[...]rooting out both, kicking through the d[...]s rolling gait. The bear scrounged and huffed around the buildings for hours.

When evening settled, the bear skirted the open pit, grazing on berry bushes mostly long past their prime harvest, but still vital calories for the massive beast. Ben perched on a slag pile and watched. The long light cast a shadow bear at the creature's feet, and Ben remembers imagining there were still two of them.

The bear knew Ben was there, it had turned his way several times during the day, swaying and lifting its nose to read the scent of him. It grazed through the twilit hours, then stepped into the dark wood lining the pit and was gone. And as easy as it was to imagine the bear and its shadow were two, Ben imagined the hollow forest without even one.

Ben cuts a step short to land on an angled tie tilting up from the ballast. The plank shifts like a seesaw and thumps in his passing. Somewhere in the bush, water burbles over a stone. The trees lining the rails grow closer to the tracks than when he started, making a tight and dark tunnel, save for a stripe of blue sky overhead. In that moment, he trips on a jutting tie and falls to his hands and knees. The gravel scrapes and the wood splinters. Sweat streams down his face, down the bridge of his nose, and drips onto the tie between his hands. It pools dark on the wood.

The wood still smells thick and greasy from the creosote they used to poison the bugs and keep the weather from destroying the ties. Stamped in the oxidized iron of the rail's web is the date '1922'. Chest heaving and throat burning, Ben sits back and rubs his hands across his thighs, then assesses the damage. He picks a thick splinter from his palm. It leaves a black creosote streak under his skin that soon becomes a line of blood. The stitching and bandage on his injured hand still seem intact.

Ben's breath hitches at a noise and he looks back. He waits, wondering if it was distant voices he'd heard, or just the thought of them made manifest in anticipation. He knows, sooner or later, he will hear them.

The forest remains quiet. Even the wind that had dogged the boughs all night and throughout the morning has stopped. The reprieve is a reminder to keep moving though; somewhere out there, the hunters draw closer. Ben struggles back onto his feet and starts moving once more, slowly at first until his legs grow numb again from the pace.

Ahead, a rusted hulk sits on the tracks. Amorphous at a distance, it becomes more distinct as he draws closer: a barrel-fronted engine, abandoned on the rails to rust. Ben veers off the tracks and slows a little as he runs past, catching a bobbing vision of aggressive metal rivets joining heavy iron sheeting together. The ladder up to the conductor's cabin has a broken rung, the handrail bristles with corrosion. The air surrounding the machine smells bitter, like coal, like burning fossils and black smoke, like energy, heat, and noise.

And then it's behind him.

Ben doesn't look back.

Through the woods, the horizon grows brighter. Sunlight seeps through ever more frequent gaps between the trees, marking the edge of the ravine ahead. Ben slows as he approaches and then stops at the end of the forest. He bends forward to placate the stitch jabbing his side, his hands propped on his knees to help ease his breathing. Looking back, the engine is barely a dot in the tunnel of trees. He turns to survey The Pinch.

The forest grows right to the lip, where the land disappears down vertical walls of limestone. A few trees lean over the void as the ground they're rooted in slowly erodes. The tracks continue on, at a glance appearing to levitate across the expanse. The bridge's limestone-grey concrete seems to have been pulled from the very cliffs that it joins together. The illusion breaks about halfway across the gorge, where one of the seven towering pillars supporting the deck has failed and a stretch of the bridge has toppled into the void below. Ben wonders if the splash was even heard from up here, when the mass of concrete tumbled into the river. He loops an arm around a tree and leans out, trying to spy the pile of concrete rubble, but a curve of the ravine wall blocks his view of the depths.

The collapse left behind a full span of wooden ties held aloft only by the rails, a crude set of stitches hovering across the gap. While the rails remain intact, they are torqued to one side, making the barest filament spanning the open air seem even more fragile, as if straining to hold the remaining portions of the bridge together.

Ben has crossed The Pinch twice before, once when training with Tomos, once when the tracker had led him to the mine on the far side.

The rocky edge is higher on the opposite side and a wedge had been blasted through it where the bridge intersects. Explosives carved a long narrow corridor back from the edge, to where the grade became more manageable for the old steam engine to labour the black rock across the gap.

A dilapidated watchman's shack, not much larger than Poppy's outhouse, perches on the high edge, overlooking the tracks and ravine from the far side. Beside it, a slag pile spills downward, a black smear into the gorge, though the moss and stunted trees have started creeping back in over the decades. Hidden behind those slopes, and through the stripe of stunted forest behind the watchman's shack, is the mine.

Ben arches some feeling into his back. His stomach aches from hunger. The sun is almost directly overhead, its light spilling down the sheer ravine walls, but never reaching the shadowed watercourse below. A cool breeze swirls up from the depths, smelling musty, of water and wet rock. The distant sound of rapids churning through the constraining walls is so faint it could be mistaken for a trick of the ear.

Ben takes his first few steps onto the bridge. Vertigo washes over him as solid ground drops away in his peripheral vision. He struggles not to think of the safety of land, moving farther behind him with every step, struggles to anchor the dizzy sensation that rushes through him. The cool breeze that drifted past while he stood on the edge now gusts up from below, powerful enough to nudge him to one side or the other. It makes a mournful lowing as it weaves past the remaining concrete pylons.

Too soon, Ben reaches the failed section of the bridge. The concrete lining the ragged rim is friable and fractured. The rails carry on through the air, most of the ties are still bound to it by rusty metal spikes. A few spikes are missing and the affected ties hang at angles, like the broken ribs of a snake. The rails sag to one side, the angle of them even more precarious when viewed from up close, before righting themselves where they rejoin the intact bridge deck on the far side.

Ben chews his lip and peers over the edge. The depths telescope away. 'Fuck me,' he whispers.

He draws a breath, hitches his backpack higher on his shoulders, and cinches the straps. He secures the chest and waist straps, drawing each one tight. Eyeing the rusty metal line slung between the two standing portions of the bridge deck, the pack has never felt heavier.

Ben sits on a rail and unties his boots. His eyes remain on the void, his fingers tremble as they work on loosening the laces.

He kicks one boot off and then the other. He pulls off his socks and stuffs them inside. Tying the laces together, Ben slings them over the back of his neck, and stands.

Ben flutters his hands by his sides as he steps onto the base ridge of the rail, pinching the head between his ankles. The iron is bitingly cold and gritty with corrosion. He takes one shuffling step forward, then another, curving his bare feet to grip the iron tightrope.

The concrete beneath the rails disappears.

The chasm drops out beneath him.

Looking down, Ben catches sight of a concrete fragment falling, tumbling through the sunlight layered atop the blackness below. It shrinks until it is a pebble, a speck of dust, and then it's lost.

Bile rises as his vision spins to one side and Ben swallows it down. Pausing to steady his balance, he brings his focus back to the rail a short distance ahead, hoping it will quell the vertigo. It doesn't help; keeping his eyes on the rail forces them to the plummeting chasm beyond. His heart batters the inside of his chest. He raises his gaze to where the floating rail rejoins the intact portion of bridge ahead and shuffles forward.

At the midpoint, the rail starts to twist and bow to one side. Ben slows, finding the centre of gravity more elusive as the rail begins to sway and bounce under his weight. A gust blasts up from the blackness below, throwing him off balance. He wobbles, the weight of the pack threatening to pull him over. In his fumbling, Ben stubs his toe on a spike. A shock of pain shoots up his leg. The spike fails. The plate and wooden tie beneath him tumble away, end over end, seemingly in slow motion and as light as ash, from the distance they fall. Ben grits his teeth, unable to take his attention off the plank, unable to keep from feeling the fall himself, until it disappears in the shadows.

Ben still feels himself falling, a dizzying sensation of twisting end over end, and he closes his eyes. The rail sways beneath him. He thrusts his arms out to the sides and flexes his knees, lowering his centre of gravity over the iron line. Slowly releasing the breath he's held trapped, Ben calibrates his balance to the sway, riding the rail like it rides the wind. Balance regained, Ben eases his eyes open again.

The cold has seeped into his bare feet. Before, he could feel the rough texture of the rail beneath them, now there is just a numb sensation of pressure. Ben can't make his feet move, his animal mind seizing to the idea that he is safe exactly where he froze in place, and moving will cause him to fall. His leg muscles begin to quiver from the strain and Ben is forced to straighten a little. That motion is enough to trick his legs into inching forward again.

Ben watches his ankles, being flayed against the rusty rail head. He doesn't dare relax the vice grip he holds, terrified they are the only thing keeping him on the rail. Skin grows back. He stares through the endless air below his feet, walking on a thread, before coaxing his gaze back to the bridge deck ahead. The rail slowly twists upright again and Ben readjusts his balance, more clumsily this time, as his muscles grow rebellious with fatigue. Still, Ben shuffles forward.

In the last few steps, he becomes reckless and steps atop the rail head, moving more boldly and trusting momentum to keep him upright. He wobbles and bends and these hurried strides take him to collapse onto the safety of the concrete again. Ben lands on his side, and rolls onto his back, reclining against his pack and putting his feet flat against the deck. The sun-warmed concrete relieves the freezing ache in his toes.

Body shaking and legs weak from the exertion, Ben looks back at the sagging track and realizes he's laughing, marvelling that the rail was even strong enough to be crossed at all. Ben pulls his socks and boots on again. He staggers to his feet and hobbles across the remainder of the bridge, relief flooding though him as land surrounds him again.

A shadow falls across the tracks where they enter the blast cut and gently angle up an incline. A shiver runs over him, the sweat between his shoulder blades driving a chill through the delicate warmth of the sun. Ben runs a steadying hand along the icy rock and cranes to see the outline of the watchmen's shack overhead, sitting dark against the unmarred sky. Its rough-hewn wood planks are warped and gapped; the tarpaper roof hangs in tatters.

Ben scrambles up the steep rock face and into the sun again. He peers through the doorway at a drift of coal dust and leaf litter. Through the window, the shack offers a commanding vantage of the ravine, the rail bridge, and a sweeping view back across to the opposite side. It is a trap though, an obvious target sitting like a tombstone, high on the bare outcrop.

Downslope a short distance, Ben scales the slag pile. The scree slides from under his feet, rolling down the gradient and tumbling into the void. At the peak, Ben turns. Behind him, running parallel to the ravine, is the rough cut of a century-old road, now nothing more than a stripe of stunted regrowth and a slightly raised roadbed with two ruts from the old mining equipment used to haul coal. Farther back, adjacent to the rails, three towering piles of rock sit under a rusty conveyor belt that angles back from their peaks, forever left waiting to be loaded onto the train and shipped out.

Loose rock tumbles down the slag pile, dislodged by Ben's descent. He wades through the shoulder-height regrowth to the old road and follows it back to the rail. He gives the conveyor belt a shake and it squeaks and rattles an uncertain response. Past the three tipple piles, the rail ends in a low mound of earth. Ben kicks at the terminus, a gravelly hump with a clear view back along the tracks, through the shade of the rail cut, and out onto the bridge.

Ben turns to face a long, low sheet-metal clad building that leans precariously to one side, a short distance from the terminus mound. He enters through a barn door that hangs askew from its rail and waits in the stale air for his eyes to adjust. The faint tang of oil and chemicals lingers. Then he weaves through the industrial detritus of conveyor belts and bulky machines connected by rust-frozen chains and brittle-looking rubber belts.

Three squat windows stretch along the back wall, the glass long since broken and scattered. They make three washed-out sunlit squares in the black cavity of the building. Ben steps up to the middle one and draws an involuntary breath. Here, the ground drops away sharply. The building rests on the lip of the open pit. Ben ducks to see the peak of the mountain that the mine is tucked up against. On that far side crouches another structure, the old log dorm house.

A thick black stripe strikes across the pit wall, like a greasy fault in the daylight. A narrow, descending track spirals around the perimeter, slowly eroding and crumbling, to give the effect it's now serrated. It would take half an hour to follow its decaying orbit down to the base.

Millions of years lay beneath Ben's feet, exposed in a short time by men with donkeys and dynamite. He can almost see the dust-black men yelling at each other, coughing soot, hear the whip-snap driving the mules underneath heavy loads, the protesting beasts hauling rattling carts, their elongated shadows cast alien against the strata. He can almost hear the thunderous boom of dynamite and smell the black powder and fine particulate drifting slowly sideways in the wake of the explosion.

At the bottom of the pit sits a black pool, where the water table had been breached. Even from the rim, Ben can see the rainbow film of petrochemicals on the surface. A huge brick of machinery sits at the water's edge, a rusted pump; the canvas piping that had been used to bail out the water has long ago rotted away.

A flicker of movement passes behind the dorm building on the far side of the pit. Ben squints at the woods beyond. He leans closer to the window frame and raises a hand to shelter his brow. As he's about to dismiss the movement as a trick of the eye, he sees it again.

A warm swell of excitement fills Ben as the bear saunters from behind the dorms. His reaction to seeing the animal is primal, is genetic, an instinctual and deep-seated mix of terror and awe. The beast's shoulders roll as he walks; his massive head sways smoothly with its gait. Its fur looks jet black, but Ben knows the distance shades the deep brown coat darker. Even so, the sunlight plays in lines across its fur, over the elegant undulations of muscle sliding beneath the glossy coat.

The bear sniffs around the corner of the dorm building, then swats at a shrub growing there. It starts digging at the base of the wall. The grunts and huffs of its efforts travel across the pit to Ben whenever the breeze drops. The bear pauses, then thrusts his muzzle into the hole he dug. Ben can't see what he eats, but he sits back on his haunches and chews. When the bear is done, he rolls forward onto all fours again.

The bear catches Ben's scent, raising his nose and weaving it through the air. The bear turns to the dorm, stands, and swipes the corner with both paws. Even from the distance Ben sees the fresh blond scratches starting where the roof meets the wall, and marring the distance halfway to the ground. Moments later, the bear disappears into the woods behind the building.

Ben watches the spot for a long time before exiting the mine shack and following the rails back past the three mounds of rubble. He veers from them and heads up to the watchman's shack. The late afternoon sun is warm and a breeze from the ravine ruffles the shreds of tarpaper roof. Ben slips the rifle strap over his head and lifts the scope, panning up and down the ravine. He chews his lip again, the skin there shredded.

He makes his way back to the adjacent slag pile and finds a divot in the debris he thinks will shelter him from view. Taking off his pack, he fishes a protein bar out of one of the pockets. Ben lays the rifle beside him and watches the ravine, chewing slowly.

He thinks back on seeing the bear, wonders at what an impossible agglomeration of atoms and chemicals and electricity and circumstance has placed them both here, on this mountain, at this time. In all the universe, over all time, they are here together, the last bear and the man who is to protect him. Ben takes the last bite of the protein bar and lays belly-down on the rise of the slag pile. The waste rock is sharp and uncomfortable. He uses his pack to support the barrel and holds the scope to his eye. The gap in the bridge jumps close.

Ben knows he will have to shoot whoever tries to cross. He won't hesitate this time. Seeing the bear again, knowing he's this close, Ben resolves that the animal will survive this.

Ben cocks an ear toward the ravine. What first seems like a trick of the air becomes a certainty within a few minutes; he hears three sharp beeps from the far side.

Ben checks the rifle. A bullet glints in the chamber. He pushes the bolt closed and leans into his scope again.

12

Ben guesses there are roughly four hundred meters of air between him and where the rail emerges from the trees on the far side of the ravine. It's not a hard shot, but he's not so good with the rifle that it's easy either. Tomos trained him, but Ben didn't practice like Tomos told him to. He never truly believed he'd need to shoot a moving human, shoot *at* one maybe, but not actually try and hit one.

Through the scope, the opposite edge of the ravine jumps close. He pans across the bridge. The rough line of the broken deck and concrete debris littering the edge are magnified clearly; then he finds the rail. Everything seems flattened with the magnification.

Ben tries not to focus on the obvious black lines floating in the scope, the reticle demarcating where a bullet would strike.

Maybe they won't cross the ravine, he hopes.

Maybe they'll fall if they try, then he won't have to pull the trigger after all.

There's movement in the trees, shadows contorting amid shadows. Vito appears first. His cheeks are flushed and the hair at his temples is curled in a wick of sweat. He holds the tracker out and stares across the ravine. He turns as Arnott and Tomos appear from the trees on either side of him.

Vito looks at the tracker again, and then back across the ravine. 'I think The Boss is back on the other side.'

Tomos clutches his rifle in hand and surveys the far side of the ravine. Through the scope, it seems that Tomos stares right at him. Ben tenses, certain he is spotted. But in the slant of light, he must appear as just another hump of slag, if he's visible at all. Tomos's gaze moves on.

Ben shifts the scope, working to steady the reticle from his pulse and breath.

Please, not another step, Ben silently urges Arnott away.

Arnott steps out onto the bridge deck. His rifle is slung over his shoulder and he has a thumb looped casually under the strap. He leans over the void and spits. A few seconds later, his low whistle bounces across the ravine.

'Christ,' Arnott says, leaning back from the ledge. 'And I thought I would shit myself when we crossed it last night with the headlamps. Better to see nothing than see this.' He contemplates the unanchored span of rail and then back at Tomos, shaking his head, says, 'Fuckin' nuts.'

'Get back,' Tomos snaps, stepping back into the trees. He kneels, brings his rifle to his shoulder, and scans the opposite side again, this time through the scope. 'You too, kid.'

Arnott and Vito look around, uncertain, then follow Tomos's

gaze. They back into the trees as the realization settles, they're easy targets.

'You think he's over there?' Vito asks.

'I don't see him,' Arnott says. He slips the rifle from his shoulders and checks it.

'That would be the point,' Tomos replies. 'I know I'd be waiting over there. Perfect spot to dig in.'

'I don't know . . .' Arnott leans against a tree and rubs the side of his scope with a thumb before bringing it up. 'Ranger Ben doesn't seem like the fighting type. The old lady said the same, said he was running back to his truck and getting out of here.'

'Poppy would say that.' Tomos glares at Arnott and jerks his chin at the bridge. 'Go on then. If you're certain.'

Minutes pass with all three watching for movement, scanning the terrain for any sign of Ben. Sunlight through the branches dapples their faces, shifting like liquid as the boughs sway. Vito grows bored of the search and sits with his back against a tree, pulls his knees up, and picks at a loose thread on his rifle strap.

Eventually, Tomos stands. He steps out onto the bridge with his rifle still held ready. In quick succession, he fires two bullets through the watchman's shack, one high and one low.

Ben flinches at the noise and hunkers lower as splinters shower down around him. Thunderous claps echo a fading barrage through the valley. Dust swirls lazily through the two ragged holes punched in the shack.

When Ben looks through his scope again, Tomos has already slung his rifle across his back and is walking toward the gap. As he reaches the free span, he peels his attention from the ravine edge to concentrate on the steps ahead.

'Cover me,' he says.

Ben peeks over his scope to see Vito scramble to take a knee, and Arnott still standing with a shoulder against a tree, both with their rifles trained across the gorge.

Ben rests his finger against the cold metal swoop of the trigger. There can be no warnings. As soon as he squeezes off a shot, they will know exactly where he is. Then it is three on one. Arnott will be formidable, he thinks. Vito will probably be less enthusiastic to pull the trigger.

Ben watches Tomos, the most dangerous of the group, inching along the free span of rail. He draws a calming breath. It doesn't work to steady his heart.

This shot has to count. Then it will be two against one.

Through the scope, Tomos teeters with one arm thrust out to the side, concentrating on the line stretching through the air in front of him. Ben leans harder on his elbows to bolster the weakness he feels in his resolve. The rubble digs in painfully and he focuses on that. The scope's black lines swarm around Tomos's body.

Ben adjusts his aim a fraction to match Tomos's creeping pace.

He doesn't want to watch, wants to close his eyes and shoot blindly. After, he could open them to an empty scope and pretend he didn't just kill someone. He draws a breath, holds it, then slowly releases it, trying to force the tension from his shoulders and steady the reticle lines that seem to shimmy of their own accord. He reaches the bottom of the exhalation.

Ben squeezes the trigger.

The rifle clicks and the bolt shimmies. Through the scope, Tomos wavers on the rail and stops to let his balance catch up with his feet. A misfire. One of Poppy's old rounds. Ben pulls the bolt back and jams it forward again, but the chamber doesn't close fully.

'For fuck's—' Ben hisses and tilts the gun to see two bullets jammed at angles in the chamber. Rolling onto his back, he shuffles below the tipple pile's edge. He reefs on the bolt, trying to free the misfire, gritting his teeth in desperation. The bullets remain wedged solid. He pokes a finger into the chamber, but can't get enough leverage to make either budge.

Ben sits up and glances over his shoulder to check his exposure. He can't see where Tomos is, which is fine because it means he can't be seen either.

Surely, Tomos isn't on this side of the bridge yet, he thinks. There must still be a minute or two.

Ben grasps the barrel in a chokehold and slams the butt of the rifle against a boulder between his feet, and then again, harder when the first strike fails to shock the cartridge from the chamber. He tilts the rifle and jimmies the bolt again.

'Fuck.'

Ben fumbles his multitool from his thigh pocket. He unfolds it to expose the pliers and then freezes at a noise. It was a quiet sound, dampened from the far side of the pile blocking him from the ravine.

Was it a shout?

Scrambling back upslope, the rocks gouging his elbows, a faint hope plays through Ben's mind that Tomos missed a step and plummeted from the rail into the dark ravine below. Or maybe the old line finally gave way?

Over the crest, he spots Tomos, kneeling on the bridge deck with his rifle aimed up the rail cut. Arnott stands at the far side, arms crossed over his chest as he contemplates the traverse. Vito is beside him. His rifle ready, but there's uncertainty in the young man's handling of the weapon, like he's hesitant to point it in any direction it could inflict damage.

Loath to take his eyes from the men, Ben glances between them, blindly trying to work the jam free. Metal grinds against metal as he tries to get a good enough grip on one of the jammed cartridges to free it. The pliers slip from the cylindrical casing and click shut.

Arnott takes his first wobbling steps over the void. He moves slower than Tomos did, arms held out like a tightrope walker.

Vito shifts from one foot to the other, his rifle angled down into the ravine and his eyes fixed on his father's progress. He tenses visibly with each wobble.

'Come on,' Ben coaxes through clenched teeth, and the pliers slip again. He can't help looking over the stunted regrowth behind him, past the shack and across the mine. The distant forest is dark under the canopy and holds no sign that the bear had passed that way, mere minutes ago. Ben wishes the bear to remain invisible forever, but he left a trail, he always does, where he digs a hole or eats from the berry bushes. They are too close to him.

The pliers slip; the pliers slip, and finally, they bite solidly on the second cartridge. With effort, it wiggles free and rings against the ground near his elbow. The pliers' nose is too thick to reach the remaining bullet. Ben drops the tool and hammers the butt of the rifle against the boulder at his feet again. The second cartridge twirls free, glinting in the light, and then rattling down the slope to settle into a crack between rocks.

Ben rises onto his knee and levels the gun at the bridge. Through the scope, he lines up the figure teetering on the exposed rail. He tenses, but seeing it's now Vito over the void, pans to the two men standing on the bridge deck.

Arnott shouts and points as Ben pivots and sights in Tomos between the black lines.

Ben pulls the trigger.

The rifle bucks against his shoulder. Ben's hearing keens instantly from the blast.

Tomos shoves Arnott to safety behind the rail cut and dives after him. A moment passes before Tomos takes a darting glance from around the corner, rage etched plainly on his features.

Ben cocks the bolt. Out of the corner of his eye, he spots Vito teeter and lose his footing. The young man shouts in fear and falls heavily onto the unsupported ties between the rails. The spikes hold for a moment and then fail, sending the ties twisting into the ravine. They slow Vito's fall enough for him to wrap himself around the bare rail, however, crossing his ankles and hugging it close, his body swaying underneath the metal thread.

'Vito,' Arnott hollers. He makes to sprint out and help his son, but is slung back into cover by a rough yank on the collar from Tomos.

Ben brings the rifle to bear again, brings the scope up. Tomos jumps close, leaning out from cover and firing. Ben pulls his trigger a fraction of a second later. The two echoes swirl through the valley. Rubble explodes inches from Ben's face. Eyes clenched, he tumbles to the side and down the rocky slope. Sharp edges dig into his knees and shoulders, lash at his exposed hands.

He hits the bottom and rolls his momentum into a blind, stumbling sprint away from the ridge. His face stings. His eyes burn. He can't see. Blinking frantically, crying to clear the debris, he tries to run in a straight line. The stunted trees rake his cheeks as he sweeps them aside with an arm. They jostle him, resist his passing.

The rustle of his frantic movement sounds from everywhere; his pounding heart, his heaving breath, all deafen him to any other noises and renew the wave of panic that fuels his thrashing, deaf and blind in a firefight. He's lost track of his foes. The clawing brush all around drives uncontrolled movement.

He senses rifle barrels pointed at him from every direction.

The blasts will tear through him any second, spin him around as they punch holes through his body as easily as they did the watchman's shack. They will knock him down at any moment. The imminent pain drives him manic.

Ben stumbles up a short incline and falls heavily to his side on the hardpack of the old mining road. He freezes, the wind knocked from his chest with enough force to make him nauseous. The pause forces sense back into his thoughts.

He's alive.

Ben rolls onto his back.

Everything is a blur. There are shapes in the haze now. His vision is clearing.

Clutching his rifle tight to his chest, Ben forces his mind to calm.

He waits.

He listens.

There's noise, but it is his own heaving chest. He concentrates on steadying its rhythm.

He blinks and thumbs grit from the corners of his eyes. The haze of dark and light clears further, black threads resolve into the stunted regrowth reaching into the bright blue sky from all around him.

He hears shouting, but it's far away.

I can lie here and they will go away, Ben thinks.

He knows it isn't true. Tomos will come for him with a vengeance now. Arnott will too, for shocking his kid from the rail. They'll come, as soon as they pull Vito to safety. This is a fight now, this is mortal. There can be no more hesitation pulling the trigger. They won't. The thought drives Ben to stand and spurs his feet to move.

The trees grow sparser and the rusted conveyor becomes visible, jutting skyward over the peaks of the coal piles that side along the rail. Ben veers in the direction of the mine shack, running in a crouch, and every few steps glancing back to where the rail emerges from the cut in the rock.

He skirts the ore piles and follows the track to where the rail ends at the mound of earth, a short distance in front of the mine shack. Ben runs over the top and slides to a halt behind it, falling backwards against the terminus. Two deep breaths and he peers over the peak.

The tracks stretch out in converging lines through the cut in the ravine ledge. There's movement there, Tomos's silhouette a bump against the shadowed rock face. The outline of his rifle is a proxy for his eyes, alternating between the top of the cut and the direction of the mine. Behind him, and fully illuminated by the high sun, Arnott lays flat at the edge of the failed bridge deck, reaching over, grappling with Vito.

Ben rolls onto his stomach and anchors his elbows on the terminus. He swipes his eyes with the heel of his hand, blinking hard a few times, then chambering a round. The spent shell pops from the chamber and pings a clear chime beside his elbow.

Through the scope, Ben watches Vito scramble for purchase on the broken bridge. He tries to hoist himself up, but can't under the weight of his pack.

Arnott sits, the sweaty line between his shoulder blades perfectly framed in the scope's sightlines. He grasps Vito by the forearm and hooks him under the opposite armpit. Using his own body as leverage, he heaves his son to safety. They lie flat against the deck beside each other until Tomos barks for them to move. Arnott is laughing as the pair scramble away from the edge, their boots sliding in the debris.

A shape flashes past the boundary of the scope's view, and Ben follows it. It's Tomos's blacked-out form shifting in the foreground. Ben loses the scope's lines in the dark figure and squeezes the trigger. The rifle kicks and the blast deafens him.

Tomos's outline jerks sideways against the rock wall. Ben

chambers another round and settles the scope again, subconsciously hinging his jaw and cocking his head in an attempt to stimulate his hearing.

Tomos's shape is lost in the shade of the rail cut and the blinding backlight. Ben lowers the barrel a fraction, estimating where Tomos must have fallen, and fires another round. Then he rapidly chambers and fires another into the same shadow.

Ben looks over top of the scope and stares beyond the end of his rifle barrel, trying to discern any movement. From this wider view, he sees Arnott and Vito on the bridge deck, both with rifles raised.

Ben ducks behind the terminus as it erupts in a swarm of bullets, spewing gravel and earth in every direction.

Ben pushes back harder against the terminus, wishing he would disappear within its cover, feeling it vibrate with each bullet that strikes the far side and sends more debris flying. The noise is a stunning, crippling barrage. Ben hunches an ear tight to his shoulder and covers his face with his other arm, trying to squeeze himself as small as possible.

The frequency of impacts falls by half, and moments later stops entirely. Ben waits, wincing in a silence so absolute it's shocking. He wonders if he's lost his hearing altogether. Slowly, his arm slips from in front of his face. The muscle contraction that his entire body has become eases.

'Tomos,' Arnott calls out once, and then a second time when there's no response.

'Yeah.' The reply is weaker, less certain.

'You good?'

Ben inches up the mound to glimpse overtop. A single shot rings out and drives him back down, but not before spotting Tomos, sitting on the ground, alone in shade of the cut. Arnott was moving toward him and Vito was covering him from around the shoulder of the rail cut. He had fired the shot.

'Yeah, fine,' Tomos says once the report fades. 'Fucker winged me. A graze though.'

'Vito, cover us until we're through,' Arnott commands. 'Then you follow.'

Ben hears grunting and the loose scrabble of the railbed's gravel, amplified by the rock cut.

They're coming through, he thinks.

Beyond his own boots, across a short stretch of bare land tufted by yellowed grass, stands the mining shack, perched on the lip of the open pit. It's his next scrap of crooked cover.

Ben glances to the side of the terminus. Figuring if he sticks to that side and keeps the three piles of ore between him and the rail cut, he could be behind cover until he reaches the shack's hangar door. The tin walls won't offer any real protection, except for obscuring him from view. The heavy machinery inside would probably stop a bullet though, if he could keep behind it.

And now is the best chance, he thinks, while Arnott's occupied with Tomos, and only Vito's rifle offering covering fire.

Ben rolls from behind the terminus. A bullet strikes the mound with a bark and a hail of gravel. Ben fires back blindly before scrambling into what he figures is the safest line. He pushes off the ground, his boots struggling for traction. With every step,

Ben waits to be struck down by a bullet, anticipates pain or blackness, and with each step the gaping door jolts closer.

At the last second, Ben veers into the line of fire and slides through the door. Two sharp pops punch new beams of sunlight through the metal siding. Ben scrambles on all fours deeper into the building, settling behind the massive bulk of an old engine.

Inside the shack, every noise is confusion. His every breath and every movement is a deafening racket, caged by the metal walls and ceiling. Each sound is louder than he wants, but still seems quieter than it should be, his hearing so assaulted by the gunfire that the volume is turned down on everything else.

Ben holds his breath for a moment, but can't hear anything over the thud of his own heart. He hazards a glimpse around the engine's edge, and then takes a longer look once he figures it's safe.

The two bullet holes angle beams of sunlight into the darkness, illuminating a jagged pile of scrap near the door and two long loops of chain hanging from a pulley, attached to hidden rafters above. As Ben's vision adjusts, the blocky outlines of other machines and piles of industry come into focus.

Anything outside is a washout of brilliant daylight. Framed by the blackness of the hangar door, the distant conveyor angles into the clear sky above the ore piles. The pale blond scrub grass between the door and the terminus mound quivers in a swoop of breeze, and then becomes still again.

Ben waits, interminable seconds stretch into interminable minutes without a sign of the three men hunting him.

Somewhere, a lose sheet of tin siding clicks whenever the air shifts strongly enough, but there are no sounds from his pursuers.

His attention darts between the three windows overlooking the mine pit behind the shack, the hangar door in front, and the dark recesses of the two opposite walls to either side.

A shadow passes a line of sunlight that seeps between two ill-fitted sheets of siding.

Ben thinks he hears movement from the opposite corner, as well.

He had counted on the united attack continuing, but realizes, as his glances around the darkened building grow more desperate, that his assailants could be anywhere.

He is trapped.

13

A bead of sweat tickles a line down Ben's neck. He shivers, though the shack is stifling. The building's metal skin acts like an oven for the air inside, still and thick and a challenge to breathe.

Two metallic crashes thunder from the darkness. Ben scrambles for cover, his panicked eyes searching for the source. A shape blinks past a thread of light between panels of siding. The sound again, disorienting, maybe a rifle butt hammering against the metal.

Ben spins and fires at the noise, piercing a new beam through the darkness. Dust motes swirl with an odd clarity, confounded out of the peaceful murk by the light.

Ben chambers another round and shuffles to the opposite side of the engine he hunkers behind, silently putting the hulk of metal between him and the new hole. He slips his pack off, sets it to the side, then settles lower to the ground. The machine is cold against his damp back, sending a shudder coursing through him.

They're playing now, he knows, testing boundaries, searching for a way to reach him in the cage that he's unwittingly allowed the shack to become. Rattled as he is, any potential movement could be a trick of overly-wanting senses. Even the sound of his own breath unnerves him, muddling vital clues.

A click comes from outside, perhaps just a phantom of the mind, but it receives a barking shot as a reply. A fresh searchlight flicks on through the metal cladding, illuminating a writhing pile of scrap in the dust.

Movement flashes through the beam. A small rodent scurries from underneath the rubble and into some other, darker corner.

Ben's trembling fingers draw the bolt back and slide it home again, slowly, to curb the chance that the grinding sound will give away his position. The silence and the obscurity offered by these thin walls are weak allies, but his only ones.

A loose panel of siding ticks and clangs an indecipherable code. The sunlight pulses in concert, scorching a washout into his vision. All falls quiet again as the wind shifts. The darkness returns. The washout turns neon violet and slowly fades from his eyes.

Ben strains for any sound, his nerves struggling with this alien new world of extremes, total silence shredded by crippling noise, darkness and light, both blindingly pure. He wants the men to go away, and as the seconds mount, he wants them to attack, anything to end the minutes that twist the atmosphere so tight that it vibrates. Ben fights the urge to run through the hangar door and into whatever is going to happen, just to put an end to waiting.

And he waits.

'Use your fucking head,' he whispers.

Another flash blots the light lining the base of the wall on the mine side of the building. The rodent sneaks through a loose panel of siding beneath one of the three long windows looking onto the hulking mountain on the far side of the mine pit. The panel makes no noise as it swings.

Ben squints in the darkness that resettles and reckons the opening could be made large enough for him to squeeze through. It opens onto the edge of the mine, and a short drop to the road that runs along the perimeter. An escape plan begins to form.

Ben slumps lower against the engine. His elbow brushes a wrench, which grinds out of the way. He picks it up and tests its weight. With the flick of a wrist, the tool spins into a dark corner. It clangs against the wall and falls to the floor with a thud.

The shack rattles with gunfire. Ben grimaces and pushes as flat as he can against the floor. New beams of light shock through the darkness. Once the riot abates, he eases his eyelids open and counts eleven new holes. From their configuration, he figures there's a gunman out front, and another to the side. With a glance at the far end, where he'd previously seen movement, he figures the third man is probably over there.

Chances are, they're all positioned some distance back from the building. Ben struggles to remember where cover could be found facing each side of the shack. Out front, the terminus that he himself had hidden behind, or the ore piles farther back, under the conveyor. As for the two opposite sides, his addled mind can't recall. Regardless, the mine side of the building seems unguarded. Over the lip of the pit, a few steps away, the curving road offers a clear run below the cover of the ledge.

Ben snakes a hand out to the side and doesn't have to reach far until it bumps against a piece of scrap the size of a brick. He quietly loops his other arm through the straps of his pack. He crouches, one hand cradling the scrap against his side, the other holding the pack above the ground so it doesn't drag through the debris.

In glances, he tries to keep the wrecks of machinery between him and the gaping hangar door. Moving silently is difficult, the murmur of detritus underfoot trips his pulse to hammer hard. After each step, he waits, certain the crunch of loose concrete or the sound of some inadvertently nudged rubble will bring a swarm of bullets punching new beams of light through the thin metal siding and into his body.

But the silence remains, and Ben reaches the loose panel. He sets his pack down and lays his free palm against the warm metal sheet. Easing it to one side, he grimaces, expecting it to rattle and squeak, but it hinges quietly open. Outside, the dusty grass ends abruptly at a drop down a steep scree cut to the edge of the track. The open mine stretches out below its threshold. At the bottom, he catches a crescent of the oil-slick groundwater, already sliding into shade.

Ben pushes his pack through the gap, onto the narrow lip of land between the wall and the drop. He squints against the blinding daylight, the contrast painful to the darkness inside.

In the distance, on the far rim of the mine, perches the dorm, its shadow stretched long by the low-angled light. With luck, he can slip out, follow the cover of the ledge above the track all the way to the dorm, and then disappear into the woods unnoticed. At worst—

Gravel crackles behind him. Ben turns to face the hangar door, dropping to one knee and bringing the rifle to his shoulder. Tomos sprints along the rail toward the shack. Ben shoots. Tomos dives behind the terminus as the bullet flicks a stone from the mound. He pops up and fires into the dark building while Ben chambers another round. Tomos's bullet pings close by, the ricochet a yellow spark.

Ben fires again, blindly this time. The second time he pulls the trigger and the hammer clicks on an empty chamber. His ammunition spent, he grabs the scrap of metal and fumbles through the loose panel. He falls to the mine pit road and lands solidly on his side, struggling for breath. Ben forces himself to his feet and lobs the hunk of metal through the window frame. As it clangs inside, he pulls his pack down from the ledge and crouches behind cover again.

Above his head, the shack is peppered with bullets. Gunfire rattles in concussive echoes, back and forth across the mine's expanse.

With the assault fading and silence returning, Ben slings his pack over a shoulder and takes a few stumbling steps along the track, then freezes. Vito hunkers twenty paces ahead, tucked against the ledge, with his back turned and ears covered.

Ben yanks the empty clip from his rifle and fumbles for another from his thigh pocket, but stops before he can withdraw it. Vito's hands drop from his ears and he twists to face Ben. Their eyes meet, Ben's terror mirrored by Vito's.

Ben pulls his empty hand from his pocket and holds it out in front as a signal for them both to stop. He extends the rifle too, barrel pointing toward the sky to show it's harmless.

Vito's rifle trembles and his face twitches. There's a dangerous uncertainty in the young man's stance, an involuntary quiver. Beaded sweat lines the downy hair of his upper lip. If he's to shoot, it's as likely to be a nervous accident as intentional.

Ben finds his voice first, and quietly pleads, 'Vito, please—'

'Shut up,' Vito snarls, but a quiver in the words betrays his apprehension. Vito hears it too, and lunges closer to compensate, driving the barrel closer to Ben's face.

Ben falls to his knees and lets his rifle drop to the ground. He holds his hands up higher.

'Please, don't,' he whispers and pats the air between them. Ben glances at the dark hole at the end of the rifle barrel before dropping his eyes to the dirt a few steps in front of him.

Vito stops, as if just realizing his power. He straightens; his shoulders draw back. His voice is firm when he says, 'Don't move. Not even a twitch.'

'You can let me go,' Ben says. 'You can—'

'Dad,' Vito shouts. He peeks over the ledge in the following beat of silence, briefly searching the side of the mine shack and the ore piles in the distance.

'Don't—' Ben starts.

'Dad. I've got him,' Vito hollers as loud as he can. He shifts from foot to foot in a ballet of anxiety. 'He's here.'

A shout returns, the words muffled by distance and the lip of the mine pit.

'Vito, you don't have to,' Ben whispers. 'You can let me go.'

He pleads not only for himself, but for what he'll have to do to Vito. Vito is putting on a tough front, and Ben doesn't want to hurt him. But he saw the hesitancy when they first met, a young man more interested in rocks and history than guns and bears, a young man caught up in his father's vision. Ben doesn't believe Vito will shoot.

Ben's hands quaver over his head and he raises his eyes enough to see Vito's boots. They're too far away, but he has to try. He has to rush Vito.

The shouts of the two men approaching grows clearer.

Ben clasps his fingers into fists to steady them.

'Vito,' he says, hoping the kid, hearing his name spoken, will be reminded of his humanity. Perhaps it will etch some respect back between them, perhaps it will steady his trigger finger for the vital second Ben needs to rush him. 'I'm going to stand now.'

'Don't do it,' Vito warns, but his voice hitches and the words come out as imploring rather than commanding.

'I'm going to. I'll go real slow.' Ben rises to one knee.

'I said don't,' Vito shouts and jabs the rifle at Ben.

Arnott's voice comes from over the lip of the mine, closer now. 'Vito?'

'Dad, I've got him,' Vito shouts back. His desperation could almost be mistaken for excitement, if not for the fear on his face and haunting his eyes.

Loose gravel crackles as Ben draws his other foot under him and stands. A glance overtop the mine's rim reveals Arnott breaking from the stunted undergrowth near the conveyor, moving at a full sprint. Tomos is closer, rounding the corner of the shack. Their eyes meet and Tomos raises his rifle to shoot.

'I said stay,' Vito yells and spins the rifle, striking Ben across the jaw with the butt.

The world hurtles sideways. Ben is thrown against the ledge and then slumps onto the gravel. His vision blurs. Blinding agony and the taste of blood confuse Ben's senses, but not as much as the sound of a rifle-shot and the warm spray that showers his face. It gets in his eyes, speckles his lips.

Have I been shot? His mind prattles feebly.

Ben licks his lips. He blinks rapidly, trying to clear his vision of blood. Everything lies sideways, the whole world at an angle, but he stares into Vito's eyes as if they both still stand upright.

Vito has fallen too.

Above and still far away, Arnott is shouting.

Ben raises his head, works his jaw from side to side. Inside, something pops and grinds. A spike of pain shoots down his neck. He stretches the shocked muscles, spits blood in the dirt; thick and deep maroon, it seeps into the thirsty clay. The sight of it is surprising, something intimate and hidden being unexpectedly exposed.

Far away, Arnott isn't shouting words anymore, just noise and anguish.

Tomos yells, too, from somewhere.

Ben frowns. The commotion sounds muffled in his ears. His vision still seems hazy. Perspective has been flattened. Everything beyond Vito's face is blurry. Ben pushes himself upright, wobbles, and sits hunched, cross-legged with his wrists resting limply on the dirt by his sides.

Through welling tears, Ben cocks his head in confusion.

It doesn't look like Vito anymore.

Its eyes are dead.

There's a weeping hole in the boy's cheek.

Vito is dead and the hole in him seems too small a thing to have made that happen.

The silence is total and unbearable.

Another shot rings out. It sounds far away, as if muffled by cotton. Then another shot. A flash of movement in the corner of his vision draws his attention. It shifts again, in the shadow beside the dorm building, on the far side of the mine complex.

Ben fumbles his rifle from the dirt and tries to stand. He staggers to the side, tripping over Vito's legs, knocking a stream of gravel over the track's edge, before he can get his feet properly beneath him.

The stones fall and splash into the water below.

All noises still sound so small, so distant, a muted wailing, the unpredictable thump of gunfire. Ben doesn't know if he's the target. He doesn't even crouch behind the cover of the ledge in case he is. He can't even think to hide. It's all he can do to make one foot land in front of the other.

Portions of the track have collapsed along the edge; other stretches have grown striped and rugged with knee-deep ruts from runoff. It sinks deeper into the mine, which fills Ben with a growing claustrophobia, more earth between him and the sky, the horizon shrinking as he descends, the weight of the rock pressing in from all around.

Ben stumbles and staggers, feeling like he can't move fast enough, away from the mine shack and toward the dorm. The gun there sparks and sparks and sparks, relentless, then he finds himself below the building. The road has sunk deeper here, and he starts scrambling up a slope three times as tall as himself.

The rock is blasted, rotten, and frail from decades of weather. A foothold collapses. He slides down clawing scree back to the road. He doesn't feel anything, just knows the pit feels like a grave he has to get out of. Clumsy and frantic, cutting fingers and peeling skin from his knuckles, he finally heaves himself over the rim.

Mechanically, he's on his feet again, running into the shadow of the dorm building. He drops to his knees, soaked with sweat, chest heaving and muscles numb, starving for oxygen.

Emma's there. Her pack, like a tortoise's shell, seems too big for her to carry. Her shoulder is braced against the corner of the building, under the bear's scratches, her feet planted wide for stability. The dorm house's wood is pocked and prickly with fresh damage. She's been taking return fire.

Emma doesn't look at him; her focus is on shooting across the mine, shooting at Tomos and Arnott. And she scowls, shoots. Her body jolts with the kickback, a tense percussion shocking her taut muscles. She pulls the bolt, takes a quick breath, and fires again.

Emma steps back from the corner and squats with her pack pressed back against the wall. She tugs the magazine free and it clangs against the three others piled by her boot.

Thirty bullets spent.

One of them took Vito.

She slaps a new clip home and slings her rifle over her shoulder. Their eyes meet. Ben's are grateful to see her, relieved. Emma's are set, anguished, her expression taut.

'We're going.' She grabs Ben by the arm.

Ben doesn't feel like his legs work anymore; there's a void where his body used to be, but Emma's persistent pull gets him to his feet again. The world becomes a confusion of whipping branches and clawing barbs, the sensation of tumbling onward through the forest, gravity's pull twisted to its side. Drawing him on, all force is now anchored to the tug of Emma's hand.

14

Sounds return to Ben's battered senses. The rustle of their movement becomes clear, the pace of their breathing, the grip Emma has on his hand as she pulls him forward. Sweat soaks through his jacket and the air is cold on his face as they run.

The sky becomes flat grey and drops closer overhead, seconds counted by their footfalls and minutes pass in a blink and a breath. Breath, it seems like each one draws less oxygen as their muscles grow more fatigued. The temperature drops steadily. Behind the clouds, the sun leaves the valley and twilight is diffused through a pall that's descended so low that it eddies and whirls through the trees. Still they run.

Ben's legs give out and Emma's hand jerks free when he falls. He wishes it hadn't, but he can't run anymore. A few steps ahead, Emma turns, a questioning expression on her face, the forest writhing around her.

'I need a minute,' Ben gasps, a shiver runs under the sweat coating his skin. He leans forward, his forehead pressed against his hands, waiting for the nausea to pass. How long have they been running? His body clenches and he vomits, blood from his mouth mixed with bile.

Emma returns to him, kneels, and rests a hand on his back. Her gaze keeps darting to the woods behind them. Every noise seems like a threat.

'What are you doing here?' Ben asks when his breath returns. He sits back on his heels and wipes his lips with the back of his hand. 'I told you to stay away.'

Emma stops scanning the woods and looks at him. 'Not your choice to make.'

'You can't be here. It's too dangerous,' Ben croaks. 'I don't know what I'd do if anything happened to you.'

Emma's scowl collapses into a smile. She gives a slight shake of her head. 'You're an idiot,' she says, but not meanly. She pulls him into an embrace.

Ben closes his eyes and loses himself in her, wanting to draw her in, wanting to crawl inside of her. Weeks of doubt and loneliness disappear and the cold place they lived is left blissfully empty. He pulls her as close as he can, desperate and rough, arms grasping. She returns his force.

Branches swirl around them as the wind shifts.

When they finally part, Emma whispers, 'That boy.'

'I know,' Ben says; when he leans back Emma is staring into the woods behind them.

'Temperature's falling,' she says and looks up into the corrugated cloud. 'It's going to snow.'

She stands, and starts off again, at a walk this time. 'Let's keep moving.'

'Keep moving,' Ben repeats, a command to his insubordinate legs. He wants to stop, to succumb to an exhaustion so deep that he would just lay down in the moss and let the night cover him in deep snow. He struggles to his feet and runs a few steps to catch up to Emma.

'We need a place for the night,' Emma tells him.

'I know a place,' Ben replies as he walks past, his hand briefly linked in hers, her fingers trailing a fraction longer after he's gone.

The snow starts as frozen pellets, tiny fragments of sky falling onto their hair and faces, pattering against the foliage and dusting the ground. Grey clouds have settled in low and solid, scraping the swaying treetops.

'Are we close?' Emma's breath is visible, and her words are half-lost in the wind. She rubs her hands together quickly, then thrusts them into her armpits. 'This'll turn bad.'

'I know it.' Ben slurs a little. His jaw is swollen and sore. His inhalation snags on the cold, so he breathes shallower, slower. He doesn't break stride, weaving through the trees, and he doesn't look back when he says, 'Not much farther.'

As if conjured by those words, they walk up a slight incline and onto firm, even ground. They veer to follow the old roadbed, too overgrown to be visible unless trodden upon. The going is easier with the hard-packed earth beneath their feet. They each follow a wheel rut, staggered a few meters apart, close enough to hear the other breathing.

They move faster when a distant crackle and tumble of thunder rolls in from the north. The cold seeps through their jackets;

damp with sweat, the plummeting temperature feels even more marked. It bites at their noses and cheeks; their eyes run from the wind that brings it. Their legs tingle, the frigid air finding a weakness in the thin fabric of their pants. It's early for such a storm, but not unheard of.

The road slopes gradually downward. The ground becomes soft and squelches, wet under a thick layer of moss. Trees grow more stunted, sparser, and then there are none at all. Ben pauses at the boundary of the clearing. Emma stops beside him. Patches of open water mirror the clouds, like the sky has been flayed and lies in tattered scraps across the ground before them.

The meadow's perimeter is guarded by a palisade of knee-high grasses with sharp edges, mangy cattails starting to bend under the accumulating snow, and the wiry interwoven branches of alder and willow bushes. Everything is draped in twilight, no shadows, only the slow sapping of colours from a steadily disappearing world.

'That's it?' Emma asks.

'That's it,' Ben confirms.

A distant pulse of lightning illuminates wavering striations in the layered clouds. They both wait, subconsciously counting the seconds to calculate their distance from the inversion's front. The temperature continues dropping severely under the guidance of a persistent northerly.

'It'll do.' Ben's tone is unconvincing, even to himself.

He leaves the trees for the tall grasses. The moss sinks ankle deep with each step. He stumbles in a hollow, icy water pouring over the rim of his boot. It feels like knives.

Even under the cover of the storm, he doesn't dare flick on his headlamp. The thought of doing so has him concentrate a little harder to parse any voices from the constant current of swirling winds; it has him scan the frail grey for any hint of Arnott or Tomos.

There are no voices and there is only Emma, shifting from foot to foot, her arms tucked into a tight hug. She has a strained expression on her face, her skin seeming lucent in the rare remnants of light.

The snow is heavier now, driven sideways, forcing Ben to squint. He raises a hand to keep it from his eyes. A white crust has already settled over everything.

A car sits at the centre of the meadow. It may once have been a colour, but is now the mottle and shred of calico rust. The bubble curve of the hood, the cab, and the trunk are a style that hasn't been considered for more than a century. Barnacles of weathering cling to the heavy chrome bumpers. The front tires are missing; one axle sits on a thick stump, the other on the ground. The rear wheels are now just rims, half-sunk into the ground and surrounded by shreds of rubber.

Ben touches the hood ornament as he rounds the car to the passenger side. It's a woman standing on one foot, her opposite ankle raised to her knee. One arm is thrust out in front, the other held by her hip. Behind her flow the certain curves of deco angel wings; her stance is of leaning into a strong wind, her posture a challenge.

The billowing curves of the hood are glazed with a rind of ice that's been sucked from the air. Ben thumps it and it crazes like broken glass.

Extinction

The passenger door is frozen shut. Ben plants a boot against the back door and levers it open. The ice cracks and the hinges shriek in protest. The side-view mirror, attached only by a wire, swings back and forth, beating a waning rhythm against the side panel.

A downdraft blasts from directly overhead. The microburst throttles the surrounding trees and buffets the car, pushing the mirror to tap arrhythmically again, dull and metallic. It's barely audible in the squall. Ben tucks his face into his arm to protect it from the renewed blast of numbing air, and to fend off the potential of frostbite.

Emma slips into the passenger seat and makes room for him to follow.

Distracted, Ben closes the door behind her and retraces his steps around the front of the car. He stands with a hand resting on the driver's side handle. There's something unsettling that he can't place. He looks out, above the trees, his vision driven to static by the pelting snow. The mountains are gone. Dark clouds scallop the sky. A purple sheet of lightning crawls through them and a sustained growl of thunder comes almost instantly this time.

Ben flinches and strains to hear anything else once it fades. It's the howling wind. It reminds him of something he hadn't consciously registered until now. The pitch is the same as he heard through the haze of shock on the mine track, Arnott's scream when Vito died, the ghost wail over a fallen child.

At the realization, Ben finds he can't command his body to move, can't feel his fingers resting on the handle. A piercing chill seeps down his collar; burning sparks of ice pellets needle his exposed skin. His breath is caught, no exhaled cloud obscuring his vision, no searing inhalation follows. The temperature drops by degrees instantly. The trees surrounding the clearing bend and writhe in a chaotic wind that shrieks from every direction.

The driver's door opens with a groan and Emma yells, 'Get in.'

Her command is punctuated by an instantaneous flash and thunderclap.

Ben shrugs his pack from his shoulders. They wrangle it over the headrests and into the back seat, where it lands atop Emma's. Ben ducks into the car and heaves the door closed, struggling with the clawing winds that fight to keep it open.

The thump of the door slamming mutes the storm. Even getting out of the wind feels immeasurably warmer, though it's an illusion of contrast. They both shiver uncontrollably.

'You good?' Ben stammers while trying to work some feeling back into his hands.

Emma gives him a distracted nod, her trembling fingers fumble the plastic brick of a hotpot from an outside pouch of her bag. She snaps it and drops it to the floor with a thump. The chemicals mix in the resin tube and the cab starts to warm.

The snow flails past, now wet and heavy. It starts piling on the cracked, lee-side windows. The metal creaks and ticks as the cold grasps hold of the car and squeezes. The glass grows opaque as their breath condenses. The worst hits. The howl rises. The outside world obscures.

Ben finds his headlamp and clicks it on. He sets it on the dash, the yellow light casting only the colour of warmth. Their breath is loud. Outside, the gusts are strong enough to jostle the metal frame around them. The seats are torn, threadbare edges and exposed foam padding. The vinyl dashboard is sun-faded, dry, and cracked to show the rusted surface under the veneer. The air smells of mould and the lingering reek of oil and gasoline.

A muted flash illuminates the passenger side window, followed by a percussive smack that rings the wrecked car like a bell. Ben pictures the shockwave rolling overhead. It is a visible sound.

The hotpot fends off the worst of the cold. Emma wriggles out of her jacket then pats her shirt to see how damp it is. She's deliberate; her expression is fixed.

Ben slips out of his jacket. He works his jaw side to side, probes for loose teeth with his tongue, and figures nothing is broken, just bruised.

Emma looks at him but can only hold his eyes briefly. She pulls her damp shirt over her head and leaves it crumpled on the dash. Her features are etched sharp by the headlamp glow. The cold textures her skin with goose bumps. Her hand is ice through the fabric of his shirt, pressed flat against his chest. She lifts his shirt over his head and her eyes well at seeing the damage on his side. The flesh feels so hot under her palm.

'Emma . . .' Ben hesitates and the word fades inside another tumble of thunder. His voice cracks and he shudders at the clumsy machine of this tongue, teeth, and lips. She killed a young man. He wants to tell her it will be okay, but knows she doesn't need a lie right now.

She kisses him and everything beyond the two of them disappears. He winces, but returns the strength of her lips pressed to his, driven by the focus the pain brings. Their fingers fumble blindly with each other's clothes. It hurts too much to part for any longer than needed to blunder out of their boots and remaining clothes.

Once shed, their bodies press and become more urgent. The grunt and moan of their joining is forceful, their movements desperate, as if they could hold each other together, with clasping arms and clawing hands, as if the hurt is a deserved punishment for such pleasure. They welcome it together, under the delusion that all thoughts of death can be erased by a reckless act of life.

Ben comes swiftly and hard, finding that being animal in this way does alleviate the trauma, if only for a few thoughtless moments. When he opens his eyes, Emma is watching him with an expression he can't decipher. He pulls her lips to his with hands on both sides of her face. He wishes he could do more.

They rest with foreheads touching, trying to fend off the loneliness as his heartbeat retreats from within her. She cries horribly and Ben draws her to him. He doesn't want her to see that he has his own tears. He holds her until the tremors ebb, minutes or hours, he can't tell, and then he strokes the back of her neck.

The world inches back in with the sounds of the storm outside. At some point, the hotpot runs out of fuel and the press of the cold returns. They unpack their sleeping bags in silence and nestle in, Ben reclining with his back against the door and Emma on her side, resting her head on his chest.

They sit in the near silence that a thick blanket of snow can create, the only sound their breathing, slow again. They listen for errant noises from outside, but only hear the shush of nylon fabric when one of them shifts. The heat and smell of their sex fades from the car, leaving a chill outside the sleeping bags.

'I shot—' Emma starts.

'I know,' Ben says and kisses the top of her head.

'I can't stand it here,' she whispers.

Emma reaches from under the sleeping bags and turns a knob on the radio. It clicks, and of course, no sound comes out; the battery is long dead, the radio broken, the car gutted. Emma doesn't seem to notice as she twists the tuning knob, as if searching the silence for the right station.

Ben watches, engrossed by the movements of her fingers. He sees the veins hovering shallow under her skin and he scowls. It's too thin a membrane to protect us, he thinks.

It sounds like Emma is whispering, barely louder than an exhalation. Ben strains to hear, but can't make out any words.

Finally, she seems satisfied. She smiles as if she has found her favourite station and it is playing her favourite song, one that only she and the rusty antenna sprouting through a drift of snow can hear. She peeks up at him, withdraws her arm back under the sleeping bag, and tucks her feet further up.

'Sounds like the wind's died down,' Emma says. 'Has it cleared?'

Ben leans to the side, resting his arm on the steering wheel. He peers through a gap in the snow at the top of the windshield, rubbing the glass to clear the condensation. Snow still drifts past, flake after flake flashing into view, then winking out of the seeping headlamp glow, like frozen fireflies.

'The moon is up,' Ben says. 'Can see its glow through the clouds.'

Emma shakes her head slightly. 'Doesn't matter.' Her features are drawn tight and her attention remains fixed on the car radio.

Ben settles back, Emma warm on his chest, his chin nestled near her ear. 'You didn't have a choice,' he whispers.

Emma glances up at him and her chin dimples. 'I can't . . . you talk.'

Ben glances at the moon once more, then looks down over their bodies, intertwined under the sleeping bags. He buries his nose in her hair, wanting to make the smell of her an indelible memory. He closes his eyes and tries to remember their first time, years ago in university, and all the times after that. They had fit well together from the start.

'Are you sniffing me?' she asks.

'I am,' he admits.

'Weirdo.'

They laugh, but the sound is sad, accommodating.

Ben rubs her arm.

'You ever heard of Earth Dreams?' he finally asks, and she shakes her head a little.

'That's what the shrinks are calling it,' Ben continues. 'Some of the first migrants are suffering them, these vivid, completely immersive dreams of Earth. Where they're in a jungle or a forest or on the plains, and there're herds of animals, swarms of insects, and the sounds of birdsong on the breeze. Life everywhere.'

'I haven't heard of this,' she mutters.

'They say the reptilian part of our brain can't handle the centrifugal gravity of the transport spinners, or the unfamiliar ones of the deep colonies. They say that it craves real gravity, craves sunlight, the familiar rhythm of Earth days and nights. It reels from everything it hasn't evolved for hundreds of thousands of years to deal with. They say that Earth Dreams are the brain's way of coping with the fact it'll never see Earth again.'

'You believe that?'

Ben shrugs and holds her tighter.

'It's still all new. A resurgence of two-hundred-thousand-year-old memories from the deepest folds of our brains, something to comfort those who go farther from home than anyone has ever been, knowing they won't be returning,' he says. 'Makes sense to me. We know how our bodies can deal with it, we don't have much a clue how our brains will. The primal brain is set up to react, not to think. It's there to make us survive at all costs. Doesn't seem out of the question that it would start taking over, fighting for us where our conscious brain has failed. "Genetic memory" they're calling it. A manifest of evolution, buried deep in our heads.'

'If it's only a few people,' Emma says, 'the shrinks can't even be sure. What you're talking about is only a theory.'

'Maybe,' Ben says, twirling his finger gently against her temple. 'They say a few people have even gone catatonic from,' he leans closer and whispers with a quavering, dramatic voice, 'the space madness.'

Emma chuckles and swats him away. 'Better than whatever madness is fermenting between your ears.'

Ben ignores her, and continues, 'It's diagnosable. Imagine that, something called Earth Dreams being considered a mental disorder.' Ben smiles and sighs. 'Sounds pretty wonderful to me.'

'Columbus never had crippling and uncontrollable dreams of Spain,' Emma says.

'Maybe,' Ben says. 'But he didn't really land in a new world, it was the same one. It had sunshine and water and air and gravity. Besides, he was Italian.'

Emma flicks a dismissive hand in the air.

'This is different,' Ben continues. 'We should expect the mind to reel with echoes from our deepest past. It takes the most extreme trauma to trigger the unforgotten forgotten. Our conscious brain says "yes", but the brain whose only responsibility is our very survival says, "fuck no".'

Emma is turning the radio dial again. Her fingers work smoothly, deliberately hunting the frequencies. Twisting the needle one way and then back again. She swims past one frequency and into the next, searching.

'You'll be down here all alone,' Emma says. 'Eventually.'

'I won't be alone.' Ben tucks a curl of hair behind Emma's ear. 'Poppy'll still be here.'

'I'm being serious,' Emma says. 'You know what I mean.'

Ben stares out the side window. Framed by a lattice of ice, the trees encircling the clearing are vague, trembling on the edge of his vision. They are softened and obscured by the condensation haze and the snow. In his mind, they are making noise, rustling and swaying, but in the car there is silence, the turbulence muted to all but one sense.

'Being left all alone,' Ben says, 'sounds like a dream. Fleeing a sinking ship doesn't make much sense. Sure, you escape, but now you're out in the open ocean with no land in sight. Doesn't seem to leave you in a much better spot.'

He reaches across and gently touches a scar on Emma's arm. It's a thin, pale line. He expects Emma to recoil, but she doesn't; she keeps twisting the dial.

He asks, 'What are you doing? It's broken. You won't get anything out of it.'

Ben can hear her breathing. Without looking up she speaks, her voice soft.

'Somewhere, right now, something has to be exactly right. Everything has a line, a circle without a blemish. I'm trying to get everything perfect. What if the radio needle was that one thing out of joint, the only thing keeping everything from fitting again? Imagine if I could get everything just right and this would be the time and place where everything is good.'

Thunder rambles across on a distant horizon, the stormfront travelling away from them now.

'Don't be mad,' Ben says. 'I'm not mad at you for going.'

Emma stops fiddling with the radio, she seems irritated by it. She could not find the right frequency. He gently guides her hand back under the sleeping bags. They hold on tight to each other because they both know that, one day, they won't be able to anymore.

'I just wanted out,' Emma says quietly. 'I wanted you to come.'

'Fuck no,' Ben whispers.

Emma leans forward and turns the radio knob until it clicks.

They no longer receive frequencies, adrift, they are deaf to the sound and float invisibly deeper into the night. At some point, Emma falls into a fitful sleep. Ben tries to soothe her when she squirms, giving quiet noises and gentle caresses. When she cries out, she doesn't wake. While exhaustion holds her firmly under, cruelly, it seems to pinch Ben whenever he drifts too close to sleep.

It's still dark when Ben eases Emma to the seat and twists out of the cab into the cold quiet night. He makes sure the sleeping bags are pulled up to her chin before inching the door closed. Emma doesn't even twinge at the groaning metal, her exhaustion weighs so heavily.

He should be shivering, but he is warm, draped in heavy, thick pelts that smell wild, like animals. He stands with an arm resting on the car's roof, staring across it in wonder. The air is clear now, the sky speckled with stars, but they're in unfamiliar configurations. The blackness between them is free from the wandering specks of satellites and the moon is full, its light striking the fresh snow incandescent.

The surrounding forest seems farther away than he remembers, a saw-toothed black line nearer the horizon. Starlit mountains rise, blue in the distance. Between the car and the trees, enormous creatures move and shift, a herd moving slowly, seemingly oblivious to his presence. One of them lets out a huff and another rumbles in response.

Elephants, he thinks, no, they're mammoths. Four adults and two babies.

A murmur comes from his side, a human voice from a figure that somehow stays hidden in the corner of his eye when he turns to look. Ben ducks behind the car. The figure does the same. The voice speaks in a language he doesn't know, but he understands.

'This is as close as we can get,' he leans closer to whisper and the flicker in his peripheral vision turns to face him. There is more than one. Ben grasps his spear tighter, to choke out the frustration that he can't pin down these lurking shadows, can't make their features or forms align into something familiar.

'This is close enough,' he whispers.

They erupt from behind the car. The mammoths turn, spooked by the sudden movement and the sound of animal-skin boots grinding through the snow toward them. Massive tusks glint smooth arcs in the moonlight. The shaggy tendrils of their pelts quiver.

Ben throws his spear. It casts multiple shadows as it flies over an unbroken expanse of snow. As four spears strike one of the baby mammoths, Ben realizes his clan have thrown their weapons as well. The little one shrieks in pain and surprise.

The mammoths become chaos. Two charge the hunters, trumpeting, and with heads swaying tusks in preparation of the attack. Two others lead the injured baby and second juvenile towards the tree line.

The ground shakes as the charging mammoths draw near, gaining a speed that seems impossible for such large creatures. Their stampede sounds like thunder. Ben spins, desperately searching for safety. He judges the car is too far away now, and with Emma still sleeping inside, he fears inciting one of the enraged behemoths to trample it.

The closest animal draws up on its hind legs. Ben cranes and raises an arm in a feeble attempt at defence. The ground cracks and slips, liquid, from underfoot. Ben falls backwards. Instead of striking hard earth, his breath is stolen by frigid water. A lake had been hidden beneath them by a thick skin of ice. The mammoths thrash and writhe, with screams that sound human.

Ben chokes on the churning waves and dives to avoid being battered to death by the beast's struggles. He swims down. His skin, struck instantly and thankfully numb at first contact with the water, does nothing to keep the creeping cold from clawing through his muscles, in search of every last shred of warmth.

Ben reaches the lake bottom, his feet prompting two slowly rolling clouds of fine silt. Above, silhouetted by the rippling glow of the full moon and framed by the jagged hole in the ice, the outlines of the mammoths slow, grow still, then start to swell as they sink toward him.

There's no air left. He pushes off the lake bottom and crawls back toward the surface. The oxygen fleeing his blood, his lungs beg for air. The weight of his pelts threatens to drown him. Ben kicks off his boots and sheds layer upon layer of skins. Naked now, he strains upward, the need to breathe a tangible ache throughout his body. Pulling on watery rungs, he passes the corpses of the mammoths as they drift toward the lake bottom. He climbs through the spangles of glittering bubbles that trail in their passing.

When he breaks the surface, it's daylight. He gasps and treads in the groundwater pool at the bottom of the mine pit. The rainbow slick of petrochemicals ripples out in concentric waves. Above, beyond the rim of the corkscrewing pit road, he sees himself held frozen at the command of Vito's rifle, then struck down.

After the rifle-shot cracks and after Vito's body quakes from the bullet passing through it, after it falls to the ground, Ben hears clearly the two words that Arnott had wailed in that moment, 'Emma, no!'

15

Ben listens to Emma's sleeping breath, watches darkness seep into her features as the headlamp's battery wanes and eventually winks out. Wind moans, a lonesome sound in the trees, until it too fades. Sometime in the early morning, the remaining clouds are ushered out of the valley, revealing stars that follow in slow smooth arcs over the jagged tree line. Black peaks loom in the diminishing moonlight.

Had Arnott really shouted her name?

How could he know her?

Ben watches everything change, watches Emma change in the growing dawn.

It all fades and sunlight blanches the mountain tops in a clear new morning.

The snow on the windshield glows white and starts to melt. A crack running through a clear corner of the glass pinches the light into a piercing thread. Ben blinks at it and tilts his head back into the shade. His jaw feels tight and swollen. His side aches horribly again. The soreness in every joint and muscle makes him realize he hasn't moved in hours.

Emma's breathing changes. She shifts and murmurs and stretches. Looking up at him with sleepy eyes, she smiles briefly before a cloud crosses her face, the memory of the day before creeping back. She turns away.

'Your jaw is purple and fat,' she says.

Ben nods. Even little movements hurt, but he accepts it in favour of the missing time of the previous night, the disconnected spell at the cabin when he doesn't remember pain and he doesn't remember his body.

'I gotta pee,' Emma says, throwing back the corner of the sleeping bag. She roots her pants from the footwell and slips her feet through. She laces her boots and bumps the door open with a shoulder.

Cool, fresh air washes in. It's clean, and only when Ben smells the dampness tinged sweet by trees does he notice the cab has grown so stale from both of them breathing it all night. Snow melts from the branches and falls like rain. It drips onto the trunk with a rhythmic, metallic twang.

Emma stands, shimmies into her shirt and pulls her coat over the top. She leaves the door open. Ben watches her hop across the clearing through knee-deep snow and she does not look back, even as the woods envelope her. There's movement between the trees, she crouches and touches the ground, and then she is gone.

When he's alone again, Ben digs the vial of painkillers out of his pants pocket, bumps two onto his palm, and dry-swallows them. He wants to ask her what she knows about the hunters but struggles, his evidence based on dreams. Or was it something real?

Bergs of snow slide down the windshield, leaving clear veins of water threading their wake. Ben lies back and slings an arm across his eyes, willing the pills to work faster. Eventually, he gathers the resolve to get dressed. Water patters all around the car, the metal shedding the melt into the surrounding moss and puddles. He rolls the sleeping bags into clumsy bundles. Everything is still cold and damp.

Ben slides across the seat and exits through the passenger door. He looks into the bush after Emma while he dresses, but sees nothing. Swiping his arm across the hood to sweep away a slushy drift, he wrestles the packs and rifles from the back seat, and stacks everything in its place. Before closing the door, Ben pauses. He checks the direction Emma had gone again before leaning back into the car and turning the radio on. He gives the frequency knob a twist, hoping it lands on the right spot, but knowing the chances are impossible.

The door hinges groan shut. Emma re-emerges, rubbing snow between her hands to wash them. She bounds from one deep footprint to the next, retracing her path back to the car. The snow spills over the tops of her boots. She cringes and grits her teeth.

Ben hands her a protein bar and unwraps one for himself.

Emma takes a bite and wrinkles her nose. 'Chocolate banana. Tastes like chemicals.'

Ben shrugs and examines his bar, not even sure what it is

supposed to taste like. The pills start softening the edges of his discomfort, but his jaw still aches while he chews.

They sit on the hood in the sun, feeling its growing warmth and watching water drip from the enshrouded branches. Their breath is invisible again. The sky is pure and the air clean. The surrounding mountains are covered in a fresh cloak of white.

Ben rummages through his remaining gear: two clips of ten bullets each, a knife, a foil-wrapped meal, a small canister of white gas, water, the walkie-talkie, other odds and ends.

'How many rounds you got left?' he asks.

Emma holds her protein bar between her teeth and pulls the clip from her rifle.

'Six,' she says.

They look at each other and Emma reseats the clip with a frown. She takes a bite and chews slowly. Ben's gaze lingers on her. Something is different, a distraction in her, a diversion; how she looks away when he doesn't.

Ben crumples his empty wrapper, then fishes the battered cigarette package out of his breast pocket. He holds it out to her.

Emma shakes her head. She glances at the pale grey hint of a moon hovering near the horizon before quickly turning away to look across the clearing. 'The snow's not so deep in the trees.'

Ben flips the pack open to see the cigarettes are mostly destroyed. Fingering through the debris, he finds half of an intact one and pulls it out. He squints at Emma, cocks an eyebrow, and lights it. He shakes the package empty beside the car. A hash of filters, papers, and tobacco flakes peppers the snow near the bare axle. He takes the filter from his lips and exhales.

'It'll all melt in a few hours,' Ben says through a haze of smoke, 'in the valley anyhow. That,' he wags a finger at the mountain peaks, 'is here to stay.'

'I know,' Emma says. 'I'm saying it'll be easier to move through the trees than it is out here, or than it will be along the river.'

Ben pulls the empty clip from his rifle and deposits it into his jacket pocket. He takes a full one from the hood beside him and slips it into his thigh pocket, then loads the last one in his rifle. There's one last drag from the cigarette and Ben drops the butt into the snow. It gives a quick hiss.

'Last one,' he says, more to himself than to Emma.

'Good for you,' Emma says, with an exaggerated smile and a hearty pat on his thigh. 'I'm proud of you. You'll live a long and healthy life now.'

Ben glances at her, but she's staring into the trees. He hoists himself from the hood and starts packing his gear.

'Oh, come on,' Emma says. 'Tough crowd.'

'Time to go.'

Emma loops her arms through her backpack straps, and starts breaking a trail northward. Ben stands in front of the rusty car, watching her go.

Halfway to the trees, she turns.

'Come on.' Emma gives an uncertain jerk of her chin. 'We can make your truck by mid-afternoon.'

Ben picks a piece of tobacco from his tongue and examines it, a dark fleck on his thumb. He swipes it against his pant leg and points in the direction of Emma's footprints through the deep snow. Stepping high into her tracks, he heads off that way.

'What are you doing?' Emma asks.

'Bear's this way,' Ben says over his shoulder.

'You don't know that. You don't have the tracker anymore.' Emma waves a hand at the forest, the horizon of mountains, the sky. 'The Boss could be anywhere.'

'Bear's this way,' he repeats. 'Don't need a tracker. This is his valley. I know where he'll be going, and the snow will make him easier to track.' Ben stumbles on the uneven ground, thrusting a hand into the snow to steady himself. 'Tomos and Arnott can't have him. He's mine.'

'Ben, wait,' Emma says, but he keeps moving. 'You think they're still going after the bear? After what happened? For Christ's sake, they'll be coming for us and we'd be wise not to be found. Use your head.'

Ben keeps trudging through the snow.

'Wait,' Emma shouts.

Ben stops at the spot where her footprints enter the shrubs ringing the tree line. He examines the ground ahead for a moment, cocks his head at another line of tracks they cross. Those have broad pads and five round toes. The impressions of the claws are still distinct in the melt. He turns to face her from across the meadow, eyebrows raised and his thoughts a jumble of conflict.

One question keeps surfacing through the confusion. How could you?

He steps back into the clearing, unable to take his eyes from her.

The snow between them is so bright it hurts.

The trickle and drip of meltwater comes from everywhere.

Emma sighs and jabs a thumb over her shoulder, to the north. 'We should go back to the dam, get in your truck, and leave.' She waits, but Ben just stares at her.

'This is nuts,' she says. 'You're nuts. They had you pinned. They would have killed you. They aren't playing.'

'You should go.' Ben shifts, like he's about to turn and keep walking, but can't make his feet follow his mind. 'You can't be a part of this anymore.'

'Seriously?' Emma scoffs. 'I can take care of myself. What's wrong with you?'

Ben plants his hands on his hips and looks at his feet, nodding and muttering, 'Yeah, you can take care of yourself . . .'

When he's finally able to force his gaze to meet hers again, he doesn't shy away. He can see her thoughts clearly; she thinks he's being ridiculous.

'You're rattled.' Emma taps the side of her head. 'I get it. Someone's dead, Ben. They'll come after us now, not the bear. Others will get killed if you keep this up. You'll get killed. And for what?' When Ben doesn't answer, she throws her arms out to the sides in frustration. 'Leave the fucking bear for them and let's go.'

'You shot that boy,' Ben snaps. 'He's dead, and you shot him.'

'Because he was going to shoot you.'

'He wasn't. He was scared.' Ben bites his lip when he sees how deep his words dig. He can't think straight. He shakes his head and continues, 'And the bear—'

'Fuck the bear.' Emma's voice cracks. 'I came back for you.'

'You misunderstood me earlier,' he says in a measured tone as he unzips a pouch and pulls out a carabiner with a loop of keys attached. He flings them across the meadow at her. They punch a hole in the snow at her feet. 'You go back to the truck and leave. I'm going after the bear. You aren't coming with me.'

'What's wrong?' Em⬛⬛⬛⬛⬛⬛⬛⬛⬛⬛⬛ys out of the drift. 'I'll come with you. I⬛⬛⬛⬛⬛⬛⬛⬛⬛⬛⬛ to the truck, but I'll come with you—'

'You lie,' Ben shou⬛⬛⬛⬛⬛⬛⬛⬛⬛ in her direction. 'Now go.'

Ben takes a few ste⬛⬛⬛⬛⬛⬛⬛⬛⬛

Emma starts to foll⬛⬛⬛⬛⬛⬛⬛⬛⬛

In one smooth mo⬛⬛⬛⬛⬛⬛⬛⬛⬛ rifle and raises it at her.

Emma freezes, shackled to the spot.

Ben's eyes are ringed with red and tears stream down his cheeks. His lips are drawn back and teeth bared. His features are pure rage, twitching with an energy that seems a struggle to control. His finger rests against the trigger.

'How do you know Arnott?' Ben asks.

Emma stands stock still, gaping. Her lips move a few times, mouthing the words before her voice comes back, 'I don't—'

'Don't lie, Emma.' His voice hitches on emotion as he shakes his head, oscillating between rage and heartbreak. 'No more. Please, don't . . .'

Ben advances a step and jabs the rifle in her direction. 'Back at the mine, he knew you. He shouted your name. How did Arnott know your name, Emma?'

A whisper creeps through the branches, causing them to sway and bob. The stillness returns as quickly as it was robbed.

He barks, 'Answer me.'

Emma flinches, too stunned to speak or even breathe.

'Why are you trying so hard to keep me from the bear?'

'I'm not. I'm—'

'Bullshit,' Ben shouts, his lips glistening. His anger quickly becomes pleading, as he repeats, 'Emma, please don't lie. I don't understand . . .' As quickly as it dissolved, his anger rushes back with one ragged inhalation. The rifle trembles as he grips it tighter, as if the rage has nowhere else to go but into the weapon.

Emma judges him for a moment, and then starts slowly across the clearing toward him.

'How do you know Arnott?' he growls. 'Why are you trying to keep me away from the bear?'

'I'm not. I promise,' she says, throwing her hands out for balance as she stumbles into knee-deep, wet pot hidden underneath the snow.

'I don't understand,' Ben says, letting the barrel drop toward the ground. He raises it again as Emma regains her footing. 'How could you? How long now?'

'Ben,' she says, as she draws nearer, 'you're not making sense. You're in shock. We both are. Let's talk.'

Emma flinches and shrinks when he swipes her rifle from her shoulder and yanks the strap free. With a flick of the wrist, he sends the weapon spinning into a snowdrift.

'Move,' he grunts, pointing into the brush, in the direction of the tracks.

'I don't need to.'

Ben grabs her above the elbow. His fingers dig into tender muscles. Emma instinctually tries to pull away, which only causes his grip to tighten. She yanks her arm again, harder, and slips his grasp.

'You saw his print, and then tried to lead me away, back to the truck.' Ben chokes, then clears his throat hard. 'What deal do you have with Arnott?'

Emma stares at the ground between them, then speaks quietly. 'I didn't think they'd try and kill you. You weren't supposed to be there—anywhere near them when they got The Boss. Tomos promised. It wasn't supposed to go this way.'

Emma looks up to find hard eyes glaring at her.

'And then you would hop on a shuttle and get your trip to a colony? You cut a deal with Arnott. Same as Tomos,' Ben says. 'Is that it? Is that's why you kept pushing for me to come with you, for so long? Were you going to tell me about any of this if I said yes?'

'I can't be here anymore.' Emma shakes her head. 'It's been too hard. For too long.'

She can't look at him any longer, not with his hurt and hateful eyes looking back, the ones that once loved her just as clearly as they now hate her. She turns and sits cross-legged in the snow. Her gaze drops from the clearing to her hands, fingers curled, resting palms up on her thighs. Dirt creases the lines of her palms. Her fingers are pale from the cold.

'All I could think about was going.' Her voice becomes small, resigned that her desire is a weak excuse. 'It's all I dreamed about, which made me want to sleep all the time, so I didn't have to be here. But when I shot the boy, I chose you. It wasn't supposed happen like—'

'But it did,' Ben says quietly. Watching her grapple with what she'd done, his rage begins to settle and a feeling of loneliness fills the gap it leaves.

'I came to you.' Emma looks up again, hopeful. 'When you said you heard their voices, I started toward you, right away. I came to help you because I was scared for you. After you called from Poppy's cabin, I ran, for hours. I ran until I couldn't feel my legs.'

'Too late,' Ben says.

Emma flinches. Her cheeks are wet with tears and her nose is running. Her chin jumps once, but she stays quiet.

Ben clutches his rifle by his side, feeling foolish for ever having raised it. Of course, he couldn't shoot her. His gut cinches with her betrayal, Emma sitting there, explaining her dreams away, the ones he'd known so well and heard so often and wanted her to achieve. Now, he's ashamed to see how they've twisted her into this shape in front of him.

Ben spits out the breath he'd been choking on since the night. The cool inhalation that follows brings clarity. He can't love her anymore, but that doesn't change the fact that he once had. The pain of that being torn away so quickly saturates him in a wave of cold sweat and nausea.

Ben contemplates Emma for a moment longer before turning to survey the surrounding peaks. He points at one far up the valley. 'Remember that?'

Emma looks up, then away again.

'You remember the meadow up there?' Ben says. 'The tiny flowers. The pissing rain that lasted a week? How it pelted down. Remember seeing the bear there?'

'No,' Emma says.

'Yes, you do.' Ben stares at the slopes, trying to spot the clearing. 'You may have forgotten for a bit, but you know.'

Ben thinks back to that day, the sounds the bear made and how it watched them back. He remembers the lock of hair that had slipped from beneath Emma's hood and curled, wet against her cheek.

'This thought,' Ben stares off into the trees, 'I've had it, too. I still do. I know its weight, the need to run away. It's so heavy. I was going to leave, as well. I talked to Poppy and I see why we're at this point. The program could never work.'

'Come with me then,' Emma says. 'This was done before it even started.'

'It wasn't.' Ben shakes his head. He frowns as he chases a memory. 'Poppy said something else. She said if humanity's the problem, then that's the thing that has to be removed from the equation. You go back to the truck. I'll go after the bear. Arnott will meet me there. He's hunting for revenge now, for Vito.'

Ben extends a hand. She takes it and lets him help her to her feet.

'I'm sorry. I'll come with you. I'll make this right.'

'You can't,' Ben says. 'You have the keys. Leave.'

In the distance, a gunshot cracks. It echoes from the direction of the river.

207

Ben and Emma stare at each other, as if to confirm they had both heard it, as if wishing neither of them had.

Another shot claps through the trees.

Ben bolts toward the sound.

16

Ben's body moves automatically, feeling like it's skimming above the ground's surface and his consciousness is merely an observer of muscle and bone. He weaves between tree trunks, like liquid, barely disturbing the branches. The snaking root mat can't trip him up and the uneven terrain doesn't need his eyes. He is distilled into movement with animal purpose.

Time shifts, becoming mercurial, like he could move this fast and forever, and if he did, maybe he'd find a time that the bear hasn't been shot yet, and maybe Vito would still be alive, a young man again, and not eternally drifting in the spaces between these trees. Maybe Ben wouldn't figure out Emma's deceit and maybe he could still love her in his ignorance.

Still, it all feels too slow.

The forest blurs in front of him. Everything that rattled his thoughts in the clearing with Emma had been struck blank by the first gunshot. The second shot sparked his body to move. Dread knotted his stomach instantly, one thought swiping all others aside: they shot my bear.

Ben's feet float over a log, his body curves around jutting branches. He lands with a sharp exhalation, not breaking stride, not even pausing. The ground undulates. The land disappears and the distance between him and the bear becomes theory, two points in space drawn by each other's gravity.

The shots came from the north, closer to the river and nearer than they ought to have been. Somehow Tomos and Arnott have moved ahead of them. They wouldn't have travelled through the storm. Everything living found shelter from a system like that, and everything that didn't was now dead. They must have started moving again before the sun came up, but that still would have been dangerous and numbingly cold; the risk of being blasted by a freezing stratospheric downdraft was high after such a storm.

Ben slows to a jog, trying to get his bearings and recalculate where the shots had sounded from.

It has to be close now, he figures, scanning.

Through the trees, in the distance, bright light shines in an uninterrupted wall, marking the open thread of the river. He veers to run parallel to it, concentrating on making his footfalls quiet and his breathing silent.

They have to be close.

The valley dips, land's edge dropping closer to the river level, but the slope still would have muffled the gunfire he'd heard, which means they are somewhere on this upper terrace. He should be able to see them.

Ben slows to a walking pace, peering through the woods, drumming an anxious fist against his thigh. He both wants and dreads to see the men's backlit figures, or any errant movement that would tell of their location. But the longer it takes to find them, the longer he can linger in a time when the bear may still be alive and he hasn't yet failed.

Where are they?

Did they hit my bear?

Two shots, he thinks. Perhaps they missed and now the bear is on the run. Maybe they drove it to attack and this silence marks their death. Or perhaps it was a call for him to come, a trick to draw him in, to be repaid for Vito.

In his mind, Ben backtracks over the path he'd sprinted from the clearing, wondering if he'd overshot their location and run too far upstream. He stops and scans a slow arc, whispering, 'Come on, come on, come on.' He wants a clue, a sound carried past by the breeze, anything that isn't another gunshot.

Were they upstream or down?

There's a logging camp up from here that was built at the turn of the millennium, closer to the dam. There is a scattering of abandoned heavy equipment there, machines with giant metal pincers that could grab twenty trees and snip them off at the base, like gathering a bouquet. Another machine has giant metal rollers to strip the bark and limbs. There are a few trucks left behind as well, their paint blistered and charred, their tires melted to scrap rubber beneath the rims. The trailers still stand where they were abandoned after the embers of a slash-pile fire had leaped to the bordering forest and sparked a blaze.

Fire had ripped through in the night, the dry deadfall from the clear-cut just north acting as tinder that burned so hot that only the mineral soil remained. The clearing had saved some of the camp, as had a few swaths cut as a hasty firebreak by a bulldozer, which still sits near the trailers. When Ben had first seen it, he could hear echoes of the diesel engine labouring through the howling scream of the inferno.

The camp is still largely intact, but there is nothing to draw the bear there, except perhaps a place to hide.

'Where are you?' Ben whispers.

Downstream, wilds stretch uninterrupted, all the way back to the mine. A few jagged tributaries have chewed through the bedrock on their way to the river. The beetle has gotten the pine trees on those slopes, leaving a snarl of deadfall and windthrows for kilometres. The understory has grown up to fill in the space left behind, and the spruce is still okay in the lower, wetter areas. There'd be plenty of cover for the bear there.

Ben takes two steps downstream when he hears a shout from behind, close, from the direction of the camp. Pulse spiking with the sound, a fresh charge of adrenaline prickling across his skin, Ben's legs start pumping again, carrying him upstream. The forest closes in, growing in a denser cluster here, clawing. Ben doesn't slow. Branches whip his face, rake his arms and legs.

Shouldering through an entangled nest of wiry dogwood, Ben sprints into a wall of juvenile pine tree regrowth. Their branches knit together and their trunks, still skinny and pliable, grow closer and tighter than they will a hundred years from now. Once the die-off happens, the victors will continue their struggle skyward, but until then they twist tight and stand barely taller than Ben does.

Moving is like swimming, Ben grasping and pulling his way through, anything to propel himself forward. Ben knew the replanted area was close, but he had lost track on his flight, and hadn't figured he'd covered so much ground. He curses the naive enthusiasm of the old logging company, replanting a monoculture of the most valuable wood species after clearing a forest of hundreds, farming by any other name. He grazes his shin on invisible deadfall and stumbles over the disturbed earth. He hyper-extends his knee, stepping into the void left by a rotted stump.

The pain adds resolve and Ben lurches forward, leaning into the branches and pushing harder, twisting from side to side like a fish in a strong current when he gets entangled by interwoven boughs, his eyes almost closed to avoid losing them to the lashing branches. The world becomes a disorienting net of clutching green. All direction is quickly muddled. And Ben pushes harder, trying to judge the closest thing to a straight line that the vege-tation will allow. He wants to yell in frustration, but keeps silent and secret, leaning more into the trees, using his body weight to push through, and suddenly all resistance is lost.

Ben trips over a thick ridge marking the boundary of the regrowth and tumbles into a barren shallow trench. He lands on his side, the breath jolted from his body, momentarily para-lyzing him. The ground is a slimy muck of meltwater and ash; it smells of charred wood. He stares down the trench, a swath chewed through the forest by the blade of a bulldozer, the shrinking line cut and back-burned to stop the fire. It worked; on one side of the line is the dense green regrowth, so much life the land is choking with it. The opposite side is populated by the thin, charred black tendrils of scorched pine, dead trunks still wriggling skyward.

And voices.

An involuntary whine escapes Ben's throat as he forces air back into his lungs and pushes himself up onto all fours. It's then he spots a line of bear tracks through the muck, and two sets of boot tracks nearby. Ben looks back in the direction they'd come from, then in the direction they were heading. Arnott and Tomos must have spooked the bear from elsewhere with their first two shots and then tracked him here.

Scrambling through the clinging muck to the edge of the trench and peering over the berm, the outlines of the abandoned logging camp become visible in the distance. The cluster of trailers crouches amid the remnant forest. Hulks of machinery and vehicles are scattered throughout.

There's movement, but it's too far to tell what it is, the charred tree trunks too obscuring.

Ben silently clambers over the berm. His boot lands on bare clay and stones, wet dust and ash burbling up from the impact. The snow is less here than in the clearing, mostly melted, creating a gluey slime everywhere.

Moving in a crouch, and slowly to hide his approach, Ben winds through the scraggy trunks. Broken branches claw at his jacket, rake his hands and cheeks, leaving comets of blood beading wherever they strike bare skin.

Ben holds the rifle to his shoulder, the barrel steady on the structures ahead. They become distinct from each other as he draws closer, three industrial trailers in a staggered line. The ruin of a raised propane tank is visible on the far side, exploded, peeled and jagged at the top, like petals of a rusting metal flower. A logging truck sits at an angle, along with a few other blackened wrecks.

There's movement at the end of one of the trailers and Ben sidesteps to break the line of sight with the bulk of a bulldozer. Ash and debris grind softly underfoot; the blaze, decades past, still lingers in the smell of the skinny, burned trunks and the layer of charred talc coating everything.

Voices come now, a few words spoken back and forth, commands from inside, muffled by the trailer walls.

A few slow minutes later, Ben rests a hand on the coarse, rusty metal track of the bulldozer and creeps to the edge of the bucket. He stops to survey the adjacent trailer. The voices have died off now, but the dim outline of a hunched figure is visible through the cracked and soot-smeared windows.

Ben hears breathing from close behind and spins, rifle ready. Ten paces back, Emma flinches and freezes on the spot. She silently covers the remaining ground between them. Ben turns his attention back to the trailer.

'What are they doing?' Emma whispers.

Ben doesn't take his eyes from the figure inside. 'No clue.'

Emma straightens to peer over the machine and Ben grabs her by the collar and drags her back down.

'You shouldn't be here,' Ben snarls. 'Can't keep you all in sight.'

Emma's brow furrows and tears swim in her eyes, but they don't fall. 'I want to make this right.'

'You can't,' Ben says.

A distant throaty huff silences them. Ben drops to the ground and peers under the machine, the trailers, and catches a flicker of movement on the far side of the spindly metal legs holding the destroyed propane tank. It disappears behind the ruin of a truck. Emma lies on her stomach beside him.

'They're using the trailer as a hunting blind,' Emma whispers and pushes to her feet. 'Just waiting for a clear shot.'

Ben sights in the trailer window, trying to spot the silhouette again, only to find it's no longer there. A quick survey of all the windows shows them empty. A muffled thump comes from within.

'Cover me?' Ben asks, shrugging out of his backpack and tucking it against the bulldozer's tracks.

Emma crouches, rests her elbows on the machine's bucket, and raises her rifle toward the trailer.

'As soon as you get a shot, you take it.' Ben stares at her, trying to judge her. 'Please don't shoot me.'

'Fuck off,' Emma snaps.

Ben skulks around the end of the bucket, his eyes locked on the trailer. The hand he rests on the cold metal quivers, and he scowls at it with mild confusion. He doesn't feel fear, at least not for himself. He pulls his hand back, the palm black with soot. Ben dashes the ten paces of open ground between the bulldozer and the side of the trailer. With his back to the heat-warped siding, he inches his way to the door at the far end. Closer now, he can hear the occasional whisper through the cracked and broken windows above his head, the words still unintelligible.

Ben reaches the end of the trailer and glances back at Emma. She remains propped on her elbows, scanning the windows over the barrel of her rifle. Behind her, stretching endlessly, the grey and black burn, charred stumps and skinny, writhing stalks of immolated trees.

Ben peers around the corner of the trailer.

Tomos stands a few steps away, on the metal stairs leading into the trailer.

Their eyes lock.

'He's here,' Tomos hollers.

Ben charges. Tomos takes two steps to the ground and raises his rifle, but the distance between them has disappeared. Ben swipes Tomos's rifle aside and brings his own up. The stock connects with Tomos's face, his head snapping back and his mouth exploding in a spray of blood. The muck slides beneath his feet and Tomos falls backwards. He grabs Ben by the collar, dragging him down. Ben twists, trying to shake the grasp and keep his feet under him.

A gunshot hammers the air as Ben lands on his back, on top of Tomos, with a grunt. Tomos wraps his legs around Ben's thighs and locks an arm around his neck. He torques Ben's head hard to one side. A spike of pain shoots up Ben's neck. Something grinds, cartilage and vertebrae, but he manages to bring an elbow up and swing it back over his shoulder, landing another firm blow to Tomos's face, leaving a streak of clotted mud in the bleeding mess there.

Ben raises his head and slams it back, smashing against Tomos's broken nose.

Tomos's grip loosens as he shrieks, a desperate, primal noise.

Ben twists onto his side, the greasy mud making it easier to slip under the pressure of Tomos's arm cinched across his neck. Tomos's breath spills across his cheek, the smell of blood comes in hot gasps as Tomos tries to keep him immobilized.

Ben stares sidelong into Tomos's eyes. There is nothing human left, only desperation and death. Tomos's nose is flattened into a blossom that chugs slow blood down his cheek. His grimace shows a mouth full of gore and jagged, shattered teeth. An ivory shard glints in the mud.

Another gunshot cracks, followed by a barrage.

Tomos hooks his fist in the crook of his other arm and levers the vice hold on Ben's neck tighter. The pressure in Ben's head builds. His pulse labours under Tomos's grip. Only a squeak of air gets through.

Ben writhes and bucks, struggling to break away. He catches glimpses of Emma shooting into the trailer. The bucket of the bulldozer sparking as return fire strikes it.

Ben raises his head and drops it sideways, feeling the pulp of Tomos's nose grind, and a shocking, shredding pain as Tomos's shattered teeth clamp onto his cheek. Tomos screeches with agony and effort. The pressure is not enough to cut the chunk of flesh clean, though the searing sting is enough to hold Ben in place.

'Ben,' Emma is shouting, he doesn't know for how long. She points and then opens fire on the trailer again.

Movement flashes in the corner of Ben's vision. There's no pain when he yanks free from Tomos's jagged bite, just a tug from deep under his skin followed by a wash of heat spilling across his cheek; the sensation of the open flap of flesh barely registers as adrenaline alters sense and time.

A lumbering form runs through the camp, the bear. It breaks from the cover of the machines and buildings and charges through the broken forest, gathering speed and ploughing through the charred remnants as if they were smoke.

Emma's rifle clicks, empty.

Arnott's hail of gunfire from inside the trailer falls quiet. Then, after a terrible moment of silence, a single shot. The bear convulses, taking a stumble-step as a quake ripples through his muscles. Momentum carries the creature onward, through a few staggered steps, and then his gait regains its rhythm. He crests an incline and disappears over the other side.

Fuelled by a wave of unstoppable rage, Ben breaks from Tomos's grip and pushes himself up. He straddles Tomos's chest, a knee pinning each shoulder to the ground, sinking him into the ash and mud. With one hand shoving Tomos's head down, the other reaches out, groping through the sludge. Ben's fingers wrap around the rifle stock.

Tomos's fists batter desperately at Ben's sides, but pinned, he can't gain enough leverage to strike a reasonable blow. They stop fluttering and raise feebly to try and block Ben's first strike.

A burbling 'No' whines from Tomos's bloody, broken mouth.

Ben clasps the rifle in both hands and brings the stock down on Tomos's head like a pile-driver. The body underneath him bucks with a single violent tremor. One of Tomos's hands curls and falls to the side as Ben raises the rifle again. The other hand flutters; while consciousness has been battered out of Tomos's body, some residual instinct still tries to defend it.

The glistening rifle butt drops once more.

Tomos's final twitch of resistance eases to the ground.

Ben stares down, numbed by shock and rage.

Someone is shouting a mess of words that his ears can't untangle.

Ben pushes off and grabs Tomos's rifle from where it landed, several steps away. He slings his own rifle across his shoulders and pats down Tomos's corpse to find two clips in his pants pocket, averting his eyes from the man's wrecked face. There's movement in the corner of his vision, and the subtle sensation of blood plucking a steady rhythm from his chin.

The metal stairs ring out with each step Ben takes. He yanks the door open to a narrow hallway that runs the length of the trailer. Doors line either side, opening onto rooms, each with a narrow bunk, a tiny desk, a window, and a closet.

The far end of the hall opens onto a common room, presided over by a stag's head mounted on the wall. Glass eyes stare down the hall at Ben and a hammock of spider webs between its points shifts with a recent disturbance. Pinpricks of light riddle that end of the hall. Emma and Arnott had exchanged more bullets than Ben remembers hearing.

He limps forward, careless of any noise he makes. In the darkness of a blink, he sees muscles ripple under fur, an involuntary contraction in response to a metal slug. Had the bear really been hit?

Ben fires a shot through the thin walls and into one of the rooms down the hall.

He pulls the bolt, chambering another round.

Through the ringing in his ears, he hears the bear grunt from the bullet strike. The crack of skinny tree trunks as the bear stumbles. There's a rattle breath, ragged lungs unfit for more than the next few minutes before they will go quiet.

The smell of gun smoke masks the musty stink of mould and decaying matter in the trailer. The smell of the long-ago fire pervades, irritating and inescapable. A fleeting movement blots out one of the beams of light at the far end of the hall. Ben yells and shoots another round at it.

From outside, Emma is screaming, a jumble of words.

Nothing makes sense.

Ben chambers another round and fires again.

Ben's halfway down the hall when Arnott returns fire, from somewhere unseen. A hole appearing in a cloud of splinters a few strides ahead of Ben.

Ben laughs and shoots back. He feels unstoppable and the madness is exhilarating.

He reaches the common room to find a side door open underneath a dark exit sign. Outside, fifty paces away, four metal legs hold up the remains of the propane tank. Its belly is still intact, but the top is a clutch of thick metal fingers splayed skyward, from when it had exploded in the blaze. A glimmer of movement comes from within. A boot strike rings metallic, and Ben fires at the tank. A spark flashes as the bullet ricochets and splatters into the ground.

Ben steps out of the trailer, pulls the bolt back and shoves it home again. He aims and the rifle clicks.

Arnott rises from within the tank and fires a shot. The trailer wall beside Ben's head explodes.

Ben frowns, pulls the magazine from his rifle and watches Arnott chamber another round. Ben fishes the fresh magazine from his pocket. Arnott rises to kneel, a stable firing position.

Ben stares up the length of the barrel at Arnott's face. One eye is pinched closed and the other is intent on the scope. Ben seats the clip and is yanked around the corner of the trailer, falling to the ground beside Emma. The trailer spews a shower of wood pulp, cottony insulation, and sharp vinyl fragments where he'd been standing.

Emma hooks her arms under Ben's armpits and drags him away. He kicks at the ash and mud to help her. Another shot echoes, and then they are behind the bulldozer again. Emma heaves Ben into a sitting position and pushes him back against the tracks, next to his backpack.

'The Boss—' she pants.

'I know,' Ben says, swiping his cheek against his shoulder, which only makes way for a new flush of blood. He passes her Tomos's rifle and the extra magazine before shouldering his pack. 'You keep Arnott here for as long as you can.'

Emma glances at the weapon in her hands, then up, staring in horror at his mangled face. 'Where are you going?'

Ben shuffles to the end of the bulldozer's track and peers around the corner, then in the direction of the swale the bear disappeared into. The few hundred meters of exposure between here and there seem infinite.

'You'll get a bullet put in you,' Emma says when she realizes what he's planning; her voice quavers but her words are certain.

Ben turns back to her. 'You say you want to make this right?'

She chews her lip.

'You did this. Buy me time to get to the bear. Cover me until I reach that swale, then hold this spot as long as you can. Start making this right.'

Emma swallows and nods.

They look at each other. Unspoken, in their expressions, is that this could be the last time they get the chance.

Ben runs.

A bullet kicks up mud and rock at his feet.

Emma stands and returns fire.

17

The incline steepens and pulls Ben's legs faster than they can keep up. He drops to his side, sliding down through the muck. Rocks and burn debris rake his forearm and leg. A gunshot pounds the air behind him, muffled slightly by the rising swale walls. Ben flinches at the noise but doesn't look back.

The bear's flight from the trailers tumbles through Ben's memory in fragments, and he struggles to distinguish reality from fear. He hears the silence again, the single shot, sees the animal stumbling through the ashen forest. Had the bear even been hit? The world was shaking so much at that moment. It hasn't stopped since.

Forward is the only direction left. Follow the bear; it's all he's done for so long.

Using his diminishing momentum near the base of the hill, Ben wrangles his feet back beneath him and stumbles into the channel. The gentle decline of the narrow swale makes moving easier, though the meltwater seeping from above has turned the footing slick.

The bear's path is easy to follow. Perfect imprints form a diagonal line down the slope and Ben intersects them, heading riverward along the channel bottom. The edges of the gully rise higher and rivulets become more frequent, funnelling meltwater down, turning the ground into a clawing mire. The clay is soon ankle-deep, clutching at his boots with each step.

The sound of Ben's breathing echoes back to him from the close walls. The lingering smell of the forest fire mixes with a sulphur stench of decay that permeates the mud.

The gully makes a sharp, blind bend, undercutting the opposite bank. A recent slump has collapsed from the wall. The jumble of earth and stone, twice as tall as Ben, blocks the channel, forcing him to clamber on his hands and knees, seeming to slide back a step for every two purchased as he struggles upward.

His chest heaving with the exertion, Ben pauses at the top of the pile. Ahead, the banks of the gully cut steeper and sparkle with more ribbons of meltwater. The drip and gurgle of water sounds from everywhere. Ben covers his nose with the crook of his arm to fend off the smell. He half expects to see the bear stuck in the quagmire on the far side, but there is only the pockmark line of his tracks trailing through a gently meandering stretch ahead, disappearing around the next bend.

Another gunshot pops from the direction of the logging camp, distant now.

The shot is answered with two in quick succession.

Ben pivots to the noise, but he is too far below them to see anything beyond the ragged rim. His distraction is fleeting and instinctual; as if swiping a fly away, his mind returns to reaching his bear.

Ben scrambles down the far side of the slump and lands shin-deep in mud. His legs quake from exhaustion and he has to torque bodily to free his feet. Each step is a crippling effort and his body doesn't feel like his own any longer.

Ben strains, forcing his aching muscles onward.

The very ground becomes an enemy, making savage sucking noises each time he pulls free. The pits left behind quickly fill with rank brown water. His leg gets stuck and it takes four jolting attempts to free it.

Ben yells in frustration.

The bear tracks punch deeper and deeper, showing the heavier animal staggering against the resistance.

Bright red drops of blood act as beacons in the remnant patches of snow lining the sheltered lee of the slope. This first confirmation that the bear is injured drives all pain and exhaustion away. Renewed, Ben lurches onward.

Halfway to the next bend, Ben veers toward the edge of the channel, thinking that walking along the foot of the slope will be easier. The angle is too steep though, and the slippery sediment forces him to his knees when he tries. Every part of him is covered in the icy muck, soaking his clothes so they cling to his body. The death stench of clay gets stuck in his nose and drives him mad, thoughtless, blind to anything but finding the bear.

He pauses beside a deeper, larger hole in the channel, where the bear had become stuck. It's full of churned, dirty water that's tinted pink. The surrounding earth is torn and ripped, scarred from the creature's struggles and scabbed with blood-tinged ruts radiating out in every direction. It is panic. It is desperation.

Ben is gripped in a clutch of anger and sorrow. His fingers ache and he looks at them through watery vision. They are balled into tight fists. He has lost the ability to unclench them.

He carries on toward the bend. His movements become more desperate, in response to the increasingly difficult terrain, his uncoordinated struggling led onward by the ghosts of the bear prints. He slips and torques his ankle, the throbbing ache shooting up to his knee drives him harder, pushes him more manic.

A short distance from the bend, Ben sinks in past his knees. He yells in frustration, yanking on his legs and clawing at the muck that hinders. The bandage on his hand unravels, the gash across his palm opens again. He throws clods of earth aside, frantic and digging like an animal. Frigid water pours into the voids he excavates.

Minutes feel like hours until Ben frees himself, finding firmer ground in the heavier sediments on the point bar of the bend. Both of his boots are missing. He can't tell his sweat from the mud and meltwater, his body aching with cold and shivering with exertion. Ben carries on, bare feet flayed by debris hidden in the mud, but the sting is invisible to him.

Around the bend, the gully cuts its deepest and suddenly opens onto an outwash plain at the river. Ben staggers onto the gravel bar. He sinks to his knees; his hands fall limp by his sides, and he stares. His mouth gapes, but there's no sound.

In the shallows, the bear lies, unmoving. Beyond, the river is wide and drifts past like an illusion. The water pulls a cloud of pale brown mud from the creature's fur, the stain spreading in the current.

A distant gunshot echoes.

Ben doesn't draw a breath until there are stars swirling before his eyes from holding it. He wails as the air enters his lungs again. Then the bear's side rises with a slowly drawn breath.

Ben leaps to his feet, sprinting across the gravel expanse.

Splashing the few final steps through the icy shallows, rocks strike Ben's numbed, bare feet. The feeling is blunt, like it happens to someone else. He fumbles to shed his pack and drops to his knees behind the prone bear. His hands hover over the slow rise and fall of the creature's flank, but he does not touch it. Heat radiates from the animal; tremoring in the narrow gap between Ben's palms and its body, is life.

Ben hesitates. He has never touched the bear. Closing his eyes, his palms connect with the thick brown fur, which billows up between his splayed fingers, the warmth of the skin and firmness of the muscle underneath. A quiver of recognition runs through that muscle, the electricity of one beast making contact with another for the first time.

The musky smell fills Ben's nose as he leans closer, thick and alive, familiar. A rain-soaked meadow of wildflowers. Emma is beside him. She pulls aside a branch and droplets fall from the leaves, a curl of wet hair from under her hood, the awe they shared.

The bear shifts under his palms, but slowly and calmly. Ben's hands make a slow circle on the creature's side, magnetic, as if dictated by the animal instead of his own will. The bear draws a quivering breath and releases a throaty groan and a whistle. Ben feels the vibrations, marvels as his hands rise and fall, and he finds his own breath aligning, coming and leaving with the same slow pace.

Ben opens his eyes to see blood.

Panic pulses tight in his temples. He runs his hands over the bear's side, searching for the source. His mind reels at the sight of the bear's blood, red the same as his, a fact so obviously known before, but a revelation when experienced so intimately.

Ben draws back momentarily, realizing the wound on his palm had opened up again and bleeds, the same blood. But there's too much of it on the bear to be solely sourced from his own wound.

The bear draws another breath, exhales with another groan and squeak. Pink froth bubbles up through the fur, just behind its shoulder. Ben swipes it away and finds a hole the size of a coin. The surrounding flesh, visible in fragments through the tousled coat, is pulverized and bruised. Ben leans over the bear and sees its muzzle is also coated with pink froth.

The bear's dark brown eye shifts to meet his, and Ben is caught, entranced. It blinks and draws another burdensome breath, the froth disappearing back into its snout and the movement lifting Ben from where he leans against the animal. As it exhales, a curl of blood disperses in the water.

The bear's eye moves again, this time to gaze across the water's surface, at the trees and mountains on the far side. The logging company hasn't been over there, neither has the beetle decimated those trees, the fire didn't cross the river; there is just forest, stretching along the riverbank, swooping back from it, uninterrupted and green, up to the tree line on the mountain behind.

Ben sits back and looks up and down the length of the massive beast. Another frothy mound forms on the bear's side with a breath. Shot through the lung.

The mesmerizing shock of the creature laying beneath his palms passes. Ben pulls his knife. Drawing the blade at a shallow angle across the bear's side, he shaves a spot around the bullet wound as best he can, and then sinks the knife blade into the riverbed by his side. Swatches of fur float away, borne atop slow water.

The bear draws a breath and trembles with the exhalation.

'You stay here,' Ben tells the bear as he tugs his pack from the water and yanks open the top.

The bear shifts at the sound, water splashes, and Ben lays a hand on it, says, 'Stay here.'

Ben finds the first-aid kit and one of his shrink-wrapped meals. Packets of freeze-dried food fly as he clumsily rips the plastic open with his teeth, silver bags bobbing in the eddy's swirl. Ben draws the knife from the water and slices the wrapper into a ragged square. He doesn't feel like he can move fast enough, the first-aid kit zipper breaks as he fumbles it open.

He spills the contents across the bear's side. A bottle of antiseptic drops into the river and floats lazily away. A pair of scissors slips down the bear's back and into the water with a plop. It sinks to the pebbles beneath, glinting as it twists.

Ben pulls a roll of surgical tape and a sheet of gauze from the pile. Tearing the gauze package open, he swabs the shaved area dry. The bloody swatch floats for a few seconds before it drifts below the surface of the water and snags on the bear's submerged leg. Ben drapes the plastic square over the wound and tapes down three sides. He drops the tape and lays his palms on the bear and looks over the length of the animal again.

'Breathe,' he commands through clenched teeth.

The bear does draw a weak and shaky inhalation. The plastic sheet sucks tight to the bear's side, creating a vacuum and allowing the punctured lung to inflate more fully than it had before. The quaking exhalation inflates the plastic. Ben places a hand against a section of the tape that threatens to let go, holding it flat against the skin.

A ripple passes underneath Ben's palms and his attention locks on the plastic sheet, willing it to pull tight against the bear's side again. Ben pushes his palms harder against the bear and whispers, 'No.'

'No,' he says, shaking the beast.

A chill sinks into him, deeper and colder than the icy water. Ben grabs handfuls of fur, still hoping in the warmth he feels there. His stomach knots.

Ben thumps the bear, and yells, 'No.'

The bear's eyes remain motionless, staring glassily across the river.

Leaning over, his chest pressed against the bear's shoulder, Ben cups the animal's muzzle and strains to twist it up from the water.

He gazes into the bear and knows there's nothing left of him. He cries. He eases the massive head down and sits back on his heels. The bite of the water passing across his thighs no longer demarcates the passage of seconds or minutes; the stillness of the bear now occupies all time.

Ben rests a hand on the body. He runs it across the fur, then begins straightening the mess it has become. Cupping water over it, he washes muck and blood from the animal the best he can.

Finally, he stares at the bloody plastic sheet taped to the naked swatch of skin, then peels it off. The hole there no longer bleeds, no longer froths; a single pink line runs from it. Ben covers the wound with his hand, his addled thoughts still hoping the bear will somehow draw breath again.

The river gurgles.

Somewhere meltwater drips.

The bear doesn't draw breath.

Ben pulls his hand back, fingers prodding between the bear's massive shoulder blades. He strokes and pinches the flesh there and draws the knife from beneath the water's surface. He slices a shallow line as long as his finger. Ben pinches the flesh and pulls out a narrow device. He throws the tracker into the river.

Ben stares at the bear, eyes travelling between the two wounds, and the bear becomes unadulterated again. He thinks it odd, how removing a piece could make the animal whole again.

Ben stands in water to his shins, and the bear lies the height of his thighs. The river drifts by, unknowing; the occasional dissipating ripple is the only proof that the water actually moves.

The air is still and the trees on the opposite bank are still. The slope behind is lit with a brilliant light, and Ben wants more.

He wants some acknowledgement of what has just happened, but the land is impartial and refuses.

Ben turns his back on the bear and looks at the ruined terrain he'd fought through to get here. The gravel fan pinches back to the gully. The land rises to a barren flat, ash-black on either side, prickly with the remnants of burned pines, a jumble of those dead trees are blown down or have fallen in various angles. A series of messy slumps line the length of the land's edge, eroding faster without the ground cover and roots to hold the ground in place.

Someone stands in silhouette, at the peak of the gully cut. Ben remains unmoving, waiting for a bullet to open him up, or not. He can't care. When the figure doesn't shoot him, he reckons it's Emma and he wonders how long she's been standing there, whether she watched instead of helping, whether she saw him cry. But what help could she offer? And what did it matter what she saw? What had he really achieved in those last moments? He did what he could, which was to hold on to hope for a duration of time after hope had long passed.

Ben stares at Emma, wondering whether the two of them together would be strong enough to push the bear into deeper water and let the current take it away. He doubts they can move its body.

Ben picks a path back to the shore. His feet ripple in the shallow water, so numb from the cold that they don't even seem to belong to him anymore, their form becoming something alien, until they are exposed to the air again. The skin is pale, except for a hash of lesions from his struggle to get here, which are deep purple.

Ben gathers his rifle from where it lies on the rocks and slings it over his shoulder, realizing he left his pack in the water near the bear.

He won't return for it, there's nothing in it he needs.

The truck isn't far now.

This is almost over.

Emma clambers down and they meet with an embrace. At first Ben resists, but the need to feel someone again, the need to allay loneliness by clinging to another life, becomes overwhelming, and he concedes. Emma's neck against his cheek is warm. He can feel the rise and fall of her chest pressed against him. Her smell is comforting, alive.

After some time, Emma whispers, 'Arnott's coming.'

Her voice is calm, or maybe resigned, and Ben scans the terrain for the hunter, nodding once in response. Then they part. Emma only has her Colt now; she must have left the bigger rifle behind.

'How many rounds do you have left?' Ben asks.

'None.'

Ben pulls a full clip of ten rounds from his pocket, thumbs out five bullets and passes them to her.

She loads her clip and says, 'There's more ammo at Cache Cave. There's more of everything.'

Ben shakes his head and looks down at his feet. They are his again and throb horribly now. Cache Cave is across the dam, past his truck, past the rockslide. They are leaving. They don't need anything.

Ben pushes his clip back into place. Five each, he thinks. 'Arnott have any shots left?'

'I don't think so.' Emma shrugs. 'He stopped shooting at me.' Her eyes remain locked on the body in the water. 'I still have some white gas. We could light up the bear, make it so there's nothing left for Arnott.'

'Doesn't much matter. Arnott is gunning for us. He has been since the mine. The bear was just a place for us to meet.' Ben scowls and looks out at the bear.

Emma nods and Ben sees by her expression that she always knew, that she was simply trying to ease his mind, to show she's with him.

'This is a good place,' Emma says, scanning the surroundings. 'We could find cover here, surely Arnott would go out to the bear. We'd have a clear shot. We could get free of him.'

'We know nothing of what he'd do. We were never here for Arnott,' Ben says, with a glance back at the bear. 'This is over.'

'And now?' Emma asks.

'And now . . .' Ben rubs the sole of his foot against his pant leg. 'Now we get to the dam, get in the truck, and leave. How far behind is Arnott?'

Emma stares at the terrace edge over her shoulder. 'We should get moving, if we're going to. He's going to dog us all the way back.'

'I know it,' Ben says.

'Where're your boots?' Emma asks.

Ben flicks a hand toward the mouth of the gully.

'Wrap your feet. I've got a few packs of clothes and some tape. We can rig up something. I'll glue your cheek shut, too.' Emma starts take her pack off, but Ben stops her with a hand on her shoulder and a glance back the way she came.

'We should get to cover first,' Ben says and starts picking his way upstream. 'There's still a clear cut to cross before we're back in trees. We'll follow the river. At least the terrace will block us from view.'

Ben is slow. His feet are battered.

A cluster of boulders eroding out of the bank gives them their sought-after cover. Using Emma's spare clothes and a roll of tape, Ben fashions some protection for his feet. Emma cleans and seals the wound on his cheek the best she can.

In the distance, the valley narrows between two peaks and the forest cover grows thick again. Though they can't yet see it, the dam sits in that gorge, a few hours away.

'What about me?' Emma asks quietly.

Ben can't meet her. 'What about you?' When Emma doesn't respond, he shrugs. 'You can't stay here.'

Ben starts moving again.

Moments later, Emma follows.

They flinch at every noise, knowing Arnott is back there somewhere, following them.

18

Ben struggles over a jumble of deadfall. He totters, his foot slips, and he falls heavily onto his side. Glancing at the terrace above, Arnott haunting his instinct, he expects to see the silhouette staring down. He scrambles back to his feet.

Ahead, Emma picks their path along the riverside through a constant snarl of stumps and toppled trees propped at angles between the bank and waterline. Over the years since the cut and the fire, erosion has gouged large chunks out of the shore, new ditches have been etched by runoff. Sprawling and uneven fans of deep, sticky muck frustrate their progress.

Ben pauses. His feet bleed; his soles feel tacky, wrapped in Emma's spare clothes that have been duct-taped with loops around his toes, heels, and ankles. He checks closer and sees he's not bleeding through the material yet, but each step over the impossible terrain is dreaded. The makeshift boots are thin and every piece of debris he steps on aggravates the injuries on his feet.

'We're going too slow,' he mutters.

Emma looks back, her expression saying she didn't hear what he said.

Ben shakes his head.

A melt-wash saddle causes the terrace to sag; a rivulet of sooty water oozes over the edge. Standing tall, Ben gets a ground-level view to the far side of the clear cut. The deforestation stretches across the flats to the mountain behind, a mess of sun-bleached waste wood, pulverized stumps, and rough ruts gouged deep into the earth by machines. Charred slash piles are mounded at intervals.

Oddly, a single fir tree is left alive, its branches swaying beside the logging road that snakes through the middle of the cut-block. The tree casts a long shadow and Ben squints at the sky; the sun has sunk low, and is less than an hour from dropping behind the peaks. At the far northern end of the cut, the land slants upslope dramatically where the valley pinches tighter, the rutted road rising and disappearing into intact forest beyond.

Ben hiked in on that road. He doesn't remember how many days ago he heard the clap of his truck door slamming. He'd left it parked at the base of the rockslide marking the end of the road, crossed back over the dam, and hooked south onto that logging road. He would have walked by that lone tree, but he doesn't remember it either. Maybe he'd been lost in thoughts or the distraction of his daydreams.

Movement catches Ben's attention, on the far side of the clearing, glimpses of a figure darting through the trees. Ben brings his rifle up and tries to anticipate Arnott's line of movement. It's easily a kilometre away and there's no shot to be taken.

Ben drops back below the terrace and turns to call for Emma, but she's already waiting, watching him.

'He's out there,' Ben says, hobbling closer, so he can be heard over the river noise. 'On the far side.'

'Of course he is,' Emma says flatly. 'He's always out there. You're parked near the slide?'

Ben nods.

Emma glances at his feet before she starts moving again. 'We have to beat him back there, or we're going to be swimming across the river. His truck is at the end of that logging road, on this side of the dam.'

Ben cranes to scan the far tree line again but doesn't spot Arnott. He grimaces, questioning if he'd even seen him in the first place, or was it just another ghost in the valley. Not knowing Arnott's location is worse than seeing him out there in glimpses; the man could be anywhere, which makes him everywhere.

Ben frantically scans the border of the cut block. 'Use your fucking head.'

'What?' Emma turns to him, her foot planted on a stack of felled trunks.

'Does he have any bullets left?' Ben asks.

Emma scowls, hoists herself up, then clambers down the far side.

'At the camp, you both stopped shooting.' Ben scrambles up the melt-wash saddle, keeping as low to the ground as he can, his nervous gaze locked on the far boundary. 'We just have to get to the trucks before him.'

'Stay down.' Emma scowls.

'We'll make better time in the clearing, even better on that old road.' Looking at Emma over his shoulder, Ben asks again, 'Do you think he's out of ammo?'

Emma shakes her head. 'I don't know.'

'It's kind of important,' Ben says. 'You stopped firing. Was it because you were both out of ammo?'

'I said, I don't know.' Emma's voice is strained. 'I was out. I slipped away and it took him a bit of time to notice. He could be out, too. We weren't exactly on speaking terms.'

Ben turns back to the clearing, then stands tall, a clear target. He wonders if he's wrong, if he'll have a chance to hear the gunshot after feeling the bullet.

'Don't,' Emma says.

Silence remains unbroken.

The upper branches of the lone fir tree weave in an invisible current and Ben can't help thinking they are trying to warn him, trying to wave him away.

He turns to Emma. Her expression is distant, empty. He knows the disconnect she feels, the numbness, moving without thought, trying not to let anything close. He feels it too.

'Come on,' he says and strikes out over the scarred land toward the road. He moves cautiously at first, his steps measured so he doesn't have to take his eyes from the tree line beyond his rifle-scope. He hears Emma following, catches her moving in his peripheral vision, her rifle raised as well.

'Was he ahead of us, or behind?' Emma asks.

Ben frees a hand to swipe the distant boundary where he'd seen Arnott moving. 'Pretty much in line.'

'We have to move faster.' Emma starts to jog over the upended terrain, cutting a diagonal line toward the road. She holds the rifle stock pressed to her shoulder but has to watch her footing rather than the tree line.

Ben runs, at first hobbling awkwardly because the chewed earth seems designed to torture his feet, with stumps hiding beneath the litter and holes in the surface that become exposed only when the debris above collapses. Frustration mounts with each step. He grits his teeth and grows more reckless, more defiant of the pain, and lets it drives him. Interminable minutes stretch out. In glimpses up from the ground, he sees Emma running. They draw closer to the road.

A gunshot cracks the silence. Ben falls, slamming into the berm of the logging road with the breath blasted from his lungs. For a moment, he's dead, and for another he's confused. The shot sounded too close. He peers over the berm to see Emma kneeling on the road. She pulls the trigger again. Her shoulder bucks from the recoil. She chambers another bullet, not taking her eyes from the distant woods. The simultaneous kick and clap of another shot.

Ben scrambles up the berm and staggers onto the road. Emma fires again. Ben tries to line up her target by following the direction of the barrel.

'I don't see him,' Ben says.

'He's there,' Emma replies, her voice unsteady. 'He won't stop.'

Ben looks at her. Her face is pale and thin lips compressed white. The muscle in her jaw twitches. The rifle is held firm. The tears rimming her lower eyelids betray her determination as true distress.

What she sees is a guess, Ben thinks. What she sees are ghosts.

'I know,' he says, and turns his probing eyes back to the trees. He squints in a curl of dust blown up from the road.

They both wait in the riffling whisper from the high branches. Ben lowers his rifle and looks over at Emma. The tears have released and drawn lines down her cheeks.

Ben scans once more, then hobbles past Emma. 'Let's go.'

After a few exploratory steps, Ben starts to run at a loping pace, his left foot more damaged than the right. Any pressure there is agony. There's a beat of silence behind him, followed by rhythmic footfalls as Emma catches up. She slows her pace to keep in step with him, occasionally glancing back.

At the cut-block boundary, the road angles upward more severely where it enters the forest. The bordering gorge is sheltered by late afternoon shadows. Emma runs ahead and disappears around a bend.

Ben stops and turns. A figure stands near the lone tree, unmoving on the road, halfway back across the cut block. Oily black creatures shift, glistening liquid in the highest branches. Carrion birds, Ben realizes. His pulse sprints and he raises his rifle at the figure, for a long shot. He draws deep breath, trying to steady his body. It seems to vibrate ceaselessly from the days of compounded trauma, and the barrel twitches with the energy.

'Arnott,' Ben hollers with a torn voice.

The figure doesn't move.

The birds ripple through the tree, as if crawling all over its crown to find the best vantage, as if eager for death.

Ben blinks, not trusting anything beyond the end of his rifle anymore, not trusting his senses to know what's really there and what are ghosts. Ben half expects antelope to bound across the clearing, a herd of mammoth to walk from the tree line, a shoal of fish to swim through the sky overhead.

There is a figure standing there, he reassures himself. It is Arnott.

But if it is, why doesn't he run?

Why doesn't he find cover?

The carrion birds jostle in the boughs.

Ben fires. The blast deafens and the recoil punches him in the shoulder. A puff of dust pops, a few steps in front of the figure.

The birds scatter, the bubbling mass resolving into six of them, wings beating hard for altitude, swooping and struggling with fright.

Ben reloads and brings the rifle back up. He squints through the scope, trying to see if Arnott is really smiling. He fires again. The side of the berm explodes, just wide of his target. The sound of the gunshot rolls across the clearing. Ben's third shot kicks up debris, wide as well.

'Ben,' Emma shouts.

Ben glances over. She's sprinting back toward him. When he turns back to the road, it's empty. He desperately surveys the wrecked earth for a push pile that the figure might be hiding behind or a gouge in the land deep enough to shelter a man. He casts his gaze wider.

Arnott has disappeared.

Emma draws to his side, labouring for breath and weapon held ready. 'Where is he?'

Ben lowers his gun.

'What are you shooting at?'

Ben opens his mouth, but doesn't have an answer.

Emma examines the clearing for a moment, and then Ben. 'Come on.'

The road draws them into the narrowing ravine as it angles up a ledge cut along one side. The sound of the river is trapped by the near-vertical walls and rumbles louder. The gloom grows more dire. Their panting breaths become visible, billowing as they run.

Emma and Ben check over their shoulders more frequently. Each feels their exposure. On the road, in the bottleneck chasm, there's no cover to run behind.

The dam comes into view, first as a scar on the opposite limestone face, where century-old blasting is still visible in the lighter colour and ragged texture. Then, the near-vertical wall of shadow-blue concrete stretching between the cliffs comes into sight.

The towering palisade spans the two mountainsides. Six massive metal tubes weep rust down the steep ramp of concrete. On the far side, a stream of water tumbles down the sluice way, frothy and white, as if in slow motion from the sheer scale of its fall. At the base, a bunker crouches, a brutal concrete building housing the generator.

In contrast to the hulking structure, impossibly delicate threads of wire sling outward between towers, running away in an orderly line that had been blasted and hacked out of the terrain. A vibration permeates the air, a feeling more than a sound, of the power of the shackled river and the drowned valley constantly pushing against the far side of the dam, of the movement of massive amounts of electricity.

'We'll be perfect targets.' Emma points at the road ahead, a straight stretch up the slope with no trees, no cover, a wall of rock rising on one side and a void on the other, where it falls sharply down to the churning waters below.

Ben looks behind them. The view is short. With the curve in the road, Arnott could approach unseen, until he is too close. Ben flexes feeling back into the crook of his arm, into his injured hand that has been clasping his rifle so tight it has gone numb.

'I'll wait here.' Emma finds a position she can see back to the bend, and tucks herself against the rock. She raises her rifle. 'I've still got a bullet. You get to the top and then cover me from there.'

Ben starts toward the crest of the dam with a worsening limp. A quick glance at his feet and Ben sees the bindings are now dirt-stained, blood-soaked rags. He grits his teeth and pushes harder. The amphitheatre created by the dam and valley walls plays havoc with sound, his breathing resonates like a crowd's, and the noise is lost in the occasional rush of water echoing up from below.

A gunshot roars from all around, in layers far and near, an entire army firing at will. Ben stumbles when he looks back to see Emma still tucked against the rock face. He reaches the crest of the dam and ducks behind the cement parapet that juts up waist-high and runs along the edge.

A small brown truck sits a distance up the access road, angled on the berm of the road. Across the dam and down a short stretch of gravel on the opposite side is his truck. Behind it, a jumble of boulders rises, as tall as a person, spilling from the mountainside and spreading across the road, a decades-old slide that there had been no purpose or resources to clear.

Ben crouches behind the parapet, using it to steady his rifle. He swallows a swell of vertigo as his vision reels, telescoping rapidly away at the open space dropping so severely to the invisible valley floor below. He has a clear view down the road to Emma.

'Go,' he shouts, the echo lost in the pulse battering his eardrums.

Emma pushes off the mountain wall and sprints, head down, knees high, moving too slowly for the effort because of the gradient.

Moments later, Arnott rounds the corner running at full tilt, mere steps behind her. Ben squeezes the trigger. The rifle bucks. Arnott drops hard onto his side, shielding his face from the debris that explodes from the rock near his head. He scrambles sideways, writhing for cover, and rolls into a shallow ditch running along the base of the rock wall. By the time Ben reloads and brings the rifle to bear, only a sliver of Arnott's prone body is visible.

The clatter of gravel grows louder and Emma's ragged breath fills his ears. Out of the corner of his eye he tracks her progress, but keeps the rifle trained on Arnott's hiding place. Emma reaches the crest and scrambles behind the parapet wall beside Ben, her chest heaving, her face slick with sweat.

Ben stands and fires another shot, desperate to keep Arnott pinned in the ditch for as long as possible, hoping for time enough for them to make it across to the truck. He grabs a handful of Emma's jacket and helps haul her back to her feet. They run.

Ben's feet leave bloody impressions on the dam road as they sprint. Emma stumbles beside him until she regains her stride. Halfway across, Ben slows to peer over the edge. Arnott is almost at the crest, sprinting uphill at a driven pace. His pack bounces, his weapon clasped in one hand, held steady by his waist, as his other arm pumps with each stride.

Ben stops and firms his rifle against his shoulder. He hears Emma's laboured pace carry on without him, growing quieter as the distance stretches between them.

Arnott reaches the crest. Ben fires as he appears from the opposite side of the parapet wall. A gout of concrete fragments sprays from the palisade near Arnott, who scrambles to stop and drops back behind the wall.

Relief floods through Ben when, in the distance, he hears the driver's door of his truck groaning opening. Emma's made it. They're so close. He turns and sprints, willing his legs to move faster than they do, but their reserves are drained from days of exertion.

Emma shimmies out of her pack and lobs it into the bed of the truck. She turns to check his progress, resting a hand on the open door. An expression of fear settles over her face. Her body tenses, and through her, Ben knows Arnott has raised his weapon. Still ten paces from the truck, but Ben knows he's caught. If Arnott has a bullet left, it will soon be lodged in his back.

A final reserve of adrenaline courses through his muscles, as if his body knows what his mind yet doesn't. Ben falls to his side, landing heavily on his shoulder and rolling to face Arnott, raising his own rifle as he does. Arnott stands in the middle of the road, weapon held ready at the end of a perfect and clear shot. Ben squeezes the trigger. His rifle clicks. All tension drains from his body, his muscles slacken and his lungs empty; the weight of gravity embraces him fully. He closes his eyes. They were so close.

Arnott's shot roars, knocking all other sound from the world.

Ben flinches, anticipating pain and hoping the world just disappears from him before it becomes unbearable. But pain doesn't come and an errant embarrassment flushes through him as a thought flees, no deep revelations or life review, just be quick and be over.

Ben opens his eyes to the sound of a weighty thump landing behind him and a road-level view of Arnott sprinting away, toward his truck. Numbed by the sound, Ben doesn't look back. He doesn't want to see the hole punched through the driver's door, a fragmented flower blooming out of the backside of the panel, and then nothing, nothing but air where Emma once stood. Her body, fallen, lies on its back, head tilted to one side, staring sightlessly at the concrete parapet. Her eyes, they don't hold her anymore.

Ben pushes himself up and watches Arnott run toward his truck. He might have more ammo in there, Ben thinks. Or maybe he took it all with him in the first place and there's nothing left. Ben stands, the shock of the bullet sunk in deep. He blinks and glances out over the valley. There's nothing left.

A thought flits through his shock, there wasn't even time, for anything . . . just sound and darkness.

In the distance, the click and hum of an electric engine starts.

Ben turns to his truck. The driver-side door is still open. There is a hole through the metal. Ben raises his eyes so that he cannot see Emma on the ground behind it. The keys chime when he lifts them from the dirt, a short distance from Emma's hand, motionless, palm up, with fingers gently curved skyward.

Ben climbs into the driver's seat, the familiar smell cocooning him, musty fabric and grimy floors, lingering cigarette smoke and the tang of a poorly tuned diesel engine, old oil.

The door moans and shuts with a thump.

Ben drapes a hand over the wheel and jams the keys into the ignition. His vision floats through the twilight dusty windshield, past the end of the rusted hood and across the dam. Arnott's pickup loops a tight turn onto the road from the side of the berm.

He's not done with this yet, Ben thinks.

Ben slumps forward and cranks the key. The engine chugs and growls, turning five times before catching and roaring to life. Ben presses the accelerator slowly to the floor. The engine chatters, threatening to stall, then growls, blasting black smoke from the rattling tailpipe.

The headlights of Arnott's truck trace a crack across Ben's windshield with a point of white light as they complete the turn to face him. The back of Arnott's truck shimmies and skips, slipping to the side a little before it gains traction and lurches forward.

He's not going to stop, Ben thinks.

With the revs still spinning, Ben drops the truck into gear.

The clutch grinds and the tires spin, rattling gravel off the underbody. Ben is pressed back into his seat. With one hand torquing the wheel to keep the truck on the road, Ben draws the seatbelt across his body with the other.

A sign flashes past, briefly illuminated by his headlights in the bluing. 'Single lane traffic only. Yield to oncoming vehicles.'

The truck bumps onto the crest of the dam, the parapet wall becoming a close blur in his peripheral vision, corralling him forward. The pitch of the engine rises and Ben shifts gears. Speed vibrates up from the road, through the steering wheel.

Arnott's truck bucks as it passes from the gravel and onto the dam's tarmac. The truck weaves to regain its traction, almost grazing the concrete wall. The headlights leap forward with the new concrete footing and the trucks careen toward one another.

Ben's focus washes out in the point of light flaring through the crack in his windshield. It grows so bright he closes his eyes. A concussive thump claps his ears and the world vaults forward. His head whips, feeling barely anchored to his neck. His chest compresses and his hips burn as the seatbelt locks. Metal squalls and shrieks. Agony grips his hand in a vice and twists. The steering wheel bends. Consciousness is battered from him momentarily, and when it returns, his face is wet and warm; one side feels swollen so tight that it might crack.

Everything falls suddenly and absolutely still.

Distance is a blur of shape and colour, but the world within arm's reach is vibrantly clear. The door groans open. The metal beneath his outstretched, steadying hand is twisted and every edge is sharp and ragged. The cold evening air feels good because his face burns. One headlight still shines, motionless and too bright. Ben squints, almost blinded, but by its guidance, he finds the door handle of Arnott's truck and pulls.

The door is twisted in its frame and takes effort. When it finally bounces open, it hangs at an angle by one hinge. Arnott slumps sideways, prone, hanging half out of the door, his waist still secured by the seatbelt. Ben examines the man's damaged face. In the headlight, red blood is black. One eye is swollen shut and the other rolls to look at Ben. In that eye, Ben sees Arnott is still in there.

Ben stumbles and backs against the crutch of the open door, slinging one arm across the truck's crazed windshield and the other along the top of the door. This gives him the best leverage to draw a foot back and kick as hard as he's able.

Just once and Arnott is gone. The eye is empty.

Ben lets himself slide down to the ground and sit.

He stares out over the deepening hues of the valley.

19

The light is blinding white. Ben sweeps a tickle from his cheek, brushing the reinvigorated wound there but barely registering it, barely inhabiting his own mind. There's blood on the back of his hand and he looks at it, questioning, then presses his palm to his aching head as if he can push his scattered thoughts back into place.

How much time has passed? It's dark now, but not full dark yet.

Thoughts of the past few days thrum a fading current through his muscles; they still ring in his ears, threatening to surface. He holds them under the currents of the immediate moment even though they struggle fiercely. He has to keep it together.

It's over now, Ben thinks, for now. Our lives are in the future, not the past. Arnott had said that. Arnott. He winces against the brightness, a single headlight shining on him from Arnott's ruined truck, then he closes his eyes to quell the beam.

The darkness inside is manageable.

The blood pulsing through his eyelids is deep red. He concentrates on that, simple, physical present. The distraction is needed. Just feel, he tells himself, become instinct.

The dizzying height of the dam, dropping out from behind him, becomes a sensation that doesn't need sight; it registers as a twinge of gravity, something the twilit atmosphere is forced to bend around. The valley stretching beyond is likewise unseen, but known, an amphitheatre so vast it pulls his hearing outward toward it, searching for any reverberation to tell where the land starts again.

From the north, a cold wind blows across the expanse of water trapped by the dam. It's not strong enough to mask the arrhythmic ticking that sounds from nearby.

The hairs on the back of Ben's neck rise. The sound stirs something he's never known, but something most deeply buried in the tissues of his mind, a primal sensation that his cells remember. He opens his eyes and brings a hand up to shade the headlight beam, the mountains and tree line lingering a hue lighter in his memory.

The sound is bird claws on the metal wrecks. The clicking hops from one ruined truck to the next. Many shapes move in the gloaming.

Look away. Become instinct. Ben repeats these thoughts, creating diversion through mantra, and feels himself stop crumbling. A memory breaks the surface, his own voice from last night in the car. 'The primal brain is set up to react, not to think. It's there to make us survive at all costs.'

Emma's fingers turn the broken radio dial. Emma.

'We should expect the mind to reel with echoes from our deepest past. It takes the most extreme trauma to trigger the unforgotten forgotten.'

Ben clamps his eyes tight and concentrates on pushing the image back under.

The hum of the dam beneath him is unnerving. His renewed instinct yearns for the time when industry will end, leaving a stillness unheard in hundreds of years, but one that was known for all time before that. The instinct wants for a time he could hear his own breathing, unsullied by the saturation of electricity and radio waves.

Above the layered mountain peaks, and framed by the dim remnants of the day, a faraway flickering bead of pure light pulls a streamer upward, like a new star rising over the eighty million years of mountains clustered beneath it. Then comes the distant and delayed tear of rocket engines, rending the machine from gravity and battering the thin film of air coating the planet.

Ben scowls and looks over the meadow tucked between the mountains and the lake, by the side of the dam. The colours are dusky and subdued. A white plastic bag rustles, draped across the branches of a low shrub. He tears up from the arctic wind skimming across the water from the distant peaks. It churns the surface. Translucent chunks of ice ride the dark water. It's not cold enough to stitch them together yet, but it won't be more than a few days before that happens.

The faint smell of chemicals taints the air. The dirt beneath the vehicles glistens wet in the headlight's glow, where the engines have leaked their guts through broken seals and twisted welds.

Gravel crackles as Ben stands and staggers backwards, away from the wrecks, and at the far end of the dam, he spies the indistinct form of Emma's body on the road.

Ben sways and covers his ears, trying to block the scream of engines that still shrieks as tinnitus. Beneath his clamped hands, his head throbs relentlessly with gunshot echoes, bang and bang and bang. Then everything is silenced by a crash that shifted his world. Though it still deafens, it doesn't seem like a big enough noise for such a seismic thing.

Ben's hands fall to his sides and he averts his eyes from the shadowed movement of the birds near Emma's body.

It's easier not to see, not to feel; neither will change a thing.

The black birds have waited for days, and now will do their work.

Ben thrusts his hands into his pockets, hunches his shoulders against the chill, and turns away, closing his eyes as his gaze passes over the feasting crows. He surveys the wreckage of the trucks and beyond, to the dark access road cut through the wild terrain. Far away, it intersects the highway, and there, there are people. There are still people. That's a strange world to him now, one he no longer belongs in.

From over his shoulder comes a ragged caw. The carrion birds squabble.

There's no hiking out. There's no leaving. He's injured and tonight he will freeze. He needs shelter and supplies. Mostly, he needs to be away from the wreckage, what they've done. Anywhere else is better.

Emma's pack is near the side of the road, where it had been thrown from the bed of his truck. In the top pouch, Ben finds her shattered walkie-talkie and her logbook. He slips the logbook into his thigh pocket. A side pocket holds the first-aid kit, and in the failing headlight beam, using his truck's side-view mirror, he swabs his face with antiseptic wipes and glues the hinged wound on his cheek closed again.

Ben hobbles down the embankment from the road and crosses the meadow. The moss is a crust of frost that gives way underfoot, but the cold is numbing. Waterlogged stumps form an uneven picket lining the shore. An ice rind rims land's edge. He unwraps his battered feet and washes them in the water, dousing them with antiseptic, and welcoming the sting that helps focus his shock-addled mind.

Arnott's boots fit a size too big. It's an easy gap to fill by taking the man's socks, as well. They are good boots with good treads, rated arctic and waterproofed better than the ones torn from Ben's feet that afternoon.

He slings Emma's pack over a shoulder, turns his back on the road out, and walks away from the wrecks. He crosses the dam, averting his eyes when the carrion birds take flight at his passing, and feels how exhaustion can outweigh sorrow, how shock can stop tears, and how relief can be unfathomable when there is nothing left to fight.

Reaching the rockslide, he veers from the road and up a shallow gully, which is run through by the glimmering thread of a creek. The gully deepens and ascends more severely. Through the trees, in glimpses, Ben keeps an eye on the mountain peak he's heading toward. It has a name, but he won't think of it; he wants it all to become nameless again, undiscovered.

At an unmarked point, he turns straight upslope, away from the creek. Night fully settles as he climbs, at times forced to drop to all fours to scramble up steeper sections in the darkness. His lungs labour and his muscles burn. When he breaks from the tree line, he glances back through a haze of breath. In the moonlight, he can make out the dam far below, a perfect line engineered into a place where perfect lines don't exist.

The black birds are invisible from here.

The cave mouth is tucked at the base of a towering limestone outcrop. It's small and blacker than the surrounding night, outlined by the ghostly blue of starlight and the waning moon. The geometric amber badge is clear, the lights of Copernicus.

Ben stops outside the entrance and leans on a metal sign riveted to a post. His chest heaves from the exertion of the climb. He stares blindly at the rolling bib of scree that spills down the mountainside, disappearing into the trees below.

Ben drops Emma's pack at his feet and roots through the main compartment. He finds her flashlight and cranks the handle. The grinding rasps too loudly in his ears, the sound amplified by the nearby wall of stone. Instinctively fearful that the hunters will hear, it takes a moment to realize they're no longer coming for him.

The flashlight grinds the night for a minute before it's charged. Ben flips the switch. He winces at the yellow beam reflecting off the sign. Threads of rust weep from the bolts that secure it to the post. Peeling red lettering on a reflective white background reads, 'Caution: Rabies. Do not enter,' underneath which is an outline of a bat in crucifixion pose.

Ben heaves the backpack onto his shoulders again and shines the beam across the cave mouth. The blackness within remains absolute. Ben shivers as his sweat-soaked clothes cool and, he realizes, with trepidation. A basal fear creeps within him, a primal flutter of adrenaline, a tingle across his scalp, warning that this is not a place to go.

The sensible child within speaks louder than the logic of his adult mind. It whispers that monsters live in caves. They always have. It whispers, 'This place eats light.'

The smell seeping out is stale and damp, a caged and ancient air. The cave mouth is silent, no chirrups or whispering wings. No small disturbances skim past, no movement flashes through the cone of light, and nothing flies by on the graceful tricks of sonar.

The colony had succumbed to white-nose fungus long before Ben and Chuck cached the gear here. The fungus had arrived with two bats hunkered in the hold of a cargo ship. It spread across the continent in less than a decade, wiping out colonies.

Only two zoologists noticed the decline of this colony, a grad student and her supervisor. One year their count took half a day to complete. The following year there were thirty bats tucked in the highest notches of the entrance gallery. Then there were none. Nothing could be done against something so fast and fatal, except witness it happen.

Loose stones rattle underfoot as Ben ducks under the rim of the cave's entrance and steps inside. He switches off the flash-light and stands still, because that's what he and Chuck had done on their first visit, when they'd stocked the cache here.

Recreating the moment is like stepping back inside himself, two years ago.

He's tricked by a blackness as absolute and secure as being stowed safely inside his own cranium. His body is gone. He has to trust the experience of his eyelids that they're actually open, that the ethereal purple shapes swooping past are some confused mechanism of his robbed vision and not some actual bioluminescent creatures that dwell deeper in the earth.

Without sound, he has to trust he's not deaf and that the subtle ringing he hears comes from within himself, tiny, damaged follicles constructing their own reality. He wonders if that tinnitus doesn't ring throughout the cave.

Can the monsters hear it, too?

Can they find me by it?

Are they on their way?

The weight of Emma's pack on his shoulders, the press of clothes against his skin, becomes deceptive. Without a grounding sight or noise to fixate on, he floats, and gravity becomes just a sensation lining the soles of his feet. The rest of him is free.

'Peaceful, eh?' Chuck said with a laugh. 'Like being in the womb again.'

Ben listens to the words in the dark, not sure if the voice is his own, or if Chuck's still echoes off the rocks, two years later.

'Yeah,' Ben agrees, and the word sounds too close. His heart beats faster.

'Life is everywhere.'

Chuck's voice again?

Had he said these words on their visit?

Ben's eyes dart, searching for the movement he thinks he spotted, but shadows can't exist in total darkness.

'If there're the slimmest conditions, if there's even the most precarious hope, it will be there.'

Ben becomes aware of breathing, close, and without reference. It sounds as loud as shouting. His scalp prickles. It's not his own breathing; his chest moves with a different rhythm.

The light clicks on and pale shapes twist in front of the trembling amber beam. It's impossible to tell how close they are without something to mark perspective. It's his own breath, a miasma swirling out from him.

'You shine that thing in here for long enough, even for a few minutes every day, these brown walls will turn green. The bat shit, the moisture, the spores, a tint of some algae or lichen, it's all here waiting for the slightest chance. Even though it doesn't sound like much, it'll be a miracle just the same.'

White teeth glint in a broad smile.

Where did Chuck go? Ben wonders.

The entrance gallery of the cave soars overhead, its limits hidden beyond the strength of the flashlight beam. Stretching out before Ben, a few bumps of stalagmites with glistening peaks, and a field of boulders, furry with silty drift, all deeply etched by the stark binary of light and dark.

Ben takes a step forward, holding the flashlight high over his shoulder, trying to push back the darkness.

'Hello?' he calls, and instantly feels ridiculous. Like a little kid afraid to peer under his own bed at night, he feels small.

The beam wobbles as Ben slips, the ground covered by a slick sludge. He doesn't look down, doesn't want to see the litter of bodies, an entire bat colony preserved by the cold and lightlessness. This place is a tomb for thousands.

Behind a boulder, at the end of the gallery, Ben finds the weatherbox, untouched since the day he and Chuck left it. The seal hisses when he pulls the latch.

A whisper replies from the distance.

Ben spins to face the sound. He swings the beam in an arc, but doesn't see the source, so he hesitantly discounts it as his piqued imagination.

Ben turns back to the weatherbox and lifts the lid. A glowstick rests at the top, propped across bulging plastic bags that shimmer in the uncertain light. The glowstick pops when he bends it and a soft green light grows brighter with each shake.

The top layer is bun⬛⬛⬛⬛⬛⬛⬛⬛clothes, an emergency blanket, a few h⬛⬛⬛⬛⬛⬛⬛⬛through strata of first-aid equipment an⬛⬛⬛⬛⬛⬛⬛d ropes, packages spilling onto the cave f⬛⬛⬛⬛⬛⬛gers wrap around what he's searching fo⬛⬛⬛⬛⬛s out the pack of cigarettes he'd sneaked⬛⬛⬛⬛⬛

Ben drops the glo⬛⬛⬛⬛⬛⬛ weatherbox lid. Nudging a few fallen ⬛⬛⬛⬛⬛⬛he sits on the box. He pats his pockets. ⬛⬛⬛⬛⬛⬛ers linger on the rectangle of Emma's logbook. On the other, he first rummages out the bullet Tomos had put in him. The slug lands silently in the debris by his feet. Ben then digs out his lighter.

The click snaps through the gallery and Ben draws a deep drag. He exhales slowly while staring cross-eyed at the glowing ember floating in front of him. Ben's focus lengthens to a gap in the gallery wall, becoming visible in the dissipating smoke. At the end of his breath, he grunts and shoves the lighter back into his pocket. They hadn't seen the gap on their first visit, but they hadn't lingered either.

The cigarette filter lands beside the bullet. Ben's grabs the flashlight and crosses to the gap.

The crevice is narrow and Ben has to sidle in. The flashlight scrapes against the rock.

20

Cold wet walls press close, sucking heat from his body. His movements fill the constricted space with whispers. He grips the flashlight tight, with a dread of dropping it and not being able to retrieve it again. He struggles onward with his palms and elbows levered against opposite walls, scared that if he stops, he won't be able to start again. The passage shrinks. His lungs feel like they can't fill up enough, squeezed by the converging stone.

The floor slopes. The next steps remain hidden because of the contortions he's forced to conduct, to twist through the sliver in the rock. Blind steps. He's terrified the ground will drop away entirely and he'll fall into an impossible crevice.

Ben loses his sense of direction. Down is discernible only by the direction that sweat streams across his face, plucking at the tip of his nose with each drip. The walls constrict more with every jostle, to a point that Ben can no longer move forward. He angles the flashlight with a pivoting wrist, swinging the beam up and down the narrow crack, the inky darkness impenetrable beyond a few feet.

'No,' Ben whimpers and grits his teeth.

'No,' the cave whimpers back.

He strains, trying to backtrack, but it's as if he has swollen and the space has shrunk. The air fills with the mist of his own strangled exhalations. The edges of the light become visible and draw closer, growing weaker as the flashlight's charge begins to fail. Ben wheezes in shallow, panicked breaths. The glow turns tawny, then fades and dies. With one arm trapped out front, and one behind, there is no way to wind the charger.

Ben tries to turn his head, but rakes his cheek against rough rock and has to give up. He breathes in tiny gulps, wanting to keep his lungs as full as possible because he fears the walls will take any opportunity to squeeze him tighter. Spittle quivers on his lip as he strains again to hoist himself forward, and fails. He slumps into the embrace of the rock.

The soft drip of water echoes. The noise had always been there, but was hidden by the sounds of his struggles.

Grey and white stars swarm toward him from the dark, the grip of claustrophobia bringing a wave of dizziness.

A high-pitched and sustained whine echoes through the darkness, choking out the constant cadence of his panting. Ben desperately wonders what of this underground world is real, and what part comes from inside himself.

Ben closes his eyes and tries to calm his mania.

The whine fades.

Ben squirms again, kicks. Pain burns from where he barks

his shin on the rock, and then the sensation goes numb. His boot scrapes are muted behind him. Or are they below, he wonders. The deafening breathing stops when he pulls, fingers clawing for a hold, scraping his knuckles raw, and eventually he shifts. Fraction by fraction, Ben starts forward again.

Minutes or hours pass, he can't tell. Time is marked only by the struggling inhalations and exhalations. Eventually, the walls diverge enough for him to bring his arms together.

Ben waits, holds his breath, interrogating the silence for any noise beyond the slow and steady drip, but there's none. The next minute passes to the sound of the handle whirring before the beam strikes out across a small chamber.

Ben steps into ankle-deep water. The reflection off the surface casts a wavering aurora, making the small chamber seem like a bubble suspended underwater. A drip swells at the end of a stalactite and falls into the pool. The sound echoes through the chamber. Between drops, when the ripples settle, the water becomes invisible.

Ben steps carefully over the slick calcium deposits and onto the shore. The ceiling is low, forcing him to crouch. He pans the beam around; the twisting light makes the chamber spin. A chill settles into him, his clothes damp with sweat and the chamber's air cold. He swipes his forehead against his arm and directs the flashlight onto his hands. The greasy mud from the cave walls beads at his knuckles with blood. The wound on his palm is clotted, but still weeping. Ben shakes and flexes his hand, turning his attention back to the chamber.

Everywhere is pale grey limestone and weeping buttery

calcium deposits, except for a black smear in the middle of the ceiling. Immediately beneath the stain is a mound of charcoal and ash. Ben shuffles from under the ledge and finds he can stand, if he hunches.

The chamber falls suddenly dark. Ben shakes the flashlight. It flickers. Something loose knocks within. A few more shakes and the beam becomes steady again.

Ben pokes through the fire pit with his boot, the damp charcoal staining the toe. A drip reverberates off the walls. Raising the light, Ben scowls at some brown and black discolorations marking the cave wall. He exhales to the side, hoping the condensation hanging in the air will clear a little, and in a few breaths, it does.

First, he discerns a figure, the outline of a broad rectangular body with short legs and arms drawn on the rock. The overall effect is of a person wearing a heavy cloak. The end of one arm is struck through by a long straight line that could only be a spear.

With eyes locked on the image, Ben moves closer. The cave blinks out. Ben rattles the flashlight, bringing the beam back. The walls swirl with long shadows cast across the uneven surfaces.

Closer, Ben sees there are actually five figures, all imposing and rectangular. Two hold their spears at the ready, with their stick arms bent back over their shoulders, ready to throw. The remaining three have empty hands, their arms angled forward.

Ben puzzles at them and the light quits the room again. In the darkness, a drop sounds.

'Come on,' Ben coaxes.

The knocking inside the flashlight sounds looser than it did earlier. The flickering spotlight shines across the painting, catching two horizontal black lines, spears flying through the air, and another one beyond them, stuck in the side of a creature drawn halfway across the wall from the figures. Ochre-coloured lines slash from where its hide is pierced. The creature has big triangular feet, massively exaggerated claws, and a swooping hump for shoulders. The beast is black, except for the triangle feet, which remain in outline.

Ben takes a few steps towards the animal, blood pouring from its wound. Shadows shift, small ripples and clefts in the rock bring the bear alive and it twists, trying to swipe the spear from its side, but it can't reach. It falls back in confusion and agony.

The flashlight strains, dimming with a buzz, and Ben wobbles it. The beam steadies, but fades. Ben shines the diminished glow back across the hunting grounds, the spears quivering with movement in mid-flight, but firmly frozen in place. The beam fades to black.

Ben shakes the flashlight again and light spills across the surface at a low angle. His cheek hovers close to the drawing of the bear. From its perspective, beyond the flying spears, the five figures loom, faceless silhouettes with endless weapons held at the ready. From the day this drawing was made, the spears have been flying toward the animal, and those strangers have been chasing it.

Ben steps back. The heel of his boot crunches in charcoal. Setting the flashlight on a boulder, he angles the beam to illuminate the scene. Ben sifts through the charcoal until he finds a twig that doesn't disintegrate. He returns to the wall, and with it, draws a gently curving line from the five figures, to the bear, giving them all a horizon to stand on. He extends the line to where the stone becomes fractured and uneven. There, he draws some triangles up from the horizon and smudges them with his fingers, shading in mountain ravines and crevasses, leaving negative space for the treeless altitudes.

Above the peaks, Ben draws an exaggerated circle and adds a few craters. On the top edge of the moon, he sketches a web of lines to demarcate the colony. He steps back to examine his handiwork. His lines are fresher than the ancient drawing, and the connection is clear where the old ones ended and his begin. Ben smiles at his obvious and childish amendment, then steps up to his canvas again, adding an ascending rocket between the mountain peaks, with lines of fire splaying from its tail.

Ben contemplates the ancient bear for a moment. He shifts so his shadow doesn't block the light, then draws three of his own rectangle men. These ones hold rifles ready, and he strokes three quick dashes, bullets for the bear he has yet to add. The same fire lines that splay from the tail of his rocket, spark from the end of the charcoal rifles.

The light buzzes, strains, and begins to fade. Panic rises in Ben, no longer for fear of being forever stuck in the darkness, but for his drawing remaining unfinished.

He sketches faster.

He bites his lip in concentration.

A short distance from the three figures, Ben uses charcoal-covered fingers to pull a snaking line out from the base of one of the mountains, and then draws his own bear beside it. The Boss lies beside the river. Ben grates his bloodied knuckle against the rough limestone, leaving a dark rust stroke where it spills from the side of the bear and onto the ground.

Ben scowls at the image, then presses his wounded palm over it. When he draws back, a splattered handprint is left behind.

The charge on the flashlight dies. The cave goes black.

It takes a moment for the image he had drawn to fade from his vision, his optic nerve momentarily inverting dark for light, leaving a negative image of the bear floating in the blackness.

Ben waits, listening to his own breathing and the slow drip of water. The cave doesn't instil the foreboding it once had and he thinks for a moment just to stay. Fearing the thought will stick, Ben fumbles his way back to the flashlight, knocking it from its perch with a clunk. Clumsy hands grope across the rocks until they find it again.

With the light resurrected, Ben sits on a boulder and stares at his work. In time, he notices the pressure of Emma's notebook pressed against his thigh and absentmindedly works it free from the pocket. His attention lingers on the rock wall as he holds the book, then eventually angles the beam toward it.

Through two charge cycles, Ben hunches over Emma's logbook, reading her words. First, he reads in wonder of this lingering artefact of her, these words written by her, shaped by her hand. He runs a finger across the markings, touching line after line, the pencil marks blurring a little. The drip sounds off the passing time, but Ben doesn't notice, immersed as he becomes.

When he reaches the last page, Ben's brow furrows.

Emma had been tracking a bear of her own, unknown to him. Angling the book toward the flashlight beam, his eyes jump back to reread her most recent entries. They outline her suspicions that her bear was pregnant, notes of changes in her behaviour. Emma knew her bear as he had known his. He fans back through pages and pages of observations written in Emma's hand.

Chuck and Emma had been wise to keep this bear completely secret.

Emma had been ruthless to betray his bear for hers.

Ben pulls his lighter from his pocket and sets the edge of the book alight, dropping it in the mound of charcoal as the flames spread. In the flickering light of the burning logbook, he grabs the flashlight from its seat and squeezes back through the gap to the main gallery.

The shallow grey of dawn seeps in from the cave mouth. Heavy clouds swirl by outside, carrying snow. Ben sits on the weatherbox, smoking another cigarette. In the packages that had fallen out, he finds a logbook and pencil. He unwraps them and tilts the pages toward the pale glow from outside. He writes about what happened, Poppy Freedom, the battle at The Pinch, how Vito and Tomos and Arnott died, and how they murdered The Boss before they did. He writes about how Emma died too, but doesn't tell of her betrayal. There is no point in that anymore.

Ben writes how all the bears are dead now, the last one ever is gone, and how he'd left one more void in a world of many. The creatures would never exist again, anywhere in time or the universe, only in memory and in the past, both of which fade too quickly.

Folding the cover closed, Ben empties the weatherbox of its bullets and rations and canisters of white gas and first-aid supplies. He takes the clothes and ballistic vest and sleeping bag. He leaves behind the spare radio and flashlight and logbook. The lid drops closed. The clamps snap tight. The pump wheezes as it pulls the air out of the box, sealing it from time. Ben hopes the lie he'd written within will be believed, if anyone even comes searching. He resolves to have a bullet for anyone who follows, no matter who.

Ben steps through the cave mouth into a swirling snow flurry. The pack weighs heavily on his shoulders. The bulk of the new ballistic vest is ungainly under his jacket, but it offers warmth when the air is so cold.

The surrounding peaks loom, hazy, through the washout. The dam and the lake are hidden by the storm. Emma's tracker beeps. Ben looks at it, slung by a carabiner to a loop on his jacket. A green indicator light flashes. A single beep; Emma's bear is out there, but still far away.

Ben squints into the driving snow, loops a thumb under his rifle strap, and starts down the mountain. Rubble spills ahead of each step, but Ben doesn't stumble, and he doesn't fall.

He disappears into the tree line.

Acknowledgements

There are many creative souls involved in getting any book onto a shelf. This is the story of those souls behind this book.

Our tale begins with a dedication to my husband Nenad, for being supportive of all the time and effort needed to pull a book from a brain and get it into this state. In my life, you are vital; you are seen and appreciated.

Anyone undertaking a journey needs a trusty gang of companions. So many thanks to these fellow authors: Ali Bryan, Paulo da Costa, Judith Pond, Robin van Eck, and Phillip Vernon, for sharing their thoughts on the early chapters. Also, a small, but mighty, portion of this book was written during my stint as writer-in-residence at the Alexandra Writers' Centre Society. Kudos, for the time.

To Ali Bryan, an ever-engaging interlocutor in rambling discussions about White Rhinos and New Pangea and the psychic drive for conservation, our muddy interface with the natural world, all things Medea and Drake and Fermi, and all the far-flung ridiculousness that was considered before I got to distilling down the thematic engine of this story and focusing on our beloved and stressed Earth-Farm. The hours pounding poutine and beers were not wasted!

Uncountable 'thank yous' are owed to Andrea Blatt and Anna Dixon, the highwire agents who, in the middle of the first wave of a dazzlingly disorienting catastrophe, went bravely forth and found this story a fine home.

In this home, this story met an able craftsman in Jack Renninson. With a keen editorial eye, candid wit, and a skillful handling of this most-delicate author, Jack and the wizards at Harper *Voyager* UK conjured this book into something beautiful.

The finale of this particular tale lies with you. Without a reader, these written imaginings would amount to naught. Stories are thoughts and ideas and discussions, and they are hopeless without you. To readers of my past stories, thanks for coming to this, a very different place. With some luck, there will be many very different places to explore in the future, as well.

The magic of the whole process hasn't waned one iota. The significance of this journey-of-many-characters is not lost on me. Thanks all.

The end.